CUBA
undercover

CUBA
undercover

LINDA
BOND

Entangled Publishing, LLC
10940 S Parker Rd
Suite 327
Parker, CO 80134
rights@entangledpublishing.com

Amara is an imprint of Entangled Publishing, LLC.

Edited by Vanessa Mitchell
Cover design by Elizabeth Turner Stokes
Cover photography by Marius Dobilas, BABAROGA, and lazyllama/ Shutterstock

Manufactured in the United States of America

First Edition July 2015

Chapter One

Rebecca Menendez burst through the doors of courtroom 5A, her pulse racing. Like a guided missile on a mission, she swerved past a rival TV reporter also pushing his way out of the crowded courtroom.

This was *her* story. She broke the news a year ago. She'd be the first to report the verdict today. Then, maybe she'd finally get that promotion into the Special Investigation unit. Her lungs tightened as she hit high gear and sprinted down the hall toward the south side exit of Tampa's downtown courthouse.

"Slow down, Menendez."

Out of the corner of her eye she caught Ike, one of the veteran bailiffs, standing rigid against the wall.

"You're going to break your ankle on those stilts you wear for shoes," he grumbled.

"Sorry." Rebecca skidded to a halt, offering a guilty shrug. "Deadline to meet." But she couldn't stop a smile from stretching across her face. She was so damn proud. "Verdict came back. Finally. I've been working this story for twelve months."

Ike nodded. "You keep speaking out for the abused, like you do."

Her breath caught at the cynical old-timer's indirect compliment. She lived for words like that. If only her mother had lived long enough to see her today, following in her father's footsteps. If her *papi* hadn't been murdered, she might have earned his respect today, too. Her chest burned with an odd mixture of both satisfaction and regret.

Ike waved her on and, at the last moment, delivered a thumbs-up along with a rare smile.

Rebecca grinned, heat rushing into her cheeks. Glancing at the clock at the end of the hall, her heart jumped. Five minutes to five. She'd make the top of the newscast if she bolted.

She powered down the hall, arms pumping in a barely controlled walk-run until she exited the courthouse. The summer humidity slapped her skin in one hot wave. Despite that blast, she took off down the sidewalk, sideswiping an attorney she knew, stumbling, regaining her balance, and sprinting to the large Eyewitness News van parked on the side of the street.

Dallas "Dawg" Jones, her longtime friend and photographer, was clicking his camera onto the tripod on the sidewalk.

"Hey Dawg," she huffed, sweat dripping down the curve in her back. "You heard?" She couldn't do a live report breathless like this. She leaned over, hands on her knees.

"Guilty of attempted murder and assault with a deadly weapon." Dallas broke into a grin. "That fool got what was coming to him."

"Sure did." She stood up, swiping the sweat off her forehead and quickly brushing a hand over her long hair, hoping to straighten out any wayward strands. July heat always made her melt during live shots. "It took the jury less than an hour to decide."

Dallas raised his eyebrows as he handed her an earpiece. "That man's days were numbered after his wife put him on blast by talking to you. No one could look at that woman's burned-off face and come back with anything other than guilty. Wouldn't be surprised if the jury sentences him to life in prison."

Rebecca nodded. "Sentencing is set for Monday."

"No matter what his sentence, you know his jail mates are gonna get that ass in prison. John Fredrick's gonna belong to a guy named Snake or the dude with the most cigarettes."

Rebecca bit back a smile. Dallas always broke the tension and made her laugh. It was his way. And on stressful days like today, they both needed his fresh, blunt humor. "The judge ordered everyone to remain silent as the verdict was read. But Adrianna cried with relief when she heard the jury found her ex guilty. No one shushed her sobbing. Not even the judge." Rebecca bounced on the sidewalk, her heels barely touching the cement. She felt a little buzzed on adrenaline. "That moment made all of our hard work on this story worthwhile." She gestured for Dallas to hand her a microphone. She wasn't missing the top of the show. No way. She had too much to prove today. She *was* good enough to work with the investigative team.

Dallas put in his own earpiece first. "You ready?"

"I've been ready since the day her jerk of an ex-husband set her on fire." Her stomach churned, recalling Adrianna's ruined face in those first weeks—looking like raw meat, blistered and oozing puss. How could anyone value someone so little they'd set him or her on fire? Rebecca still had nightmares about it, but she couldn't let her personal fears show now, so she pushed her shoulders down.

Dallas handed her the wireless microphone, a knowing

smile lighting up his eyes. "Thought you reporter types were supposed to remain unbiased."

Rebecca quickly clipped the microphone on her suit lapel. "Impossible in this case." She lifted her chin. "There are some stories that *don't* have two sides. Those stories simply *have* to be told." She pointed a finger at Dallas, hoping her words resonated with her ambitious young friend. "No matter what the cost."

"You're damn straight." Dallas nodded. "You hear Sandy?" He kept fiddling with a cord leading into his news camera.

As Rebecca shoved her earpiece in, her producer's voice from back in the studio came through. "Two minutes till the top of the show."

"Got it."

"Stand by," Sandy said.

Rebecca blew out a breath, wishing the fingernails of anticipation would stop scraping up her insides. *Focus. Don't get all nervous now.* Turning back to the camera, she took a deep breath and wiped her forehead again.

"You've got two minutes total," Sandy said.

Two minutes of airtime to sum up a year's worth of work on Rebecca's part. She rolled her shoulders. She didn't need to explain the devastating physical damage to Adrianna. That would be obvious. What Rebecca wanted to share with her viewers was what they *couldn't* see in two minutes on TV, like the way Adrianna flinched whenever she saw fire or blanched whenever a man raised his voice. Or the way she never made eye contact with strangers, or always held her head down. These were the details that still affected Rebecca as a reporter. *As a human being.* Adrianna felt worthless, and the man who supposedly loved her was the one who made her feel that way. She wanted her audience to realize some scars couldn't be healed, and some stories weren't just surface deep. They affected one's *soul*. Her breath caught in her throat, and for a moment she couldn't swallow.

Rebecca closed her eyes. *Focus on the moment. Make everyone watching care about Adrianna and the bigger issue of domestic violence. No one should feel worthless.*

Ever.

She opened her eyes, and the red light on Dallas's camera turned green. Her heart stutter-stepped. The main anchors threw to her, and with a deep breath, she began to recount what she knew would forever be one of the best stories on one of the best days of her life.

. . .

Not even fifteen seconds after Rebecca's live shot ended, her cell phone vibrated. She pulled it out of her pocket. It was Samantha Steele, her fellow reporter and best friend. Rebecca answered. "Okay, Sam, tell me you were watching."

"I was. I'm stuck up here in Spring Hill, waiting for my six p.m. live shot. Watching from the live truck."

"Sorry." Spring Hill was two hours away. Sam wouldn't get home until eight tonight. One of the downsides of being the station's top reporter. "Think Stan will be impressed enough to give me the investigative reporter job after my story today?" Her news director was supposed to make a decision on the position in the next week or two.

"You rocked that live shot, and the emotion in that story made me tear up."

Her heart beat faster. Coming from Samantha Steele that meant a lot. Sam had just uncovered a murder-for-hire plot at a local adventure vacation company, making *national* headlines. "Thanks."

"So, listen." Sam sounded a little distracted. "I'm calling about that party at the governor's mansion coming up. You in?"

"Hell yeah, I'm in." Breaking national news had its benefits. Sam had just scored an invite to the biggest charity event in Tampa. Samantha knew how much Rebecca longed to finally meet the governor face-to-face, so she could lobby for him to sign a bill sitting on his desk right now. The bill would secure funding for her favorite charity, Tampa's domestic violence shelter. Sam had invited her to go with her and her fiancé, Zack Hunter. Hottest guy in town. A twinge of envy hit Rebecca's heart. She longed for the kind of romantic, *I'd do anything for you* kind of love Samantha and Zack had. "I can't wait. I just got my Alexander McQueen gown cleaned." After renting it from Luxury for Less, a consignment store in Tampa. Everyone assumed Rebecca was rich because she worked in TV. She made good money, but not enough to buy a thousand-dollar gown. But she wanted to fit in, look like the classy, South Tampa elite. No one would know it was rented. After a childhood of wearing hand-me-downs, Rebecca certainly knew how to play the part without spending the money.

"All right, then. I'm off."

"Thanks, Sam."

"You bet."

Disconnecting, butterflies tickled Rebecca's stomach. She looked skyward. Too bad her mom hadn't lived to see her daughter cross over Kennedy Boulevard into the South Tampa elite, succeeding both personally and professionally. Rebecca would soon be dining with the governor, for goodness' sake. Her throat tightened, and she hoped both parents were somehow watching. She was so close to achieving all of her dreams. And she had established a platform to do good for others in the process. She liked to think her parents would be proud.

"You gonna shake a leg, Becca?"

She jumped at Dallas's voice.

He snapped his fingers at her. "Let's do this."

"Sorry." She swallowed. They still had another live shot and package to prepare.

"You got that story for the six written?"

"No."

"Girl, get on it." Dallas's eyes widened.

"What?" Why was Dallas bugging out? "You know it won't take me that long to write the story."

"What in the Halle Berry is that all about?" Dallas stumbled back two steps, both hands shooting out in front of his big frame. "Behind you! Get the hell outta the way!"

Rebecca jerked around. *Coño!* A white construction van was jumping the curb and speeding down the sidewalk toward her. Her heart sprinted, but the muscles in her legs locked up.

The van skidded to a stop, so close she instinctively stumbled back to avoid being hit. The scent of burning rubber whooshed up her nostrils. The side door slid open and a man jumped out. Tall, muscular, wearing shorts, he had tattoos covering his entire left arm. *Dear Lord.*

And he had on a mask.

Oh shit! "Wait. Don't." Rebecca threw out both hands. Her heart was racing so fast it hurt. "What's going on?" She could barely catch her breath.

A second man sprang out of the passenger's side of the van. This guy was beefy, also wearing a ski mask. He gripped what looked like *a gun* in his hands.

Holy shit! The hair on her arms stood up, and her throat tightened.

"*Metete en la camioneta!*" the tattoo man grunted.

"Get in his van?" Rebecca spun around, sure the tattooed man must be talking to someone behind her.

"Oh, my damn." Dawg stood next to his camera, a statue

on the sidewalk, his face frozen, mouth open.

A handful of other media members cluttered the walkway, gawking at the men from the white van. One reporter screamed and started running. *Good idea.*

"Rebecca." The tattooed man's voice remained calm. "I'm talking to you two."

Rebecca jerked back around.

"Just do what they say." Dallas's voice rose. "What these masked dudes want with my big two-hundred-and-fifty-pound ass, I do not know."

She was too scared to turn and see what Dallas was doing, but she knew her cameraman would protect her if he could. She also knew better than to get into a vehicle with an armed person. You do, you're dead. *My watch!* She took off the Tag she'd recently splurged on. "Here, take this. Please, don't shoot."

"You're coming with me." The tattooed guy gestured with the gun.

"Hey, someone's being robbed. They've got guns," a high-pitched female voice squawked from somewhere behind her. "Call 911!"

The robber's eyes flickered to a spot over Rebecca's shoulder.

Finally, a chance. Every nerve in her body fired. She dashed for the news van, expecting the hot sensation of a bullet to tear into her skin at any second. Blood pounded in her ears, drowning out all other sounds. She ran hard, toes pinched in her stilettos. One heel sank into a crack, and her ankle turned. Reaching out, her palms broke her fall. The pavement tore at the pads of her hands as she skidded across the sidewalk, her skin heating like an iron.

She pushed up with a grunt. Someone yanked her back by her hair, pulling her off balance. She stumbled and screamed, "Let me go," crashing into a big body, tattoos visible on the man's arm. He smelled like onions and sweat. Gagging, she pushed away.

"Man, what the hell are you doing? Let her go!" Dallas yelled.

A damp cloth clamped over her face. *What the?* She tensed. The rag stank of something chemical but sweet. Chloroform? Tattoo guy forced the rag hard against her mouth and nose. She couldn't breathe. Panic flooded through her. Her fingers started to tingle, and her head was spinning.

Lashing out, she dug into the man's arms, tearing his skin, feeling his warm, sweaty flesh lodge under her fingernails.

"Ready to go to Cuba?" The man dragged her backward.

Cuba? She'd die before she set foot in Cuba. Damn government would never silence her like it'd silenced her father.

Jerking her off the ground, the tattooed man stumbled toward the van. She had just enough freedom, and just enough air left, to drive her heel back up into his groin. Awkward and off balance, she missed.

A gunshot rang out. Rebecca's heart froze. A woman screamed, but it sounded so far away. Rebecca kept struggling and blinking to keep her eyes open. *Jesus.* Her arms felt like steel appendages, impossible to lift, and her eyes were having trouble focusing.

The man yanked her head back. Assaulted by the sickeningly sweet smell flooding her mouth and nose, Rebecca retched. Her feet suddenly hit the ground. She stumbled, slamming her shin against hard metal as the gunman pushed her through the van's open door. She hit the van floor with a grunt.

"*No la lastime.*"

That was a new voice. Ordering the tattooed guy not to hurt her? *Too late.*

She strained to see who was talking, but her vision kept

narrowing. The chaotic mixture of sound and movement shrank from a long tunnel into a small black dot. She was going to pass out.

Someone gently brushed the hair away from her face and helped maneuver her into a more comfortable position.

"I won't hurt you."

The new voice spoke in English this time.

Her heart pounded harder, but the sensation of a different man's soft touch faded.

And then…nothing.

Chapter Two

Rebecca woke with a start, gasping for air.

What the hell just happened?

She tried to peel her eyes open. *Dark*. She blinked again. She couldn't make out anything.

Then, mental images of her kidnapping flooded her mind. She'd been thrown into a van. Jerked out of it. Pulled into some smaller vehicle. The tattooed man had set the van on fire. *Holy shit.* She could still smell the burning tires. Her pulse drummed in her ears. Where had the tattooed asshole taken her now?

Sweat snaked down her skin. She couldn't still be smelling burning tires. Burning wood maybe? *What the…?* As she hauled herself into a sitting position, a sharp sensation ripped through the left side of her chest. She froze, unable to inhale further. She held her breath until the pain passed.

In that brief moment of silence, someone else took a deep breath.

An electric wave of fear shimmied over her flesh. "Who's there?" She sprang up, rocking back on her heels. "Dawg?"

No answer. Her heart stalled.

"Dallas? You okay?"

"My name is Antonio. Antonio Vega."

She recognized the voice from inside the van. The man with the *gentle* touch. Still, the hair on the back of her neck stood up. "Who are you?" Her gaze darted back and forth. "What's going on?" She felt like a cornered animal. Squinting, she tried to make out her captor's face, but her eyes were still adjusting to the dark. "What do you want from me?"

"I need your help."

"Are you kidding me?" Confusion whipped through her. "*You* kidnapped *me*. I'm the one who needs help."

Laughter erupted, but at a distance. She stilled and listened. The other voices sounded male. To escape, she'd have to get past them, too. The other men were outside, but outside what? "Where are we?"

"In a tent in the Everglades."

Hope for an easy escape evaporated. "That far?" They'd changed vehicles so they could hit the highway. Smart. The Everglades. Wow. That explained the heat and the smell of campfire. "How long have I been out?" She swatted away a piece of hair plastered to her cheek. The humidity was thick. Suffocating.

"Hours, Rebecca."

He knew her name. Of course he did. "Okay." She bit her bottom lip. What else did he know? "Why did you kidnap *me*?"

"You're Cuban."

Nausea churned her stomach.

"You know the language."

Ay dios mío…

"You know the culture."

She balled her fists until her acrylic nails pierced her injured palms, causing her to yelp. She hated where this conversation was going. "What happened to my photographer?" Her voice cracked. She needed water.

"He's here. He came with you."

"At gunpoint." *Not willingly.*

"He's fine."

"Fine?" She looked down at her scratched-up hands. They stung, and her throat still burned from the chemical residue on that rag. "Fine, like, like, I'm fine?"

Antonio didn't respond.

She ran her fingers over her left eyebrow, pressing them against her throbbing temple. "I want to see my friend. Please."

"Not right now. You and I have business first."

"You have a story for me." She knew that much. Her eyes were starting to adjust. She could better make out her shadowy surroundings now. The flap to a large, houselike tent was to her left. Closed. You couldn't lock a tent, right? "What kind of story?" She glanced back at her captor, hoping to see him better. Size up the enemy.

"You're going to document a rescue." This Antonio guy had a strong jawline and pronounced cheekbones. He was young. Maybe a little older than her, probably around thirty.

"What kind of rescue?" *Keep him talking.* She continued to study him. He had dark, disheveled rock-star hair, curly, almost to his shoulders, a thin goatee, and dark eyes. Now that she could better make out his features, he looked like a young Che Guevara, the infamous Latin American revolutionary. Handsome for sure. But maybe just as deadly.

She shuddered as a memory of her childhood crept in. She rubbed a flurry of goose bumps away, bullying the unwanted images down. "My photographer needs to hear these details, too." Her head kept throbbing, right above her left eye.

"Not now."

She swallowed. In the minimal light, she could *feel* the intensity of his stare. Her stomach was all knotted up. Could this Antonio guy sense her fear? Could he see her legs trembling? Uncomfortable with the silence, she shifted her gaze away.

It was definitely night in the Everglades. Little light to see the snakes and alligators until they were right up on you. She shivered, sweating at the same time. God help her.

Antonio sat in front of her, on some kind of metal box. He looked fit, rather muscular and lean. If she ran toward the flap he'd probably be on top of her in less than two steps. Besides, there were other men outside. And Dallas to consider. "Fine. Where is this rescue going to take place?"

"In Cuba."

"Cuba?" Her idea of hell. "That's it. I'm done." She took off for the opening, almost diving in her haste. Stumbling and half bent over, she managed three steps when his arms came from behind and wrapped her into a bear hug. With one leg, he swept her feet out from under her, the momentum pitching her forward. Her knees hit the ground, but he used his own body to stop her from face-planting. Then, in a huff, he twisted his body so his back hit the ground first, taking the impact. He quickly rolled them both over, forcing the air out of her lungs as he settled atop her. He had the power, but he wasn't hurting her. She was sure that was on purpose. It's the *why* she wasn't as sure of.

"Stop," he growled into her ear. "I don't want to harm you." Instead of violence, he seemed to lean into her with a controlled firmness, as if he still held much of his weight and anger in check.

Her stomach fluttered.

"The swamp is a dangerous place at night," he said.

"I can't breathe." Shivering again despite the humidity, she wiggled and adjusted her body beneath his, but moving only made it more difficult to breathe.

He pressed into her, his long body like a rock wall. "Even if you managed to get away, where are you going to run?"

There had to be a road somewhere, right?

"You're in the middle of nowhere, unarmed, and surrounded by gators, snakes and panthers."

And kidnappers.

"If you stay, you won't be hurt."

Her pulse rocked the side of her neck, and she became very much aware of his long legs wrapping her in a human cage. He didn't have an ounce of fat on him.

"And it's about to storm like hell." His breath fanned softly against her neck.

"Get off me." Pushing against him, she used as much strength as she could muster, but she barely budged him. "And I promise I'll listen." She forced the words out in short puffs. Her breath stilled. Something hardened against her hip. *Oh, Jesus.* Panic flooded her, and she bucked.

In a flash, he rolled to one side, but kept a hand clamped around one of her wrists, his breathing fast and loud enough to hear.

Her lungs expanded until it burned. "This is crazy," she spat as she sat up. "I'm not going back to Cuba. Ever."

His grip on her tightened. "I understand your hatred for our country."

"Your country, maybe. Not mine." She attempted to scoot away.

His grip tightened, but not enough to actually cause her pain. Interesting how he could control himself like this. Holding her, but not hurting her.

Still, she jerked against his show of power, her gaze scurrying around again.

"We'll be in and out quickly."

"Right." She snorted, and then covered her mouth with

her free hand, heat rushing into her face. "I meant *I won't* be able to get into Cuba quickly. Even with all the changes and loosening of travel restrictions, I'm still a reporter, and the Cuban government still controls who *reports* in the country."

A flash of lightning illuminated the tent, slapping harsh shadows across Antonio's face, but even the hard light couldn't mask his striking features.

Jesus. His pupils are so black. Maybe it was just the dim light. Either way, his eyes only made him look sexy. Strange that she would be thinking that in light of what he was putting her through.

The ominous rumble of thunder followed, vibrating through her. She had to get through to him. "Look, even if I wanted to go to Cuba, and I want you to understand that *I don't,* my family members were not friends of the government. So forget it. I'll never get an entry visa as a working member of the media."

She paused, her gaze memorizing his defined cheekbones and prominent nose so she could eventually give police an accurate description. He was almost too good-looking to believe he could be a bad guy. She looked away knowing that thought wouldn't help the police. Or her.

"You're not going to need a visa for this mission." His fingers dug into her flesh, dragging her attention back to him. "We're going in undercover."

"If we go in *illegally* and we're caught, you will be hurting me. We could go to prison. It doesn't matter that Cuba and the U.S. are all of a sudden making nice." Then a harsher reality punched her in the gut. "We could be killed. Used as an example, or we could just disappear." She tried to plead with her eyes. "Please tell me you don't believe all those recent photo ops out of Cuba. The government there still isn't cooperating. It needs our help but isn't willing to *really* change its ways to get it."

"I know."

Her throat tightened. "And you still want to go?" *He's crazy.*

"I've got no choice." His chest rose and fell as if he'd just run an obstacle course. "I have to rescue…my sister."

His sister. The hesitation in his voice, the soft, tortured way he'd said those two words, connected with something deep in her core. Someone he loved was trapped on that poor, isolated island, which time and former allies had all but forgotten. She was sorry for that. Could even relate to his pain. But she wasn't going to help him. She could lose too much. Everything she and her mother had spent a lifetime working toward. And then there was her father.

Words boiled up and burst free before she could swallow them. "I'll never go back. Those government bastards killed my dad. Just for what he believed in and had the courage to say out loud in public. For telling the damn truth." Hot tears burned her eyes. "Damn it." Flushed and paralyzed at having shared a secret she'd held so tightly inside with this stranger, she rolled her lips inward and pressed them together, determined not to let more details slip out.

Despite the rush of blood through her veins, she fought to sit still. The tent became so quiet she could hear footsteps outside and feel the buzzing of a mosquito whizzing by her ear. A hissing sound, and then another flash of lightning lit up the tent. She jerked back. Scary shadows danced across the siding.

"What makes you think your father is dead?" Antonio finally asked.

Thunder rattled the tent poles.

What the hell was he talking about? "My mother told me the Cuban government killed my *papi*." He'd been a hero, jailed, tortured, and murdered because he spoke out against political atrocities, and because he believed in free speech and a free press. Her mother wouldn't have lied to her about *that*. That truth had been the foundation on which she'd built her entire career.

"I have proof your father is alive and still living in Havana."

Her heart skipped. *What?* Antonio couldn't have dazed her more if he'd thrown a left into her chin. She couldn't breathe. The air was suffocating her like a thick, warm blanket. She studied him. Years as a journalist had taught her to assess and sum up people's veracity quickly. He didn't look away. He didn't fidget. He didn't wring his hands.

As Antonio's words settled in, despair slowly transformed into hope. Her heart picked up its pace. Her father might still be alive. *Alive!* She might actually get a chance to meet him. "Show me the proof."

He let go of her wrist and sat back, a slight rise to his left eyebrow.

He must have known his words would paralyze her. She couldn't run now, even if her life really did depend on it. She *had* to know the truth. If her *papi* still lived, why hadn't he tried to contact her at least once in twenty-six years? She bit her lip. Maybe her *papi* was still imprisoned?

As a kid, she'd worn a fatherless child's insignificance like a dirtied coat off the rack of their neighborhood Goodwill. She'd spent years shedding that feeling of worthlessness.

A ball of emotion lodged in her throat. If she could find a solid object, she would launch it at the stranger, hurting him for bringing all these buried emotions back to the surface, raw and blistering.

And yet he was also offering her the possibility of a new future, one that could erase the hurt of her past. If her father still lived, if he was a prisoner of the Cuban government all these years, she could find and rescue him, maybe even bring him to America now that the two countries were trading prisoners. Her life story could become one of her greatest news stories.

"Here's the deal, Rebecca." Antonio's smug voice signaled his confidence.

He knew she'd take his bait. Instantly, she hated him for his arrogance.

A knowing smile played on his lips. "I get your cooperation in exchange for my information."

Chapter Three

The reporter was staring at him like a caged animal on the verge of a breakdown. Her long, dark brown hair fell partly over her flushed face, and her full lips remained partly open, and fuck if she didn't look sexy. He looked away, annoyed by another unexpected physical rush of attraction.

He had to focus on the plan. She hadn't known her father was alive. That he was sure of. Should give her a good reason to work with him in Cuba without being a pain in his ass.

He studied her again and watched hate flash in her eyes. *Good*. He'd expected as much. In fact, he was counting on it. Hate, he knew well. He could deal with it. Made it easier to predict a person's actions.

Lightning lit up the tent. He counted to five before the roll of thunder followed. *Damn it*. He glanced at the buckling tent flap. The storm was approaching faster than he'd anticipated. He still had work to do outside.

Rebecca hadn't jumped at the lightning this time, but she did pull her legs to her chest. She was resting her chin on her knees with her eyes closed, rocking back and forth, her lips moving like she was talking to herself.

He clenched his fists as a wave of regret slugged him. He didn't want to cause any woman this kind of emotional distress, and he certainly would not physically hurt her, but leaders did what leaders had to despite the toll it took on others. He looked away. *I'm not watching this. She's going to cry.* If she didn't hate him now, she'd want to kill him when this trip was over.

Another burst of brightness lit up the tent. He had wanted to be on the road to Miami before dawn, but none of them would be going anywhere in this weather. So he leaned back against the storage unit he'd set up in the center of the tent, letting his gaze drift slowly over his "guest."

Rebecca's eyebrows bunched together, and her lips rolled inward as if processing the bomb of unexpected information he'd launched at her.

She was skinnier than she looked on TV. Fragile even. He hoped she could endure the rugged terrain and lack of basic necessities required to accomplish his mission. They weren't going to be staying at the Ritz.

She opened her eyes, and her gaze locked onto his. Despite the darkness, despite the distance, they connected. Something in his center shifted. There was a question mark in those big dark eyes, like she knew she shouldn't trust him. *Smart girl.* "Okay." Her voice sounded firm and resolved. "Tell me what you know about my father."

Okay? He looked back at her, surprised she'd gotten on board so easily. *Maybe she's bullshitting me.*

She wiped the back of her hand across her nose and mouth and then squared her shoulders. Okay, so she was probably pretending to be brave and unaffected. *That's good.* She was a decent actress.

"Tell me about my father."

"Not yet. But to prove to you I'm not playing around..." He pulled a picture from the right pocket of his jacket. "This is a recent photo of your father." He leaned toward her, holding the picture out, holding his breath.

"A picture of the man you *think* is my father isn't proof." Rebecca reached for it.

Antonio jerked the photo away from her. "This man is your father." She had to understand who was boss here. "Does the name Arturo Menendez Garcia mean anything to you?" Antonio dangled the picture just out of her reach. "This is him, and there's no denying your blood connection. You're his spitting image."

Rebecca seized the photo, bringing it close.

He reached into the storage unit behind him and pulled out a lantern. "You'll strain your eyes." With the twist of a switch, artificial light filled the tent. Antonio wanted Rebecca to see the similarities, like the shape of their dark eyes, the same full lips, high cheekbones, and thick hair.

She squinted. Blinking a couple of times, she held the picture at arm's length. Her eyebrows snapped together. "This is all the proof you have?"

Are you kidding? She had to see the resemblance. "You're the reporter. When we get to Cuba, you find more proof. Or find him. If you're good enough to track him down."

Her eyes narrowed. "Finding him has to be part of the deal." Rebecca's shoulders flew back, but she held her facial features in check.

She had a poker face. Important, if they were to succeed. Antonio cleared his throat, a guilty taste lingering in his mouth. He knew so much more, details she wouldn't want to hear about her dad. He hated these kinds of games. And he really had no desire to damage her. He just needed her. It could be no one else.

He was going to rescue his sister with this reporter's help, or die trying. It was time.

Another yellow stab of light exploded outside the tent.

South Florida thunderstorms always kicked up the earthiness of the Everglades. The aroma of damp dirt and burning wood smelled like home to him. The air was so heavy now he knew it was only a matter of minutes before the skies would burst with the weight of the rain. He had to get moving.

"You picked me because of my father?" She waved the picture at him. "You thought *this* would blackmail me into doing something illegal and stupid?"

A thunderous explosion followed. But it wasn't the sound that jacked up his blood pressure. "I know you don't give a damn about freeing my sister," he yelled above the storm, "but I thought you'd at least be curious about your father. Don't you wonder why your mother lied to you about him for twenty-six years?"

"What are you talking about?"

Antonio's shoulders tightened. He drew them back when her expression didn't change. "If I were to believe all those stories you put on the news, I'd believe you were an advocate for the abused and needy." He shook his head, looking away from her. "I should have known you'd never risk ruining your picture-perfect life for a cause greater than your own well-being."

"Listen, Antonio."

He detested the way she addressed him in such a familiar way. Like she *knew* him. She did not. "So, that show of compassion is just for the TV cameras?" They had nothing in common. She was a spoiled American. And the way she was shaking her head at him reminded him of one of his high school teachers who used to address him as if he were just a worthless, stupid Spanish-speaking illegal immigrant. His blood pressure rocketed up another notch. He clenched his fists and took a long, deep breath trying to force down his growing contempt.

"You're like so many Cuban exiles I know," she continued. "Your heart is scarred by hatred, and that's affected your judgment. We can document your mission, but it's not going to change a damn thing. Don't fool yourself."

He shot to his feet, hesitating, trying to keep his anger in check. "Don't insult me or my mission." He kept his voice controlled.

She still flinched.

He wasn't going to grab her again. He detested violence and what it could do to women. He'd warned Ignado not to ever be that physical with the reporter again. "I know what I'm doing. I'm not trying to bring democracy to Cuba." But he had to win Rebecca over, convince her to help him, willingly. "I just want freedom for my sister."

Rebecca stood slowly. "If we follow your plan, we're not going into Cuba as *tourists*, Antonio. And even though the U.S. is kissing Castro's ass right now, the government over there will shoot us if they feel threatened. Don't you get that? They're still *Communists* dressed in *Socialists'* clothing. That has *not* changed."

So, she did feel passion about the politics of their home country. But her insulting tone was forcing his body temperature up. He had to get out before he did something he'd regret.

He stormed toward the exit, but out of the corner of his eye, he caught her blanching. Was that out of fear of him, or fear of being left alone in the swamp with a nasty storm on top of them? He reached for the flap.

"Okay, okay. Wait." Her voice raised a notch. "Tell me about your sister."

Antonio took deep breaths, staring at the flap. He should leave. The blood was still launching through his body, extra adrenaline making his muscles tingle. He forced himself to inhale and exhale until he felt his heart rate slow down. Taking his time, he turned and walked back to where he'd been before. He had to be in control here. Letting emotions rule was dangerous. Staring into the ground, he sat down, attempting to compose himself, waiting until she took a seat as well.

When he sensed his body temperature dip back to normal and the tension leave his shoulders, he looked up at her.

She was staring at him with her mouth wide open.

Good. He'd gotten her attention. Now she knew how much control he actually had. How disciplined he'd become. Maybe she'd respect that. "My sister is about your age." *And she used to be as feisty. Now she's just beaten down.* "She still lives on the family farm where I was born in a little town about fifty minutes south of Havana called Güira de Melena. My family used to own our farm, about eight acres, until the revolution. Castro's government took ownership of our land. Now they own everything and allow my family to work what used to be their soil. In return for that *privilege*, the government takes most of what we grow."

"*We* grow?" Rebecca asked.

He admired her intelligence and the way she was not afraid to speak her mind. But right now the way her eyebrows were arching was pissing him off.

"You speak as if *you* still own that land."

He withheld the razor-sharp comment on the tip of his tongue. *Concentrate on the plan.* "My sister is beautiful." He paused, wondering if he should share all of his thoughts. The reporter reminded him a lot of his sister. Even though he hadn't seen Maria for over ten years, he'd seen pictures, and his sister's letters used to have the same feistiness and determination he'd witnessed so far in the reporter. They were both exotic and beautiful. And at times, vulnerable. If he had met Rebecca under different circumstances... Not good to go there.

"And?" Rebecca regarded him shrewdly.

"And the head of the local CDR is in love with her. He wants to marry her." The muscles in Antonio's jaw tightened.

"Antonio."

He lifted a hand to stop her. He could tell by the pity in Rebecca's eyes that whatever she was about to say would only piss him off more. "My sister tells me she can't go anywhere without someone in the CDR watching her and reporting back."

Rebecca's back straightened. "What's the CDR? Reporting back to whom?"

"The Committee for the Defense of the Revolution." Damn, she should already know this. Antonio exhaled, shaking his head. So much time had passed, and the younger generation of Cuban Americans did not care enough to learn the details of their country's history. He was counting on Rebecca to help him change that. "The CDR members report counterrevolutionary activity to the government. The leader of each neighborhood CDR has to know the activities of each person on their block or in their section of town."

"They still do that secretive, Big Government kind of stuff?" She shrugged, then shook her head. "Not surprised." She glanced at him with real concern in her eyes. "So, how does that affect your sister?"

"A report from the CDR can be the difference between freedom and persecution. Basically, they're the neighborhood snitches. And this Communist bastard is trying to *persuade* my sister to marry him. If she doesn't, it's been implied the whole family will suffer."

The reporter cocked her head like she couldn't believe what he was saying. Maybe Rebecca wasn't a real Cuban. Looking at her dirtied designer clothes and her ridiculous high heels, he turned away. American elitist. Disappointment rushed through him. Maybe that's all she was.

"Why doesn't your sister just book a damn flight and leave? Travel restrictions have loosened."

"It's not as easy as your news reports make it look." At least her curiosity was still intact. That would help him achieve his goal.

"Meaning?"

"Your friend who had her face burned off."

"You know her?"

"I know what happened to her."

"And that's what's happening to your sister?"

"That's what could happen to my sister if we don't get her out. You of all people know that a woman who is the victim of domestic violence can't just 'book a flight and leave.'"

"So, what's your plan?" she asked. "How do you expect to smuggle us onto the island with all our camera gear? You know how much the Cuban government loves the American media."

Antonio resented her sarcastic tone. "I'll make that happen." He ground his teeth. He was trying to keep it professional, but she wasn't making it easy. Antonio preferred to work alone for this very reason. "You speak the language, know a little bit about the country." *Not nearly enough.* "You look like our people, and you'll blend in. Then, when the time is right, you'll capture the abuse and the rescue so no one misunderstands. I want the world to know I'm not taking my sister against her will. I'm not the criminal here. Even if people won't believe me, video does not lie."

Rebecca took a deep breath and folded her hands as if in prayer, touching the top of her fingers to her nose. "Why the big show in kidnapping me?" She pressed a hand to her stomach. "Why did your goons have to grab me so violently, and so publicly? Surely you know police are already looking for me. My TV station will make me the lead story."

Exactly. "You wouldn't have come to Cuba willingly."

"No."

"And I knew that. Kidnapping you in public was all part of the plan." He pointed a finger her way. "This kidnapping will get the public fired up. Your TV station will *continue* to make you the lead story. The headlines have already started. I've read a few online. Want to hear them? *Kidnapped Correspondent. Menendez Missing.* There's already a ten-thousand-dollar reward for information leading to your whereabouts. Everyone wants to know who kidnapped the pretty TV news reporter and why. If there's no other breaking news, cable TV will keep your story as the lead, and they'll show your kidnapping instead of the staged video ops of American tourists arriving in Cuba, like it's fucking Jamaica or the Cayman Islands.

"The cops are already looking for you, but they started locally. My plan was to be out of the country tonight. The storms have delayed us, but not for long. We'll leave Miami by early tomorrow morning on a private yacht out of a private marina. As soon as we're in Cuba, I'll let you drop your media friends a few hints. That will keep you the lead story until we return. Then you can show them the truth of what's still going on in Cuba once the video ops are over."

Rebecca's mouth fell open, but her eyes shone with what looked like a new found respect.

A sense of accomplishment swept over him.

"You know a lot about how the media work. You've spent a lot of time thinking about this, haven't you?"

"Every single day of my adult life." If she only knew how hard this desire drove him, she'd find a way to break free. So his obsession didn't break her, too.

Instead she nodded, two fingers covering her lips.

"When we get back, the whole country will be dying to hear everything you have to say. They'll be hungry for all the video you have to show." *And my family will finally be together and free.* Antonio watched as the look in her eyes changed from reluctant admiration to annoyed realization.

"And you expect me to spoon-feed them *your* version of the story. What if things really *are* better in Cuba now that

Obama's loosened restrictions?"

"I expect you to do your job." She wasn't getting what he was all about. He'd always been a firm believer in the truth. "Document what happens and report *what you see*. Do that, and you'll be a big star." Antonio paused, watching her shake her head and look away. "That is what you want, isn't it, Rebecca?" She seemed a bit put off by that simple truth, but weren't most TV journalists somewhat vain and ambitious? He was counting on her drive to play in his favor.

She bit her bottom lip and stared at him. Her big eyes bored into him with such force he almost looked away again, uncomfortable from the effect she had on him. She was making him feel guilty. *Damn it.*

"I'll do this on one condition."

Like she had a choice at this point. She was too valuable to his mission. The reporter was coming to Cuba whether she agreed to or not. But he'd play along. For now. "Let's hear your condition." He preferred to have her and her photographer's compliance rather than continue to force them at gunpoint. Another stroke of lightning flashed outside, making her jump. The angry growl of thunder followed fast on its tail. Antonio glanced at the door. The tent siding bucked repeatedly.

"First, I want to know everything you know about my father, including where he is in Cuba." Rebecca turned her gaze back to the picture. "And before we find your sister and document her rescue, you have to lead me to my dad."

His stomach hardened. *You have no idea how long I've waited to face that man. He murdered my father.* "If I can."

"Oh, you can. And you will, or we don't have a deal."

Antonio smiled at her bravado, but a sense of gloom tugged at him.

"Secondly, I want a guarantee of our safety."

He raised his eyebrows at that. "I thought you said *one* condition." He couldn't stop himself from scoffing. "I can't promise your safety." He pushed himself off the ground and turned to open the storage unit. "I can't even guarantee that for myself or my men. The plan *is* dangerous. And I have no idea what to expect. Haven't been back to Cuba since…well, awhile." He thought he had stored rain gear in there.

She made a rustling sound.

What the hell was she up to now? He turned, waders thrown over his forearm and boots in one hand. She stood right in front of him, chest puffed up and heaving again. He smelled the faintest hint of jasmine coming off her. The combination of her courage and her scent aroused a curious sensation in him. He ground his teeth, irritated that she could attract and distract him like this. It had never happened before. He prided himself on being the most disciplined of men.

"I'm talking about our safety among your group." Rebecca's hand flew to point at the tent flap. "I don't want me or Dallas to be threatened by your men. Especially by that big tattooed guy. He hurt me." She rubbed her neck.

"Ignado?" Antonio nodded. "I've already told him to stop." He couldn't resist adding, "But you can't provoke him. He has a short fuse. As for your photographer, he's a big man. I imagine he can take care of himself."

She rolled her eyes.

That kind of disrespect would have to stop.

"And I get exclusive rights to all video we shoot while in Cuba," Rebecca said. "You don't own it. You don't even touch it."

He couldn't believe the size of her cojones. "You don't have that kind of bargaining power."

"Oh, I think I do." She raised her chin. "Or I wouldn't be here in the Everglades, in this pup tent on steroids, talking to you about some insane plan. You do need me. So don't play games. And I want to contact my news director and let him know what's going on. I want at least one person here in the

United States to know where we are and what we're doing. I'll make him promise not to report that fact until we're out of the country."

"That is not happening. At least not right now. And let's not forget who's the *comandante*." He'd taken her cell phone earlier while she'd been unconscious. Let her try to call anyone. Antonio stuck out the hand not holding his gear. "You've got a deal."

Rebecca hesitated, looking down at his outstretched hand as if the answer were scribbled in ink somewhere on his flesh. When she looked up at him, he didn't see conviction in her eyes, but she verbally committed. "Deal."

Good. He was glad she'd agreed to document his sister's rescue. He would have hated to force her to comply. The cameraman, too, although once the young man had calmed down, he'd made it clear he was going wherever his reporter was going. They were close friends. That was obvious. Better to have them both on board.

A quick slap of light, followed immediately by a thunderous explosion, startled her. She reached out and grabbed his extended hand, maybe to steady herself, maybe out of fear, but the unexpected connection sent electricity shooting through his fingers and up his arm. What the fuck was going on? He'd never had this kind of visceral reaction to a woman he'd just met. *Get a grip.* In his haste to end that powerful contact, he dropped his gear. He leaped back, breaking their connection. "I've got to go."

She tensed. "Go where?"

"I need to take care of a few things." Antonio leaned down and grabbed his stuff, trying to avoid her eyes. "You'll be safe in here." But as he strode out of the tent, he knew that neither one of them would be safe until they got in and out of Cuba—

alive.

Chapter Four

Rebecca jerked awake.

Her head was throbbing at a jackhammer's pace. What the hell was that noise? It sounded like engines grinding. She rubbed her eyes. Where the heck was she *now*?

Engines grinding? Boat engines. On a boat heading to Cuba. *Cuba! Holy shit*. She pushed herself into a sitting position. *The mission has begun*. She was one step closer to meeting her father.

How the hell had she fallen asleep? Once they'd left the marina in Miami, Antonio had disappeared topside on the yacht. One he'd left, Dawg, who had joined them on the way to Miami, had recounted his memory of their abduction, including Dawg being tossed into the van right after her. But the big guy hadn't been physically hurt, and once on the yacht, he'd gone to the galley looking for food for them both.

After eating crackers and cheese, she'd finally been able to relax. The boat had rocked in a lazy, comforting rhythm. She remembered resting her head on a pillow on the couch in the salon, swearing it would only be for a minute. She remembered nothing after that.

"Antonio, *ven aquí*."

The tattooed man's voice. Rebecca faced the cabin door. That jerk must be on the top deck, too, because that's where his voice was coming from.

"We've got people on our dock."

What did that mean? *Crap.* Had they been discovered already? She jumped up, grabbing on to a counter as the cruiser swayed unexpectedly to one side. She hung on and shuffled toward the open doorway. Her stomach somersaulted in anticipation. She couldn't wait to see where they'd landed. They were really in Cuba, the "forbidden" land. At least, still forbidden to her. Before her mother had died, she had forced Rebecca to promise that as long as a Castro was alive and in charge, Rebecca would never visit Cuba. For any reason.

"*No disparen!*"

Rebecca froze. *Hold your fire?* That was Antonio's voice. Oh dear Lord, they'd been caught by Cuban police? Her heart skipped.

Tiptoeing onto the deck—she'd escape and make her own way home if she had to—a layer of wet heat smacked her cheeks and assaulted her body. *Better than a bullet.* The glare of a full moon threw a blanket of light on a rocky shoreline and a rickety pier that reminded her of the gnarled fingers of an aging woman. *This can't be Havana?*

"*Mantengan sus manos adonde las puedo ver!*"

Keep your hands where I can see them. Her gaze shot in the direction of Ignado's voice. Standing straight as a rod, the tattooed man held a black revolver in front of him. She swallowed, her gaze darting down the line of his intended fire. On the dock below them, a young man and two young women stood, hands in the air like victims in a James Bond movie.

The young people, who were bathed in the glow of a

large flashlight beam, couldn't have been more than eighteen or nineteen years old. They wore dirty, mismatched clothes and their sweat and mud-streaked faces were animated with wide-eyed fear. One of the women held on to a toddler, who sucked his thumb, blinking into the blinding light.

No telling what that asshole Ignado would do. Her heart rocked with fear for all of them.

"Turn off that light," Antonio ordered. Rebecca whipped around to find him, but the light clicked off instantly, and a strange, anxiety-filled silence hung over the group. The tiny hairs on her arms prickled.

The toddler started to wail with such desperation it brought tears to Rebecca's eyes. She wanted to comfort the kid, and shut him up, but she feared his mother might be packing a weapon, too.

"How do we know the kids aren't armed, Antonio?" Ignado, switching back to English, echoed her thoughts.

"They're *kids*." Antonio stomped across the deck. She could tell by the vibrations on the flooring that he was coming closer to her.

She started to tremble.

"Amigo, even kids kill to survive," Ignado grumbled.

"Not here, they don't." That was the same dismissive tone Antonio had used on her earlier. His footsteps stopped a few feet away.

She took short, shallow breaths and prayed she wasn't breathing too loudly. She didn't want to give away her fear.

"We're not going to hurt you." Antonio spoke to the teenagers in Spanish. "Be on your way."

No answer, but the toddler abruptly stopped screaming as if one of the young women had slapped a hand across his mouth.

At the same time, Rebecca felt fingers dig deep into her upper arm. "Holy shit." She jumped, spooked by the unexpected touch from behind her.

"I can't believe this shit."

It was Dallas. She blew out a breath. "Dawg, you scared me." She placed a hand over her heart. "I'm having enough trouble breathing right now."

"Look, I've traveled to Afghanistan and Haiti, but this time I don't think I have a damn pulse any more." Dallas stuck out his wrist. "Check me. Check me."

She smiled and pressed his right wrist. "You're still alive."

"We in Cuba, right?" He made a show of stepping up next to her and putting his hand over his eyes as if searching for something. "Where's Fidel? Where's Raul? Don't bring me Elian."

Rebecca laughed despite herself. "Thank God you're with me. I'd be having a heart attack right now. Instead, I'm laughing." Dallas always knew when she was anxious and used his humor to calm her nerves.

"Even if they hadn't convinced me with a gun pointed at my big head, this photographer wouldn't have let them take you alone."

She believed him. Dawg always said they were like butt cheeks. Always stuck together. She smiled. "Did you get a chance to call the news director?"

"Hell no. They took my iPhone."

"Mine too." So, no one, no one, knew where she and Dallas were. "This has to be Cuba, right? But this can't be Havana." All she could make out in the early-morning darkness was a shoreline of twisting trees and palms. Where were the hotels and buildings she remembered from pictures of Havana?

The angry bellow of an animal erupted from the darkness, sending new pinpricks of worry down her spine.

"What the hell was *that*? Sounds like something out of the zombie apocalypse," Dallas stated. Then, pursing his lips, he said, "We're dead."

"A buol." Now that was a voice Rebecca didn't recognize. The answer came from below, so it had to be the boy on the dock. He spoke English with a heavy Spanish accent.

"A bull?" Without thinking, she responded in Spanish. "As in a *farm* animal? At the beach?"

"What, we running with the bulls now?" Dallas asked.

"Shut up. Both of you." Ignado stomped his foot, vibrating the deck, and heightening Rebecca's fear that he'd redirect his weapon her way. "Now."

Ignado was such a bully. She knew from experience there was only one way to stop a bully. "You can't tell me what to do." She barely made out the tattooed man's form, but could tell he still had his gun pointed at the kids on the dock. "You don't control me."

Dallas suddenly shuffled away. A draft of warm air pressed up against Rebecca.

"But I do." The empty space filled up instantly with Antonio's larger-than-life form. "And you *will* listen to me."

Oh boy. She flipped around to face him. "W-what's going on here, Antonio?" She could swear he was grinding his teeth, but it was hard to tell in the moonlit night. She took a step back.

"I'll let you know as soon I know," he growled.

Antonio had pulled his hair back into a tight ponytail, slick and wet, as if he'd just gotten out of the shower. In tight black jeans and a short-sleeved black T-shirt, tonight he looked more pirate than revolutionary. A gorgeous one at that. Her breath caught in her lungs, and she dropped her gaze, suddenly conscious she was staring. "I should be documenting this." Out of habit, Rebecca placed a hand on his arm. The *touch*, as she called it, usually won over reluctant interviewees. "Isn't that why you brought me with you?" Another spark of energy jumped between them.

Antonio jerked away with such force, she stumbled backward.

"I brought you with me to document my sister's rescue. Not this." He gestured toward the dock below.

"Why not?" Rebecca stood taller. "*This* is part of the problem, isn't it? Your sister can't simply fly to America out of Havana because the government won't grant her an exit visa. Right? Because of her abusive boyfriend?"

He didn't respond.

"So, despite all the real or fake pleasantries between our countries now, she and these kids are still reluctant residents here." She turned and walked to the cruiser's railing, leaning over for a better view of the kids on the dock below. "Even though restrictions on travel from Cuba are lessening, for your sister, stealing away in the middle of the night like these kids are doing would be her only alternative, right? Which is why we came here. To help her escape, safely." She searched for Dallas. He was standing on the deck to her left. "Flip on your camera light for a second."

The stark white spotlight landed on the kids' boat, which was tied loosely to the other side of the dock, banging back and forth in the white-tipped waves. "Your sister would have sailed off in…" Rebecca squinted. "What is that? That thing won't make it to America." The vessel couldn't have been more than twenty-some feet long, and only four feet high, with no seats inside. Where the hell were these kids going to sit for hours in the hot sun while they crossed the Florida Straits? Why risk their lives? Now that the two governments were getting along? They were crazy. Or desperate. What could possibly be that bad here in Cuba that these young people would chance death to escape? Her chest ached at that thought. But the answer would make a great news story, especially now. And she could be the voice for these people. Probably the only way they'd ever be heard.

The boat looked like it was made out of wood and aluminum. It had a big engine in the middle and some long tubing extending to the back of the boat. Definitely handmade by someone. It would surely sink before it made it out of Cuban waters. "Antonio." She turned back to face him. "One of these girls could be your sister."

"Turn off the light." The way Antonio emphasized each word left no doubt he was trying to control his anger.

She swallowed, remembering she wasn't in Tampa anymore, making ballsy decisions to get the news, knowing no one would get hurt. Ignado was armed. Defying Antonio longer in front of his crew would be risky. "Okay. Turn it off, Dallas." She spun around and stepped closer. "That's not even a real boat."

"Etts a real boat." The same kid who answered her question about the bull spoke again. Even with his heavy Spanish accent, Rebecca recognized indignation in the young Cuban's voice. Maybe the kid made the boat himself? *Wow.*

The reporter in her took over. She had to take the risk to get this once-in-a-lifetime story. Surely Ignado wouldn't shoot her in front of witnesses. With Dallas shooting video. Right? She gestured for Dallas to follow her off the yacht. They'd stumbled onto a gold mine. She'd never actually seen a video of young Cubans making their escape from Cuba. Didn't think they had to do this anymore. But maybe that had all been political propaganda on the Cuban side. Because why else would these young people be here, so willing to risk everything to flee? The questions began lining up in her mind, one right after another. "How'd you make the boat?"

"From parts at *mi abuelo*'s farm, and pipes I bought from a local farmer." The kid beat on his chest with one fist.

"Antonio," Ignado growled.

Rebecca flinched.

"What the hell is she doing? This isn't the time for an

interview. I should have killed you, you stupid bitch."

Her mouth went dry, but she ignored the bully and continued questioning the boy. "And the motor?" The kid was shaking, poor thing. *Her* hands were shaking, too. She gestured for Dallas to flip on his camera light. She laced her fingers together and squeezed them to better control her nerves. Would Ignado really hurt her in front of Antonio and these kids?

"Already rolling," Dallas said. "Don't need the light." He moved in front of the young boy. "We've got night vision. It'll be grainy video, but viewable, and I don't want to give our position away, know what I'm sayin'?"

"At least one American is thinking." Ignado's voice shook with anger, but the hands holding the revolver were still as lake water.

The tattooed guy had nerves of ice.

Antonio reached out and forced Ignado's arm down. "Put down the gun and start the unloading process. I've got this."

By "this" Rebecca assumed Antonio meant her. Bristling, she knew he'd try to shut down her interview next. She turned to the kid, taking the handheld microphone Dallas held out. "My name is Rebecca. I'm a journalist from the United States. I'm here to do a story on why citizens like you still need to go to these extremes to leave Cuba, while our countries tell everyone they're repairing their broken relationship and allowing more residents to travel back and forth."

"*Por favor, no converse con ella.*" The skinny woman, with the toddler in her grip, hissed in barely audible Spanish. "*Ni una palabra.*"

"*Que te preocupas?*" Rebecca asked the woman what she was afraid of and why she was instructing the boy not to speak to her. She held the microphone in her direction, but the mother cast her eyes downward and wouldn't respond.

The toddler, however, started to snivel again.

"*Mi nombre es* Domingo." The boy beside her puffed up, ignoring the toddler's distress. He wore, ironically, an iconic American T-shirt, a size too small. The Nike swoosh was almost washed out, but the words "Just do it" were still readable. "The only thing I'm afraid of is never being able to leave Cuba."

Those words resonated in her gut. Up close to him, she saw that the young boy was unusually skinny, with elbow and wrist bones that protruded awkwardly from sticklike arms. His dark hair was shorn unevenly around his forehead as if he'd cut his hair himself. She wondered if Dallas's video would be able to pick up those unique markings on this specific kid at this particular moment in his life. They'd help tell the story without her uttering a single word.

The dock shook suddenly. She reached for Dallas to keep from stumbling. The weight of Antonio's body landed right behind her, throwing her further off balance. He didn't have to jump to get her attention. She knew he was there.

"You have five minutes, and we're moving on." Antonio's breath brushed her cheek. "This is not safe, you understand me," he hissed. "Why do you think these kids chose the middle of the night to walk miles through the woods to get here?"

He had a good point. There's no way she would have done the same thing.

"There's a military base nearby in Mariel." Antonio grabbed her arm with enough force to remind her who was calling the shots here. "We make too much noise, and you'll be conducting interviews with the cockroaches in a military jail cell."

She shivered. "Got it." She jerked away from his hold. "Shouldn't you be unloading our supplies, so we're not stuck out here like sitting ducks?"

He pursed his lips and widened his stance. "Ask your questions. But make it quick."

Geez, he acted like a government watchdog himself. Fine, she'd get on with the interview. Under his suspicious gaze. *Whatever.*

"So, you made the boat yourself, Domingo?" she asked again in Spanish, swatting a mosquito off her shoulder.

She could sense the pride in the boy's eyes as he turned and gazed at his vessel. "I built it in me shed in de woods with no power tools or electricity. Took fifteen days." He answered in really bad English. Interesting. She wondered where he learned the language. Obviously, he'd been preparing for his trip.

"And the motor?" Not that she knew anything about boat motors, but this looked like nothing she'd seen, and it sat in the middle of the boat, not in the back. What was up with that?

"I used an old engine from a Honda."

"As in a *car* engine?"

"It's all I could find."

She'd heard Cubans had to be resourceful, but wow, she couldn't help but be impressed. She didn't know a single kid his age in America who could have created the same boat. She wanted to ask if he'd tested his invention in the water, but thought he'd find the question offensive. "How did you four get the boat here?"

"*Los toros.*"

The bulls. "Really? How did that work?"

"We put the boat on a trailer and the bulls pulled it."

"Because?" She followed with what was to her a logical question. "Wouldn't it have been easier to use a car to pull the trailer? And you could've taken a road."

"We can't be seen on the street."

Those words summed up so much. "If you all are so afraid

of getting caught, why didn't you run when we arrived?"

Domingo shrugged. "I knew you weren't Cuban."

"How?"

The sullen boy broke into a grin. "Your boat is too nice." His momentary playfulness vanished, and he put both hands on his hips. "We have come too far to go back." He lifted his chin at her.

"Why can't you just go home? Try again another day?"

"No money."

As he shuffled his feet against the top of the dock, she noticed that his tennis shoes were filthy and had holes in them. They were too dirty to distinguish the brand.

"It cost thirty thousand pesos to make me boat. If we don't go tonight, I lose me money. And that's why I can't just fly out to America. No one here has the money to buy a plane ticket."

"Thirty thousand pesos. What's that in American dollars?"

"About one thousand dollars." Antonio had been so quiet she'd almost forgotten he'd been eavesdropping right behind her. He leaned in and whispered against her ear, "That's not a lot of money to a rich, American woman. I bet you spend more than that on a single trip to the mall."

Or to rent a stupidly expensive evening gown to wear to an event aimed at raising money for the poor. Blushing, she refused to look Antonio's way.

"But for a Cuban kid, that kind of money is impossible to make, even in a year."

Okay. Antonio had drilled home his point. And she did feel guilty. She took a step away from Antonio, addressing the young man again. "So, if you can't afford a plane ticket, how did the four of you come up with a grand?"

"There are many more of us. I charge for coming on de boat."

The woman standing stiffly next to Domingo let out a slew of Spanish expletives that Rebecca knew would have made her blush had she recognized all of them. Her heart fluttered. Whoa, they'd hit a nerve. She glanced back to make sure Dallas was capturing all of this.

He nodded at her.

"I only see four of you." Glancing around, a chill shimmied down Rebecca's spine.

"There's twenty-three," Domingo gestured toward the woods.

Twenty-three? She looked where the kid pointed. They'd been silent throughout all of this? Were any of his friends armed?

A flashlight flipped on. She held her breath until she realized Antonio himself beamed the small light across the shoreline, moving it by the tree line in search of more faces. "Come out. We won't hurt you," he said in Spanish.

Slowly, the brush at the edge of the forest began to move, and Antonio's small light flitted across dark-skinned faces and bodies tangled within the vines and grass of the woods.

"Oh my God, there are so many of them." Rebecca scratched her head as she turned back to look at the handmade vessel rocking precariously against the dock. "These people aren't going to fit in that boat. They'll sink it if they all get on."

The light flipped off.

"What are you doing? Antonio? They need to see to make their way toward the dock." This was all way too dangerous and crazy.

"Your interview is over. Grab your backpack and gear and let's go."

Was he kidding? "Let's go?" He was just going to leave the kids here?

"That's right. If you don't grab the bag I packed for you,

you can leave with nothing but the clothes on your back. I don't care. That's all these kids have."

She threw her hands up. "You can't possibly be such an asshole."

In two steps, he was in front of her, pulling her into him, his voice in her ear. "Don't ever disrespect me that way again. Or…"

She stiffened.

"Or I'll toss you onto your friend Domingo's boat, and let him take you back to America."

Her heart clenched at the thought, knowing if she was forced onto that poor excuse for a boat she'd never make it back to America alive.

Chapter Five

"Señor, señor. We go now. *No violencia. No violencia.*"
Domingo's voice shook.

Antonio stilled, paused, and then gently pushed Rebecca
away from him. *Damn it.* If he continued on this track, he'd
be no better than the asshole who was abusing his sister.
He had to control his emotions better. But Rebecca had an
unexpected way of spiking his blood pressure and stirring up
unwanted feelings. He hadn't planned for that.

"I'm sorry." Rebecca held up both hands as if
surrendering. "I just...I'm scared and confused."

"About what?" Antonio growled at her. While he
admired her strong personality, he had to put some distance
between them, keep her aware of who was the boss here. Stay
in control. Of himself. And his reactions to her.

"Your intentions."

"What about them? They haven't changed." Where was
she going with this? "We're leaving."

"Fine." She gestured for Dallas to move back on board.
"So, basically your sister's life is worth more than the lives of

these twenty-three people."

Ah, that was her intent. To make him feel guilty. *Impressive.* It was working. She was actually making him stop to think before acting. And now he was thinking maybe she was right. These kids were willing to risk their lives for a reason. Maybe they weren't being abused as his sister was, but something bad was going on here, or they wouldn't be willing to take such a chance with their own existence. Antonio stopped suddenly.

Rebecca ran into his back.

"Damn you, Rebecca." He spun around to face her. *Damn you for reminding me of my moral compass.*

She took a step back. "Well, I just feel like we're playing God here."

He glared down at her, the full moon reflecting in her big brown eyes. Eyes he could get lost in if he allowed it. But he wouldn't.

"We came to Cuba to save a Cuban who wants to leave this country and come to America," she said. "But we're willing to walk away from all of these people who want to do the same, knowing they probably won't survive?" She swept a hand through her hair. "Are you telling me you can live with that?"

Antonio exhaled and paused, amazed at how silent the entire coastline had become. Only the hypnotic sound of the waves whipping against the shore and the constant banging of Domingo's pathetic boat disrupted the eerie silence.

He knew what he had to do. But it had taken Rebecca shaking him out of his zone of personal obsession to make him see it. No way in hell would he allow these kids to die if he had the power to prevent it. And he did. "I'll send the cruiser back to America right now, with all of them on board."

He thought he saw relief sweep over Rebecca's face. Hard to tell. He reached for her wrist. Her pulse was accelerating.

He bet the artery at the base of her neck was also throbbing. Something about the way he could affect her heart rate—as she affected his—excited him. Heat transferred from her skin to his, and he felt desire stir his center. *Jesus. Now was not the time.*

"No, wait." She pulled out of his grasp. "But don't *we* need the cruiser?" she objected.

"Isn't it obvious?" Antonio stepped back, taking a few deep breaths. "If I send *La Libertad* back with all of these kids on board, it won't be back to Cuba for another day, maybe longer, depending on weather conditions." He wondered if she picked up on the irony. He'd named his yacht *Freedom*.

She was blinking now, as if trying to clear an eyelash or maybe in this case, a bad thought. "But didn't you say that we were going to be here less than twenty-four hours?" She glanced at *La Libertad*, looking like she was anxious about letting her safety net motor away.

"In and out quickly, remember?" *Will she pass the test? And do what's right for the greater good?* An odd sense of hope filled him. While planning this mission, he'd prayed she would be the kind of woman who was brave enough to do the right thing, even if it meant risking her own personal safety. He was about to find out.

"And if the boat isn't here when we're finally ready to leave?" she asked.

"We wait."

Her gaze darted from *La Libertad* to the kids on the dock and back to him. "We'd wait here in the woods? And if we run into problems, we'd have no other way to escape, right?"

A backpack slammed against the deck. "Stop wasting your time with this bitch." Ignado hauled another backpack over his head and launched it at her.

She jumped out of the way as it crashed next to her. "Are

you crazy?"

This shit was going to have to stop. Right now. Or someone really was going to get hurt.

"The cruiser stays. We stick to the original plan." Ignado glared at Antonio. Moving swiftly, trying to tamp down the growing rage at Ignado's interruption, Antonio jumped from the dock to the deck of *La Libertad* and within seconds was up in Ignado's face, finger pointed. "Enough. You don't make that call." If Ignado defied him again, he'd leave him here to suffer the consequences of his hot temper and mean-spirited actions.

Dallas cleared his throat. "Oh, Vega, oh boy." Dallas pulled the camera off his shoulder. "That Cuban boy and his harem, they can take that thing they built and leave. Have you not seen the shit they float on to get to America? As long as it's got an engine and it's smoking, it can move. I think…"

"Rebecca is going to decide." Antonio interrupted Dallas. "If she wants me to send these people to America on *my* yacht, I will."

Rebecca's eyes popped wide. She was obviously shocked to learn he could own a yacht. Pride made him smirk. As far as she knew he had no job other than angry revolutionary. He was so much more. Maybe after this was all over, he'd get a chance to show her what he'd been able to accomplish. Him, the poor Cuban immigrant. Alone, without a family. God bless America. It was indeed the land of opportunity. This yacht of his cost over a hundred thousand dollars. And he'd bought it with cash. "If she wants *La Libertad* to stay docked here in case we run into trouble and need to leave immediately, it stays. The captain works for me. He'll do as *I* order."

The air escaped Rebecca's lungs in one long audible rush. She glanced at Dallas, who looked pissed off, with both hands over his face.

"Rebecca, Rebecca." Dallas sighed. "Girl, what are you? On a fever? You let that yacht leave and all we got is smoke signals if we need help. What we gonna do? Dance around like a bunch of Cuban Indians?"

This time Rebecca didn't laugh. Instead, she looked at Ignado, who was pacing back and forth. Finally, she looked at Domingo, who rocked the sniffling toddler in his skinny arms. "I refuse to play God. I think maybe we should take a vote," she whispered.

Not the answer he'd wanted to hear. In two strides, Antonio moved to the handrail of *La Libertad*. "This isn't America, Rebecca." He put both hands on the bar, his feet wide apart. She wasn't going to take the easy way out. He wasn't going to let her. He'd push her just like she had pushed him.

"Oh, that's right. We're in a Communist country now, and I'm dealing with a tyrant," she said.

Rubbing her chin, probably in a reference to Fidel Castro, she had to know her actions would only further push his buttons. The woman had balls. "Come up here, Rebecca." He smiled down at her, but his heart was pounding against his rib cage. "That is an order, not a request. And I dare you to defy me." What a strange effect they were having on each other. Because although he needed her to acquiesce to him right now in front of his crew and these kids, part of him enjoyed her defiance. And he loved the idea of getting closer to her, under her skin, so close he could, with skills he hadn't used in a while, bend her to his will. And watch her dissolve in pleasure underneath him.

• • •

Gulping at her own audacity, Rebecca moved toward the ladder, knowing whatever Antonio was about to say or do to her, she probably deserved it. She took each step slowly, stopping only at the unexpected bellow of the bull hidden somewhere in the woods. Taking a deep breath, she moved topside. When she stopped, he motioned with his finger for her to move even closer.

Biting her bottom lip, she obeyed.

When she was close enough to see his chest rising and falling, he reached for her, his hand snaking behind her neck, pulling her closer until they were face-to-face with their breaths intermingling. A strange electric jolt of energy shot down her center, making her knees go weak. But not from fear. Strangely, she wasn't afraid he would hurt her. And she desperately wanted to know what Antonio was going to say or do next.

"You need to feel what it's like to be a leader and have lives hanging on your decision. This is your decision to make, no one else's. There will be no vote." He never broke his stare as he spoke to her, low, in control, his words no doubt meant for only her to hear.

Feeling faint, and some other unwelcome emotion, her knees finally did buckle. Antonio caught her with his other arm, pulling her up and against him. His mouth brushed her cheek on its way to her left ear and he whispered, so even Ignado couldn't hear. "I'm curious to see if you value your life more than theirs."

Touché. His words brought heat and tears to the back of her eyes. She blinked to keep from crying in front of him. Why would he put this burden on her? She gulped. Because she'd backed him into a corner in front of his men, that's why.

"Rebecca," Dallas's strained voice drifted up to her. "Keep the boat here. What good would the video do if we die in some remote area of a third world country?"

A snort from Ignado followed. She pulled back, and Antonio released her neck, giving her space and allowing her to breathe again. Holy cow, this man could make her heart race.

She looked at the toddler, bathed in a warm half light of the moon's glare. Then she noticed his feet. He had no shoes. The girls must have carried him through the woods or his feet would be torn up and bleeding. How would these kids survive even if they did make it across the Florida Straits? Did they have family waiting for them in Miami? Who would buy shoes for this little boy?

Her viewers back in Tampa didn't really understand how poverty was still plaguing this island. They probably just watched the president's press conferences on the opening of a dialogue with Cuba and thought everything was okay now. Maybe she had a chance to prove otherwise. To peel back the curtain on this isolated island and give her viewers the truth.

Domingo was staring at her with worried eyes, hugging the child to him like a shield. They both deserved a chance. The toddler's mother was willing to risk their lives to give her child a better future. Her own mother had done the same, and look how much richer her life had become, both literally and figuratively.

But if she let the cruiser go, she'd be stuck here, literally stuck in a country whose government still committed atrocities. Well, according to Antonio, anyway. She could soon find out firsthand if they didn't get moving. She glanced at Antonio. He had stopped and was glowering back at her. An acrid brew of dread and anxiety scrambled up her already-upset stomach.

"What's it going to be, Rebecca? Will you save these people, or make sure you have a way to save yourself?"

Chapter Six

The bumpy ride into Antonio's hometown of Güira de Melena, in the front seat of a rusted-out, stinky construction truck, was shaking Rebecca to the bone. Getting physically tossed around in suffocating heat minus air-conditioning, with the scent of exhaust whooshing up her nose, was also making her nauseous. Rebecca's goal: get to Antonio's sister's home without throwing up and causing even more tension between her and Antonio.

They'd been driving for about thirty minutes after hiking out of those brutal woods that had left her legs a patchwork of scrapes and scratches. One cut on her ankle kept bleeding on and off. Her $250 Elie Tahari suit had stains that might eventually come out, but rips that could never be repaired. She brushed a hand across the silky, smooth fabric, swallowing a cry. She loved this outfit, stupid as that sounded now. And had saved hard in order to buy it.

Dallas and Jose Carlos, the bald kidnapper, sat in the open bed in the back of the pickup truck. She could only imagine the bruises they'd have after bumping around back there. And they'd both probably stink by the time they stopped. She could already smell herself.

Ignado had jumped into a different truck at the edge of the woods and driven away. *Thank God.* Antonio hadn't questioned his actions, and Rebecca had secretly cheered. If she never saw that big bully again it would be fine by her.

Glancing at the road ahead of her, she choked on the dust the truck kept rustling up. She'd pay a thousand dollars for a hotel room, a hot shower, and a nap right now. Her pink sling backs had two broken straps, and her feet were cramping from the effort it took to walk in broken high heels. Not to mention the blisters.

Yep, she'd pay every cent in her meager bank account for a chance to wash, bandage a few of the cuts, and change into some sensible, comfortable clothes. And grab a bite to eat. Somewhere. She'd pay even more if Antonio would say something. He'd been silent the whole trip, even when their bodies kept banging into each other with every new pothole or bump.

He kept staring out the open passenger's side window. Strands of his hair, which had been slicked back, escaped and smacked him in the face. She had no idea if his silence was in response to her decision to send the *La Libertad* back to America with the Cuban kids on board, or if he was simply apprehensive about a reunion with a family he'd left more than a decade ago.

True to his word, he'd honored her decision, and sent the Cuban women and kids to America on his yacht. Domingo had been insulted, insisting that he take his own vessel. A handful of men, who'd been hiding in the woods, had motored off with him. She'd watched as Domingo's contraption puttered out of view at the break of dawn. She'd prayed for him and everyone else on board both vessels.

The truck driver next to her kept rambling away in fast

Spanish, interrupting her conflicted thoughts. The old Cuban farmer swung from bittersweet tales of his aging friends to outbursts over new political difficulties.

Sweat stung her eyes. Boy, could she use some ice-cold water, and she'd run out of her lukewarm supply. She knew better than to ask to stop. What was the point, when she hadn't seen a convenience store anywhere along the way? Where did you buy stuff in rural Cuba? So far she'd seen nothing but unfarmed farmland. Had to be a story there, too. Why wasn't anyone *using* this fertile land? Made no sense. Maybe because they didn't have the equipment to work the land? Or the gas to power the equipment? How sad that would be for all the people who lived here. And lived hungry.

"We're here." As the farmer took a sharp right turn, she slid into Antonio's side again. His thigh contracted on contact. With bunched shoulders and balled-up fists, he looked like a bundle of explosives ready to blow. She didn't want to be the one to ignite him.

Shifting farther away, she sat taller, straining to see out of the dirty front windshield. The street they'd turned onto was one of many in the small farm town. It was flooded with activity. Kids, in what looked like faded school uniforms, played street games and listened to music. A few even danced on a sidewalk as they passed by. Adults congregated in groups on front porches, sipping afternoon drinks. She glanced at her watch. One p.m. *Don't people here work?*

Small homes, jammed together, reminded her of the clutter of public housing in the Ponce de Leon project where she grew up in Tampa. Homes there were made of concrete slabs that had little in personality and even less in the way of comfort. Here it was probably the same.

Her heart ached for the little ones playing on the dusty streets, knowing at their age they probably wanted nothing more than another hour to play, but also understanding eventually that a good time with a stick and a tennis ball wouldn't fill their rumbling stomachs. The lack of the basic necessities would eventually leave even the most carefree child yearning for more. She sighed, remembering how she and her friends had gathered on the curb of the concrete parking lot looking for ways to play away the bad things that happened at home behind closed doors.

"Antonio." She talked over the farmer, who still hadn't stopped to take a breath. "Is your family expecting you?" She had no idea if their visit here would be a surprise. She couldn't believe she'd forgotten to ask. So much had happened so fast.

"My sister knows. So does my grandmother." He inhaled and exhaled slowly. "I told them not to tell anyone else."

She nodded, strangely relieved. They were here illegally. "And your mother?"

He turned to glare at her, but his eyes appeared to go out of focus. "She's dead."

Rebecca licked her dry lips. "I'm sorry. I…"

"She died of a heart attack shortly after our local CDR member shot and killed my father in our front yard."

"What?" Was she hearing right?

Antonio had spoken those awful words casually, but she could feel anger rolling off him. His heated energy made her scoot farther away from him.

Antonio turned to stare out the window again, and she barely made out his next sentence. "My father and I were throwing a ball in this street when he died."

Rebecca's breath hitched. He'd witnessed his father's murder. *Dear God.* That one nugget of information explained so much about his hardened personality. His coldness had to be a defense mechanism, because who the hell could be normal after watching their dad die? Oh God, this trip back must be so bittersweet for him.

She reached out to unravel his white-knuckled fist. His

skin, which should have been hot thanks to the tropical temperature, felt clammy instead. She tried to pry his fingers apart, but he jerked away from her in a manner that left her afraid to look at him, much less speak again. His fingers were unmovable, like marble.

Cold and hardened.

. . .

Her fingers felt warm against his chilled skin. She was trying to pry his fist apart, unravel him, loosen him up, maybe even force him to let go. He wasn't sure what she was trying to do, could be something as simple as offer him comfort. Wouldn't that be a first? Someone comforting him.

An odd ache roared within him.

He hadn't let anyone, especially a woman, get that close to him since he'd set his plan for revenge in motion. And he couldn't let Rebecca get close to him at all. He couldn't let her reach that part of him he kept so carefully controlled. He had a mission to fulfill here. And that mission was to kill her damn father. So despite his pounding pulse and another rush of physical desire that would surely need to be satisfied soon, he pulled away.

Her gaze flickered over him. She looked nervous, full of anticipation. For them to reach their destination?

Or for something else?

The truck hit another bump.

She slid into him, her right thigh colliding with his.

She gripped the dashboard with her left hand, her gaze locking onto his, like she was waiting for his reaction.

He dropped his gaze to her throat, fascinated by the artery throbbing in the crook of her neck. How he'd like to kiss her right there, feel the way her pulse was rocking. Make her heart rate rise even more.

She inhaled sharply, shuffling on the seat, putting distance between them.

Did he say something out loud? Or was she simply able to read his thoughts?

Yes, he desired her. No use lying to himself about that anymore. The woman was not only beautiful but also brave and gutsy, and the combination turned him on.

She'd passed his test earlier, deciding to send the kids back on his yacht, risking her own safety in doing so, and that decision had resonated with him so deeply he'd been shaken by it. They had more in common than she'd like to admit right now. If she was willing to make such a sacrifice for strangers, then she'd help his sister once she met and got to know Maria. His sister would become Rebecca's next Adrianna, *before* suffering the same fate.

They might be able to do real good here if they could just get past this...this...whatever it was between them.

Rebecca kept her gaze glued to the road ahead of them, twirling a piece of her long brown hair around one of her fingers.

He couldn't take his eyes off her.

Damn it. He was fast losing his focus.

She laid her head back against the seat and closed her eyes. What was she thinking? And why in the hell did he care so much to know?

. . .

Letting her head fall back on the seat, Rebecca closed her eyes and sighed, hoping to control the desire to look over at Antonio and see what he was doing now. Was he still staring at her like he wanted to devour her? He'd gone hot, then cold, then hot again so quickly.

God, that hot look made her so nervous. What was he

thinking when he looked at her like *that*?

She concentrated instead on creating the image of her own father's face. She'd never seen any pictures of him, because her mother hadn't brought any with her from Cuba. Said the government workers had stripped her of everything but her clothes at the airport. The features that materialized now were those of the man in the picture Antonio had shown her. How Rebecca longed to meet her dad, if he was indeed still alive. The need stirred in her like a never-ending fire.

One Antonio kept carefully stoking.

Why?

The driver suddenly leaned forward and laid on his horn, jolting Rebecca back to the present. She sat up and stiffened. They were rolling up to a home with a flurry of activity in front of it. About half a dozen adults were gathered in a small front porch area surrounded by a peeling white wrought iron fence.

In the gateway, an elderly man, who must have been at least sixty, suddenly raised both arms and began to wave at the truck. The man had on khaki pants that failed to cover his ankles, a faded striped shirt, and a Tampa Bay Rays baseball cap, and he smiled as if he were ten again.

"Who's that, Antonio?"

"Pedro. He's my uncle on my mother's side." Antonio's voice broke with emotion or maybe stress?

Before the truck could come to a complete stop, Pedro ran over to the passenger-side door, jerked it open, and pulled Antonio out of the front seat, yanking him into a full embrace. "Hey, Americano."

Antonio tensed in the hug, his arms hanging like dead limbs beside him.

So much for Antonio's family not knowing he was coming.

"Pedro, it's good to see you." Antonio finally reciprocated

the squeeze. Sort of. The man kept patting Antonio's back like a super proud papa, and a grin danced madly across his weathered tan face. But it was the sparkle in the old man's brown eyes that Rebecca liked.

Glancing back at Dallas, she was glad to see him already moving. They needed to capture this emotional reunion. Dallas jumped out of the truck's bed. He grabbed the small video camera and walked around the growing group of family members. No one questioned who Dallas was, or why he was shooting video.

She wasn't quite sure what she should be doing right now. Asking questions at this point would only break the spell woven around the family, so she got out of the truck, grabbed the backpack Antonio had provided her, and observed from a distance.

After a few minutes, Antonio stepped out of the swirl of octopus arms. His face appeared flushed, and for a moment he looked like a lost boy looking for his parents. "*Donde esta mi abuelita?*" he asked Pedro.

The crowd suddenly parted, and Pedro pointed to an old lady hunched over in a metal rocking chair in the corner of the porch. "There's your grandmother."

Rebecca strained to see over the adults still partially blocking her view. When the old lady looked up, Rebecca gasped. The frail woman had one eye missing, a nasty scar in its place. Her pockmarked face was stained dark brown, probably from too much sun, and her lips looked like they were peeling. As the old woman tried to stand on her stick legs, she began to shake.

"No, no, *mi abuelita*. Don't get up." Antonio rushed to her side. Dropping to his knees, he gently assisted the old woman back into her seat.

A lump formed in Rebecca's throat at the gentleness with which Antonio helped her.

His grandmother's hands cradled Antonio's cheeks. Maybe her one good eye wasn't good either, because she felt along his face as if reading Braille. Mesmerized, Rebecca watched the old woman's fingertips trace over Antonio's sharp features. Antonio remained perfectly still, but his chest rose and fell with trembling breaths.

Rebecca held her air in, waiting to see if he would allow the old woman to continue touching him, or if he'd jerk away like he always did when she touched him accidentally.

"You are so handsome. So handsome, mi Antonio." His grandmother spoke in Spanish. Her hands left his face and moved over Antonio's shoulders. "You have grown into a strong man." Continuing down his chest, the woman placed one palm flat against his chest, right over his heart.

Rebecca wished she could feel how fast Antonio's heart was beating. Hers was racing like mad.

"And you have proven to be a man of your word." The old woman's voice cracked. "You came back for Maria as you promised."

The air Antonio let out was audible, even from where Rebecca was standing, and for a minute, Rebecca thought the strong man might finally let go and cry. Heck, her throat was constricting. Mainly because Antonio was turning out to be the kind of man she'd dreamed her father would have been, desperate to return to his family, willing to do anything to help them. Even kidnap a reporter and enter a country illegally. Antonio had already proven he'd do whatever it took to help his loved ones. That's what any good man *should* be willing to do.

Instead of letting his emotions go, though, Antonio took another deep breath and fisted his hands again. How could he not rejoice in such a touching and heartfelt moment? What was wrong with him? At some point, the pressure would force this bottled-up man to explode.

"I should have come years ago, *abuelita*. I tried, but—"
Antonio shook his head.

Ah, he was burdened, weighted down with guilt. Rebecca
felt his frustration at not being able to rescue his sister Maria
sooner. She knew emotional baggage like that could be an
unbearable load. This man was not all bad. Antonio actually
had love in his heart. And that love was what drove him here.
It's what brought her here today, too, her desire to feel this
kind of emotional reunion with her own dad. Reluctantly, she
admitted to herself she and Antonio had that in common.

The old lady pulled Antonio's head into her lap. He didn't
fight her. His grandmother began to stroke his hair, probably
as she had for Antonio as a child.

"No, *mi amor*. You could not come back until you had
made your own way. You are a hero to me. And now that I
feel how healthy you are, and hear the love in your voice, I
know my Maria and her Tonito will be safe." The old woman
sighed and lifted her chin. She placed one of her hands across
her own heart and whispered, "Things are changing here, but
not fast enough. Not fast enough to save Maria. Now I can die
in peace knowing my two loves are safe."

Antonio sat up, staring into his grandmother's eyes. He
closed his own eyes and inhaled. When he opened them, he
reached for the aging woman, enveloping her in a hug that
could have crushed her brittle bones, but Rebecca knew this
big man was a master at restraint. He was surely using that
control now. His grandmother lowered her head, hiding her
eyes in the crook of Antonio's neck. Her bony shoulders
began to quake.

His eyes looked skyward, and Rebecca wondered if
Antonio, the control freak, was actually praying to a power
higher than himself. Her heart yearned to hear the thoughts
swirling around inside his head, to learn what made him such
a force of nature. Now, why would she think that? Why would

she even care?

Rebecca realized it was because she already felt a connection to Antonio's family like none she'd known before. How strange that she could feel intimacy with complete strangers.

She searched for Dallas to make sure he was capturing this emotional moment on video. Always a true professional, Dawg was standing close enough to get a good angle and pick up the conversation between Antonio and his grandmother, but far enough away to remain out of their circle of vision. Just a silent fly on the wall, watching.

A skinny little boy, who couldn't have been more than six, broke through the crowd, tugged on Antonio's sleeve, and spoke in Spanish. "Are you going to take me to America?" Antonio stiffened. Carefully, he unraveled his grandmother from his embrace and turned to look at the little boy.

"Tonito." An attractive woman, wearing skintight pink hot pants, squatted next to the young boy, pulling him into her. "We don't speak about that, remember?" She placed a finger over her lips.

Okay, even the kid knew about their "secret" mission. Was that Antonio's sister? She looked older than Rebecca had expected.

"Tonito?" Antonio stared at the kid as if he had witnessed the materialization of a saint. "His name is Tony?"

"Maria named him after you." Once again the grandmother spoke with awe and reverence in her voice. "This boy will be like you, Antonio, a brave and responsible man. He deserves a name of honor."

A name of honor. *Wow.* Rebecca's eyes watered at the sentiment. She didn't know the family's backstory, like how often Antonio had kept in touch with them. He must be doing something to earn such adoration from people he hadn't seen in a decade. Did he send them money and food monthly, like most Cuban Americans? It had to be about the money. Why else would these people love someone they didn't even know anymore?

Antonio pulled something out of his pocket, an awkward move given his crouched position. The young boy's eyes lit up as Antonio held out a tiny toy to the kid. "I brought you a gift, Tonito. You like cars, no?"

"Yes." The young boy jerked the old-school SSP Racer out of Antonio's hand.

Rebecca laughed at his youthful eagerness. When was the last time something so simple had thrilled her? She couldn't even remember.

Tonito rolled the red-and-black sports car around between his fingers, licking his lips, completely focused on his new gift.

Finally, Antonio placed his hands gently around the boy's hands, disengaging the kid's fingers so he could get at the car. The little boy frowned, and Rebecca guessed Antonio had about one minute before the boy burst into tears.

"Pull the cord like this, Tonito." Antonio pulled a plastic cord out of the car's center. He set the toy on the ground, and the little wheels spun as the car took off on the porch, stopping only as it crashed into the cement next to the gated opening. The boy squealed in delight.

Geez, she'd never fully understand the opposite sex, but what she did get was the connection these two strangers were making. She wondered if that toy car had been Antonio's prized possession as a child. She didn't see this type of toy sold in stores much anymore. To give up such a precious possession was meaningful, even selfless. The small gesture made her want to know Antonio better, to see beyond his hardened shell.

Antonio smiled. Rebecca stepped back, her hand over her heart, her insides melting. The look of happiness on the grown man's face literally took her breath away. His whole look changed from angry dissident to loving father. At least that's the image that resonated within Rebecca. She shook her head, knowing it would be better if she continued to see Antonio as her captor, a man who was easy to hate, rather than a man who might be capable of unconditional love. She chalked up her thoughts to her emotions. As a reporter, as an advocate for the less fortunate, it was her job to search out the truth, to connect to the oppressed, to use her voice to bring them justice. But in order to do that, she had to find the heart of a person first. And she was seeing Antonio's right now.

Antonio stood and walked over to the toy. Picking it up, he brushed off the dirt and inspected it for damage. "Where's your mother, Tonito?"

She held her breath. So the woman in the skintight clothing wasn't Antonio's sister.

"In the house." Tonito responded in Spanish. "Again." He pointed to the car.

"Okay." Antonio reinserted the cord. "What's she doing?"

"Crying." The boy reached out with tiny stub-like fingers.

"Crying?" Antonio cocked his head to one side. He pulled the cord and sent the car flying at the boy.

"Yes." He clapped his hands in joy, watching the car rip across the pavement. It flew between his legs before crashing into the side of Grandma's rocking chair.

The old lady didn't laugh. "Maria is crying because she's scared."

Antonio's eyebrows shot up. "Scared we'll be caught leaving?"

Rebecca wondered if Cubans still got in trouble leaving the island. Hadn't that changed, too? And she wondered if anyone ever doubted Antonio's abilities before. He always acted with such confidence.

"Maria says she's waited ten years for this moment." The old lady's voice shook. "And now that it's here, she's afraid to see you. She's afraid you won't be real, or you won't be able to pull this off, and she'll be disappointed again."

A knot of emotion lodged in Rebecca's throat, her muscles straining until it hurt. Images of her father materialized in her head. Would she be disappointed, too? If they left immediately, now that Antonio had found his sister, she wouldn't get a chance to look for her dad. If her *papi* was still alive, and she was able to locate him, would he embrace her when they met and speak to her with pride in his voice? Or would he look at her with blank eyes, unable or unwilling to recognize their blood connection? Her throat was tightening up so much it was now impossible to swallow.

Despite that, she must have let out some kind of pained sound, because when she looked up Antonio was staring at her, his face paler. When their eyes met, he immediately looked away.

Her gut twisted when he failed to hold her stare. There was more about her father Antonio wasn't sharing. She sensed it. Either that, or this was all a cruel lie to get her to do his bidding, and now that he was here with his family, he was suddenly locating his conscience. She bit her lip, angry with herself for not being able to figure out which it was.

"Ay, *que linda*, what is your name, beautiful American?" The woman who had come with Tonito enveloped Rebecca into a hug, kissing both of her cheeks.

Stunned at the display of affection from a woman she didn't know, it took Rebecca a moment to realize her cheeks were wet. She stepped back, untangling herself from the woman's hold, trying to figure out which one of them was crying.

"Are you okay?" The woman's eyes were wet, but Rebecca had a feeling her own were as well. "You look like you're about to pass out." The Cuban woman steadied her with a firm hand on her back.

Dallas was at her side a split second later. "You need to sit down."

Rebecca ignored Dallas's raised eyebrows. "You need to keep shooting." She had to keep it together here, and so did he. Who knew how long they'd be here, or what other chances they'd have to capture the truth from deep inside Cuba. White dots were spinning in her line of vision. "Shoot video of Antonio." She shook the dizziness off. "This whole story is about him rescuing his sister. We need that emotional reunion on video." If seeing his grandmother again made Antonio drop to his knees, no telling how he'd react to being reunited with his sister. If she, a seasoned reporter, was mesmerized watching Antonio, think of how her viewers would feel, especially those with a connection to Cuba.

Dallas dropped the camera from his shoulder. "You're more worried about the damn video than your own health? No video is worth dying over, especially in Cuba."

Throwing up her hands, she exhaled in exasperation. "We came across the Florida Straits, into Cuba *illegally*, to document this rescue." A rush of adrenaline shot through her core, and her whole body started to tingle. Not good. Maybe she did need to sit down.

"Antonio, your girlfriend is ill." The woman in the tight pants continued to hold on to her.

Girlfriend? Is that what his family thought?

Antonio glanced her way, his mouth drawing down. "Esmeralda, can you help her? She has cuts on her legs that need to be tended to."

So he *had* noticed.

"I need to go inside." He stalked off, leaving her in the arms of a woman she didn't know.

A slow burn of annoyance fired in Rebecca's belly.

"Dallas, follow Antonio. He knows why we're here." Screw him if he got mad.

"My name is Esmeralda. I am the second cousin of Antonio." The woman next to her glanced at her as if she could read her mind. "Do not worry. Antonio is not angry with you. Most men don't deal with emotions well." Esmeralda shrugged. "I will help you, and you help me, *si*?" Then she pulled Rebecca down the narrow alley between the two homes.

Rebecca stumbled along, past windows with faded shutters open to the air. The run-down homes were packed together. One neighbor could probably see and smell what another cooked for breakfast. She tripped over a rock protruding from the weed-wrecked lawn and barked out a cry.

"Hurry." Esmeralda jerked on her wrist, forcing her to pick up the pace. "Maria is in the back bedroom." As they rounded a corner at the end of the house, Esmeralda pointed to open doors leading back into the home. "Listen." She placed a finger to her lips.

Dallas bolted past them, scattering three noisy piglets. "Holy three little pigs. Where's the big bad wolf?" Video camera still in his hands, he slipped quietly into the open doorway. He looked back and winked, then disappeared from her view.

"I don't hear anything, Esmeralda." *Except the squealing pigs.*

"Sometimes there is meaning in the silence, no?"

Still a bit dizzy, Rebecca limped forward, grabbing on to the doorframe. *Ouch.* The palms of her hands still stung with road rash from her kidnapping. Her nose twitched at the unusual scent within the home. Drawn into the room by some silent, invisible energy, her gaze landed immediately on a skinny, worn-looking woman sitting on a bed next to

Antonio. The young woman wasn't looking at him, though. Instead, she kept smoothing out a red cotton shirt lying across her lap. The shirt looked like it would fit a teenager, but the color had faded, and it was wrinkled. The woman was rubbing it with what looked like reverence.

Antonio sat close to her, but the two didn't touch. His gaze was also anchored on that little red shirt. Rebecca swore his bottom lip trembled. She froze in the doorway, embarrassed to be gawking at the big man's vulnerability.

"Do you remember this shirt?" The woman had to be Antonio's sister, Maria. She spoke in Spanish. She had a scratchy voice and thin, bony fingers, which shook as they continued to caress the red top.

"No," his reply, barely a whisper.

"This is the shirt you wore the day before you were sent to America. I took it out of your room and have kept it here under my pillow ever since." She picked up the shirt and gently held it against her cheek. "For a while it still smelled like you. The scent made me less sad and more certain you weren't abandoning me forever."

A deep, guttural sound erupted from Antonio, and he looked away from Maria and his old shirt.

Rebecca's own chest hurt at the raw sentiment.

"It's okay, Antonio. You can help me exchange this memory for many new ones." His sister reached out and placed her thin hand on Antonio's back. "I want a new start, far away from here."

When he turned back toward Maria, his cheeks were wet, and the pain of more than a decade of guilt could be seen in his furrowed brow and tightly pressed lips. "I would have come sooner," he groaned.

"Tony, if not for this…" She laid the shirt back down on her lap and caressed it again. "If not for this shirt, the money you've sent monthly, and your promises to return in person, I would have given up thinking about a future a long time ago."

Antonio sent money every month! He'd been supporting this family for ten years?

And she hadn't heard a word, much less seen a dollar, from her father in all that time. In all fairness, maybe her dad hadn't been able to send help?

Rebecca shuddered, feeling hurt and guilty at the same time, like a vulture circling over the heads of two wounded souls. She caught Dallas looking at her and reluctantly gestured for him to continue shooting. If the sincerity of this emotional moment translated onto video, the world would better understand what a revolution and a dictator had done to so many families. How the fallout continued even today. And she wouldn't have to write one word.

"The clothes Tonito wears are the gifts you send regularly. They always fit, Antonio, always. I've been amazed at how well you've taken care of us from so far away. I've never doubted your love or commitment."

Wow. How ironic that Antonio took such care of his sister and her Tonito even though he'd never met the boy, and *her* father, if still alive, hadn't made one effort to reach out and see if she needed anything. But she had no idea what her father's life had been like. What if he'd been ill, or in jail? If she'd known he was alive sooner, she would have reached out herself to find out.

She turned away from the touching scene in the bedroom, suddenly feeling lonely, although surrounded by people. A thought crept into her head. She tried to flush it out. But not before it resonated deep within her.

Antonio would make a good husband and father.

Pedro bolted past her, slamming her backward into the doorframe. "The CDR is coming."

Rebecca jumped to get out of the way in case someone else was following him.

Maria looked up, eyes widening. "Angel?"

"Si." Pedro stopped midroom, staring at Dallas and his camera.

"Angel always works at this time." Maria's hand flew up to cover her heart.

"He knows." Antonio hit the bed with a balled-up fist.

Maria bounced away from him.

Her brother eyed her. "I told you not to tell anyone else, especially your fiancé."

"I didn't tell him." Flinching, the sister scooted farther down the bed, glancing at the door.

"We have to leave now," Antonio ordered.

Old, bossy Antonio had returned.

"You," Maria whispered, pointing at him. "*You* have to go."

"Not without you."

She shook her head, her gaze darting around the room. "Angel will know if I'm not here. He'll hunt us down."

"He knows anyway. You're coming with me, Maria." Antonio grabbed her wrist. "I won't leave without you and Tonito."

"No." Maria pulled away from him, blinking back tears. "Angel doesn't know for sure you're here unless he catches you. And if he does, he'll kill you and arrest all the others."

"Wait a minute. Arrest us?" Dallas dropped his camera, letting it sway at his side. "I've always wanted to visit Guantanamo Bay, but not to live with the al-Qaeda brothers."

He may have been delivering a joke, but the look on Dallas's face told Rebecca he was about to freak.

First, they were both kidnapped at gunpoint. Now maybe they'd be arrested?

"I think…"

"If we leave now," Antonio cut Dallas off, "we can outrun the bastard."

"If Angel catches us, he'll punish me by separating me from Tonito." Maria's ashen face froze with fear.

Glancing around the room, Rebecca realized Maria's son must still be up front. Not good.

"He's done it before," Maria whispered.

Antonio's face paled. "We'll go."

Rebecca pictured little Tonito playing with his toy car, maybe even showing it to the man Angel, telling him about the Americano who had just given it to him. Her stomach flip-flopped. They were screwed.

"Go to Tio Juan's farm." Maria pointed toward Esmeralda. "She can take you."

"I remember Johnny's farm."

"I'll meet you there, I promise." Maria sprang off the bed, passing Pedro and Rebecca to stand in the center of the hall. "Johnny will hide you. I'll be there, with Tonito, tomorrow." Her anxious glance found Antonio. "I promise. Angel works all day tomorrow."

"Angel is coming inside," an unknown voice shouted down the hallway.

"Esmeralda, take them to the bike in the back. Don't start it. You'll have to walk it out the side."

"Down that skinny alleyway?" Rebecca knew they'd get caught if they had to go back out to the main street. They'd be seen for sure.

"That's right." Esmeralda pulled on her hand, jerking her out of the room.

Antonio blocked Maria's escape. "You better come tomorrow, Maria. If I have to come back here to get you, and Angel's here, I'll kill the son of a bitch. As God is my witness."

Seeing the red in Antonio's cheeks and sensing his anger bubbling out of control, Rebecca grabbed his arm. "Let's go." They needed to leave. She wasn't going to get arrested. Not for him, not for his sister, not for some damn cause that had never been her own. "Now, or we're leaving without you." But her fake threat didn't sound convincing, even to her own ears. Where would she and Dallas go? How would they get back to America? In that instant, Rebecca realized she had put her entire life in this angry, bitter stranger's hands, and today his judgment was clouded by emotions he'd kept bottled up for years.

Dallas angled past her. "I'm with you. Let's go!"

"You need to stay." Antonio's arm shot out, blocking Dallas's retreat.

"What?" Rebecca jumped in. "Leave him alone. My photographer is *not* staying."

"His job is to document what's going on here. And only two can ride on the bike."

"Oh my God." Antonio was serious. Her heart felt as if it had just dropped into her stomach.

Facing her now, his cheeks flushed, Antonio tried to reason with her. "Listen, Dallas can stay here. Angel doesn't know him. He can be Esmeralda's new boyfriend." Then, dismissing her concern by turning his back on her, Antonio dropped his arm but still blocked Dallas's path with his large frame. "Stay, and use that undercover camera in your backpack to prove what kind of man Angel is. He abuses my sister." Antonio leaned into Dallas, who shuffled back, almost stumbling over his own slow feet in an effort to retreat. "I want any violence documented on video."

"Look, dude." Dallas tilted his head in that way that said *I've made up my mind.* "You can do what you want, but I want out."

Bile rose into Rebecca's throat. "Antonio, it's too dangerous." She wasn't leaving Dallas here.

Turning slowly, Antonio drilled her with that knowing stare of his. "*You* want to stay and shoot the video instead?"

She froze.

"Well, Rebecca, what's your answer? You have less than a second to decide."

"I'll stay." What else could she do? Dallas was here because of her.

"No, no, Becca. You go. Angel, or whatever his name is, is less likely to mess with this big black man. I've got this. Just come back for me, you hear?"

She threw her arms around Dallas, squeezing him despite his bulky camera. "I promise."

She'd be back for her friend.

No matter what.

She glanced over at Antonio.

No matter who might try to stop her.

Chapter Seven

As she roared up to the Morro Castle, a picturesque fortress guarding the entrance to Havana bay, dust from the road stuck to Rebecca's damp skin. Antonio rode with a lead foot the whole fifty-minute drive in from the country, maybe due to his adrenaline-fueled personality, or maybe in response to their close call with that government watchdog guy. Either way, Antonio's need for speed had left her no choice but to keep her arms wrapped tightly around his middle.

His lean, well-defined middle.

She'd been praying silently the whole time that they'd make it to Johnny's farm without getting busted by the Cuban police.

Sun-driven heat smacked her cheeks as they buzzed down the road. Antonio hadn't said a word the whole way. Not that she would have been able to hear him from the back of this beat-up motorcycle. The old machine roared, and the wind kept whipping up a sound barrier.

Acid churned in her stomach, her discomfort increasing with each new bump in the road. She prayed again they didn't get pulled over. Did Cuba even have speed limits? No signs, and the few 1950-looking cars they'd passed on the road didn't seem to be going very fast. They'd ripped by all of them.

Antonio took a sudden turn to the right, squealing into a dusty parking lot. She gripped his center, his midsection hardening as he clenched his muscles. She couldn't help but marvel at how little body fat he had on him, another sign of his disciplined nature.

She gripped his abs tighter as he spun the bike in a circle. The cycle's back wheel spit up muck and then fell silent.

"So much for trying not to draw attention to us." Wow, how his mood had changed. Where was the gentle, loving man who'd dropped to his knees and cradled his grandmother in his arms? What was up with this sudden overdose of testosterone? "Okay, I'll ask. Why are we *here*?" She glanced around the empty parking lot. An abandoned overgrown lot was to her left; that freaking huge castle was on her right. "Obviously, this isn't your uncle's farm."

"I want to show you something." Antonio flipped the bike's stand down, motioning for her to get off.

At least he held out a hand to help her. "Show me what? The castle?" She put her fingers in his, and a spark shot between them.

He dropped her hand as soon as her feet hit the ground. "Havana." He whispered the word like the name of a lover.

"We just drove through Havana." But he'd been speeding like a bat out of hell, so she saw nothing but the expressway. They'd taken a bypass around the bay, she assumed to get to Johnny's farm, but after exiting a tunnel, the city had vanished, replaced by this fortress and this abandoned neighborhood.

"You haven't seen Havana this way."

"Should we really be *sightseeing* right now?"

He ignored her.

Sighing, she decided against arguing with him. He'd been through a very emotional reunion. Apparently, his compassionate and tolerant mood had evaporated somewhere between Güira de Melena and Havana. She pulled her backpack off her back and dug in for the GoPro camera Antonio had packed for her. "Okay, let's go." Anything to get away from the heat his body had been putting off.

And the effect that was having on her.

She followed him to the edge of the tall stone wall dividing the parking lot near the castle and Havana bay. Did he expect her to climb that thing? Looking up, she shaded her eyes from the blinding glare. She estimated the wall was about two feet taller than she was. She'd need help. Even in the tennis shoes she'd finally put on.

As if reading her mind, Antonio cupped his hands for her. She put her foot into his man-made step, reaching for the top of the wall. Gravel cut into both palms, still smarting from her injuries, but she strained to lift her own body weight. Her arms wobbled, and her left elbow started to give out, but with a push from Antonio, she hoisted herself to the top.

He handed her the GoPro camera, and she reached out to help him, but he jumped, scaling the wall like Spider-Man. Good thing, since her hands were sweaty and slippery, and one of her injured palms was starting to bleed again.

"Turn around." His voice was deep and breathy, and she wondered if it was from the burst of energy it took for him to leap up this high, or from his intense feelings for this forbidden city. His black eyes bored into hers with the same kind of heat his body had been transferring the whole ride over here.

Inhaling, she did as he requested, turning toward the city, mostly to hide from his probing gaze, which made her center all shaky. The view of Havana from across Havana bay hit her full force, pushing the air out of her lungs in one long whoosh.

She'd never in her life seen a skyline quite like this, except maybe in Miami. "Oh my God. It's beautiful." The blazing July sun bathed the city in the most perfect light, as if she'd thrown up big TV reflectors and directed sunshine right onto the city's tallest buildings. Against the brilliant blue sea, the white buildings stood tall and proud, and the city seemed to stretch on forever, looking very much like a thriving resort destination. "I...I..." Her heart fluttered like baby butterfly wings. "I didn't expect this."

"Why not?"

From this distance, the city looked so pretty and polished, like it belonged on the front of a tourism brochure. But she knew better. "I've heard stories of how Havana continues to rot. That it's crumbling away." The eclectic mixture of architecture was dying because no one had the money to take care of it. Not even the almighty government. From across the bay, she could make out the diversity of the city. Two- and three-story neoclassical buildings. Art deco high-rises like the ones in South Beach, and the real-life castle on her right. It would be a shame to let such a unique city die.

"Beauty in decay." Antonio moved up behind her, so close her body flooded with warmth.

The top of the wall was so narrow, she was afraid to move for fear she'd touch him. As it was, her nerves were on high alert. "Beauty in decay. That's what you see right now?"

"From here"—his breath tickled the hair above her left ear—"what I see is perfection."

She shivered. Was he still talking about the city? She held her breath, afraid to exhale. She didn't want to set off another jolt of electricity. The charge might send her off the wall and face-first into Havana bay.

"I wanted you to see your birthplace from here first to fully appreciate its potential. Once you get up close, you'll remember Havana in another light. But from here, you can be touched by its rare exquisiteness and limitless potential."

Antonio was quite well-spoken for a rebel who hung out in the Everglades. "You sound like a man in love."

"I *am* in love with Havana, with the city, the people, and our culture."

Our culture. She didn't feel the same connection. Never had. One thing had always been standing in the way. "But you hate the government."

His body tensed, and he took a step to the side, putting distance between them. "Yes, Rebecca." That condescending tone had returned. "You know how I feel about the government."

For so many of their people, the problem came down to one man and his family, the hate so strong Cuban Americans could see nothing else. Her own mother had forbidden her to even say *his* name in the house. "Is this a Castro thing?" As if she had to ask. Antonio had the hate, and he had it bad. It had been tattooed all over his face from the moment she'd met him.

He stomped away, putting even more distance between them. "It's a *Communist* thing." He gestured toward the city. "First the government takes away religion." Turning back to face her, a fire ignited in his dark eyes. "When you do that, you strip people of hope and separate them from their morals and values." Crossing his arms, he stared across the bay. "Then you shred every iota of what makes a person unique, under the pretense of making everyone equal, but when you do that you take away drive and desire. You create a complacent society, weak from dependence, unable to dream and unwilling to raise a hand toward change."

Jesus, he spoke like a politician, if a notably scruffy one with his goatee and strands of his crazy rock-and-roll-style hair blowing in the hot Havana breeze. Despite the fact that his words were resonating deep within her, the reporter in her automatically played the devil's advocate. "Do you think you speak for everyone here in Cuba, or are you just speaking on behalf of the angry Cuban Americans back in Florida?"

He twisted toward her, nailing her to the space where she stood with a stare as hot as glue from a gun. She knew she'd touched a nerve, and she didn't know why she felt the urge to push him like this. Honestly, this was not a man she wanted to piss off. Like it or not, Antonio was her life raft back to America. And after witnessing him with his family, she was actually starting to like him. At the very least, she admired him. Not every man would be so steadfast in his devotion to his family, risking life and limb to care for and liberate them.

Then there was the way he looked at her at times, with a heated gaze that made her insides quiver. And whenever they touched...

"Let me ask you, do you make more money than your coworkers?" he asked.

Unexpected question. "Most of them. Yes."

"Do you think you deserve to?"

Now she knew where he was going. "Yes."

"Why?"

She should probably change the subject, because his fists were balling up again, but words stomped out of her mouth of their own free will. "I have a four-year degree from the University of Florida. I have four Emmys for various stories. I speak Spanish. I broke the biggest story of the year last year by exposing corruption in the school board, and I helped a woman who was burned by her husband get her justice."

He pointed a finger at her. "All of that is what makes you unique, gives you value and equity." Gesturing across the bay he continued, "But in a country like this, they would take half of your salary and divide it among others who don't bring equitable skills to the job." He drilled her again with that intense stare. "Eventually, Rebecca, even you would give up here. You'd start punching the time card and fall in line." He walked toward her slowly.

She couldn't really back up because she was at the end of the wall. "Maybe you should run for office. And bring about change yourself."

Two steps. That's all it took for Antonio to tower over her, using his height, she was sure, and the precariously thin stone wall as a way to intimidate her. "If I did run, would you vote for me?"

The hope in his eyes forced her back a half step. She teetered, feeling breathless and dizzy. She reached for his arms, hoping he would anchor her.

His hand flew behind her back, pulling her toward him. "What's it going to take to make you believe in my mission?" He leaned down to whisper in her ear, "What's it going to take to make you believe in me?"

She rocked back on her heels, but the pressure of Antonio's hand kept her from falling. "I...well." She swallowed and swayed again. Antonio was holding her too close. He had to be able to feel her heart racing at this proximity. She placed her hands flat against his chest. His heart was pounding, too. Too close. They were too close, and she couldn't breathe.

Antonio reached out and drew one finger slowly down her cheek, tracing a path to her chin, which he cupped in his hand. "We could do good if we worked together."

Her breath caught in her lungs, and she couldn't move. She could smell Antonio's musky aroma, mixed with the dust from the road. His hold on her chin forced her to see the truth in his gaze. Although he didn't say anything else, his dilated eyes confirmed what she wanted to know. *He values my opinion. He's attracted to me.* His thumb brushed over her lower lip. She inhaled sharply, and raw desire shot through her. *And I am attracted to him. Crazy. This is crazy.*

For the first time in twenty-six years, someone other than her mother believed she had value. She wasn't sure what turned her on more: the realization this impressive man appreciated *her*, or the expert way he touched her, with that controlled restraint, despite all the intensity she knew remained bottled inside him. The skin all over her body bristled. She could only imagine what it might feel like should they both let go.

His gaze rested on her mouth, his chest rising and falling. She had no doubt he was also being swept up in the odd chemistry between them. But she couldn't do this with this man. He was a revolutionary. Maybe even a killer. And when they got back to America, he'd also be known as her kidnapper.

The public would think she'd lost her damn mind. "I can't kiss you." *Holy shit, did that just come out?*

Antonio blinked rapidly. He was still breathing hard, but this time when he inhaled, he retreated, putting the usual distance between them. As he backed away, she watched the passion drain out of his eyes.

"We need to leave. Do you want to take pictures or video first?"

"Video?" *He's thinking about video?* "Sure, right. With the GoPro?" What the hell had just happened? She finally exhaled, still shaken by that powerful brush with intimacy.

"Yes, with the GoPro, Rebecca. It is a video camera." The distant, authoritative tone reentered his voice.

"Right. I know." Holy cow, she felt about thirteen again, fumbling for words, embarrassed, ashamed. *Oh God, I'm shaking.* She pulled the GoPro out of her pocket and handed it to him. "Can you shoot?" She didn't want to shoot video herself, fearing he'd see her jitters and know how much he'd just affected her.

"Can I shoot *video*?" He raised both eyebrows, and she

wondered if he had a gun on him. What else would shooting mean? He didn't question why she wouldn't shoot the video herself. He just took the camera. Maybe he welcomed the distraction, too.

"I met Esmeralda, your cousin." Changing the subject would help her get her footing back. "What does she do?" Her heart was still racing.

He didn't look at her, pointing the GoPro camera toward Havana. "She studied to be a dentist."

"So she practices in your hometown?" She kept taking deep breaths.

"No, she raises pigs."

"Pigs?" Not the Esmeralda she met. The one in the pink hot pants?

"Esmeralda lives with my grandmother. So do her pigs."

As shocking as that fact was, it did explain the smell in Antonio's grandmother's house. Imagine eating in the same place a pig pooped.

Her silence must have indicated her shock. He stopped shooting, looked at her, and grinned. "They keep farm animals in the house sometimes so they aren't stolen at night."

That also explained why two chickens had waddled through the hall while they were there. "I can't picture that sassy woman raising pigs."

"You do what you have to do to survive here. Even if it's risky and illegal." He finished shooting video. "Here you go. Video of Havana." He handed her the camera. "Esmeralda makes more money selling pigs than she ever made as a dentist working for the state."

Well, that explained a lot. As their fingers met, that electricity jumped from his flesh to hers again. "She wants to come with us," Rebecca blurted.

"I know."

"There's room on that big yacht of yours." Rebecca

fumbled with the GoPro, debating whether she should risk taking video of Antonio. She wanted to ask him a few questions about that emotional reunion she'd just witnessed. She'd pay a treasure chest in gold to know what he'd been thinking while watching his sister caress that little red shirt he used to wear. After this was all over, she wanted to remember him. "By the way, how can you afford such a spectacular yacht? I didn't think you even had a real job."

He shook his head, glancing at her out of the corner of his eye. "You never asked me what I do for a living."

True. "Okay, well, I'm asking now." She raised the GoPro slowly, pointing it in his direction.

His brow furrowed, but the rest of his features remained unchanged. In fact, he actually looked a little amused.

"How about an interview? About your reunion with your family."

His jaw stiffened. "Absolutely not. You're not going to pull a Barbara Walters on me."

Dallas already had him on video crying. "What's wrong with showing a little emotion?" She cocked her head and gave him her best *you know you want to talk* look.

He turned his back on her. "Let me ask you a question. Are you really willing to become a smuggler?"

"What?" Now *he* was interviewing *her*? This was an odd dance they'd started. She couldn't keep track of who was leading whom.

"You want to bring Esmeralda with us. To do that, we'd have to smuggle her into America."

"Is that what you do for a living? Smuggle Cubans to America?" She placed her hand over her heart. "*I'm* not a smuggler."

He laughed, but the chuckle sounded very controlled, not heartfelt. "You are if you take an active part in recruiting people to come with us."

Throwing up her arms, partially in exasperation, partially to proclaim her innocence, she became very aware of the irregular beat of her heart pounding in her ears. "I'm documenting *your* mission."

"You've been trying to *influence* my mission, whether you realize it or not."

Why was he always challenging her, even challenging the image she had of herself? Uncomfortable, she shuffled her feet, loosening a pebble on the stone wall top. She kicked it into the bay. She didn't trust the strange feelings Antonio unleashed in her. "I don't want to argue with you." She let her shoulders drop, but the tightness didn't go away.

Antonio had moved closer and now stared down into her eyes. "I don't want to *argue*, either."

Oh God, that hot look was back on his face, and his eyes looked a little stoned—on desire.

The same physical charge crept into her center, warming her with want. Damn it, she couldn't trust herself to stand this close to him. This was going to be a problem. She cleared her throat. "Can we keep this professional?" She put both hands on his chest and gently pushed him away.

As he took a step back, he caught both of her wrists, steadying himself, and stopping her exit. "What is it you want most in the world, Rebecca?"

"What?" She jerked against his hold. She was having trouble keeping up with his changing direction.

"What are your desires?" Sweat beaded on his forehead, and his dark eyes dilated further.

She bit her lip. "What's with the random questions?"

"What's wrong? Are you afraid to answer?" He forced her arms down slowly, using his strength to move them behind her back, making her take a step closer to him in order to keep her balance.

I want to be me. "I want to be happy."

"What makes you happy?"

Good question. She hadn't been so sure lately. *I want to be respected.* "I want to get married, have a family."

"Family is important. I'd do anything to protect mine."

She believed him. "Your loyalty to your sister is admirable."

"I'm glad you feel that way." He smiled, but it didn't reach his eyes.

She'd also witnessed his threat to kill that government watchdog. Was Antonio really capable of murder?

"And you love your family?" he asked.

Rebecca dropped her gaze. "Well, my mother died last year." Antonio knew so much about her, he probably already knew that, too. So why make her say it? She tried to swallow, but her throat had gone dry.

"So you're all alone in the world now."

A chill snaked down her spine. She detected the shift in his tone and felt his changing energy. What did Antonio want from her? Maybe it *wasn't* the obvious.

Anger flushed through her, and the image of a man in a picture materialized. "I'm not alone in the world. According to you, I have my father." She lifted her chin. "You say he's still alive."

"He is." His stare, heated only moments ago, turned cold.

His new disposition gave her goose bumps, and not for the right reasons. Why did she feel like a fish about to swallow deadly bait? "He lives here in Havana?"

"He does." Antonio tightened his hold on her wrists. "Your father works here, too."

The blood slowly left her fingers. Pretty soon her fingers would be numb. "You're hurting me."

He lessened his hold, but only slightly.

She swallowed and looked out over the beautiful sun-kissed water. "He's working here, today? Right now?" She could find her father. He was only a bay away.

"I can take you to where he usually works."

"You can? I mean, you know exactly where my father works?" Her heart danced, but her insides quivered with uncertainty. "We can go right now?" So that's why they'd come here before Johnny's farm. She was right to be thinking maybe Antonio wasn't such a bad guy. He *wanted* to take her to her father.

He looked directly at her, as if he'd been waiting for this moment all of his life. "Yes."

The energy around them crackled, but this time it wasn't lust or excitement overwhelming her, it was fear. Antonio had gone arctic. Even his fingers, still holding her hostage, had an icy feel to them. What was going on here?

"You can walk right into his office building and ask for him."

"I don't know." His changing moods were confusing her.

"I'll be with you." He barely moved a muscle as he spoke.

She shuddered. Maybe the reality would be better than she had dared to dream as a child. Or maybe it would be worse. Her *papi* could reject her. "What if he won't meet me?" What if he didn't believe that she was his blood? Or worse, what if he did, but didn't care? Worry ripped through her stomach.

"I bet he's as curious about you as you are about him."

That did make sense, but the odd way Antonio said it made her heart clench. Something wasn't right. His eyes looked hooded. Still, she couldn't resist jumping at this once-in-her-lifetime opportunity. "Let's go," she whispered, even though she felt like Alice, the heroine in her favorite childhood story, tumbling headfirst down the rabbit hole.

Chapter Eight

As they rumbled into Havana, Antonio watched his speed, knowing that where they headed was far more dangerous than where they'd just been. He didn't want to be killed before he had his chance at revenge. His heart thumped against his chest as he realized how close he was to achieving this lifelong dream of revenge for his father's murder.

Rebecca gripped his waist as he guided the bike into the Plaza de la Revolución. She squeezed him, her heart thumping against his back. If she knew his true intentions, she wouldn't be nervous, she'd be furious. And terrified.

He tightened his thighs around the bike seat. The moment was finally here. He would have his chance to confront that bastard of a man, Rebecca's father. Why didn't he feel more satisfaction? Because he was letting his personal feelings, his desire for Rebecca, get in the way. Emotions! This is what happened when you let them influence you. He jerked the handles, the bike rising onto the edge of its tires as he turned into the parking lot.

Rebecca gripped him even tighter, gasping.

Her heart was beating faster, pounding between his shoulder blades where her chest pressed against his back. He could feel it. So was his. He needed the adrenaline spike. He was going to kill the son of a bitch. It was now or never.

He'd secretly made Jose Carlos promise to take his family and the news crew to the dock to wait for the yacht if anything bad happened to him. But what if the "bad thing" happened to Rebecca as well? He'd brought her here as bait. He shook off the thought. *Concentrate on the plan.*

Antonio had seen pictures of the plaza before, many of them while doing research online. The buildings circling the plaza were exactly as he expected. Each had been stripped of anything that made them unique. He grunted. They were ugly concrete. Sterile. Typical Communist style.

The only two exceptions, as far as he was concerned, were the statue of José Martí and the iron sculpture of Che Guevara. The statue of Martí looked across the plaza at the face of Guevara hanging on the front wall of the Ministry of the Interior.

He didn't remember ever coming here as a kid, so, although he'd seen plenty of pictures of the marble tower with Martí's statue at its base, actually being here caused bumps to rise up on his skin.

He'd finally made it. But being in the center seat of what he thought of as true Communism, illegally, with a weapon in his bag and revenge in his heart, was crazy, even for him. A knot lodged in his throat, and when he swallowed, it wouldn't go down. Could he really do this? With Rebecca watching? He'd be damning her to his same fate. To watch a father fall from the bullet of an enemy. The thought brought actual pain to his chest.

He jerked his head to the right, forcing sweat to roll away before it landed in his eyes. Motoring the bike into a parking place, he kicked the stand down, his gaze quickly sweeping the plaza. A handful of people mingled around. A couple with khaki shorts and cameras around their necks had to be tourists. No threat. What in the hell did they think they'd see here? Fidel or Raul, roaming around giving out autographs? He spit on the ground as the tourists walked by. They didn't even notice, which fueled the fire of his hatred even more. *Idiots.*

His father had come to this plaza many times to hear Fidel Castro speak. He did remember his father complaining that the government would strip him of a day's pay if he had refused to go.

But today, the plaza had a lonely, empty feel to it. A flock of birds took flight, their squawking the only sound. He could change all that in a matter of minutes. He could give these few tourists something shocking to post on Facebook. If they could even find internet service around here. He could shatter Rebecca's perfect little world with one well-placed shot.

His stomach knotted. Would revenge finally kill the hurt in his heart? He jumped off the bike before he could change his mind. He couldn't be a coward. Not when his father was counting on him to avenge the wrong done to their once poor but happy family.

He glanced around. A handful of uniformed officers were walking a beat around the plaza. The one nearest to him packed heat. Antonio laid his hand on the bag at the side of the bike, itching to open it and get on with his plan before he could be stopped.

"Wow, is this Cuba's answer to Mount Rushmore?" Rebecca jumped off the bike, pushing off him as she did. She stared at the opposite side of the square, at the image of Che. "Until the everlasting victory, always." She read the wording beneath the giant face. "That's Che's saying?" She turned to look back at him, her face lighting up and camera in hand, like one of those idiot tourists. Awe colored her voice, making his chest burn. She had no idea what went on within the buildings in this circle. She should *not* be impressed. He frowned, but bit back a sarcastic reply.

"Why does he get his face on a building? Why not Fidel?"

He cringed at the sound of *that* name. "That 'man' is still alive. The piece of art went up as a memorial after Che's death." He didn't want to sit here and talk Cuban history. He wanted to change Cuba's future. His fingers itched to touch metal.

Rebecca glanced back at him, eyebrows arched, studying him in silence. He wondered if she was catching on to his intent. A metallic taste coated his mouth. He had imagined revenge would taste sweeter.

"What's that building?" She turned away from him, pointing at Che.

"The Ministry of the Interior." His heart sped up. Watching her closely, he anticipated her reaction to his next words. "That's where your father works."

"It is? Wait." She turned slowly, facing him, understanding etched in her wide eyes and pursed lips. "My father works *there*?"

What did she expect? That her sweet *papi* rolled cigars on a street corner? "He works for the government."

"Oh." Her shoulders dropped, and she threw up her hands. "Well, no big deal. Everyone here works for the government."

Obviously, she had no idea what working in the Ministry of the Interior meant. He couldn't wait to school her. "He used to be an undercover informant for the MINIT, the security force of the Ministry of the Interior. Now he's one of their higher-ups. Probably has an office on the top floor." *And a key to the torture chamber in the basement.*

Her mouth fell open. "He works directly for Fidel?"

Why did she keep saying that man's first name? Like some

regular guy she knew and even admired? Heart drumming against his ribs, Antonio tried to keep his movements around the bike casual, choosing not to look Rebecca in the eye. "Well, technically he now works for the brother." He would kill both Castros given the chance. "He works for a group of people who use surveillance, intimidation, and even torture to keep the Cuban people isolated, ignorant, and in fear."

The humming of a tour bus's generator filled the silent pause.

He kept his back to her, but his muscles tightened. What would she do now? Had his passion scared her off? Or would she do what he needed her to do and draw her father down to the square, out in the open, where the murderer would be an easier target?

"I don't believe you." Her haunted whisper interrupted his train of thought.

He tried to pull off an indifferent shrug. Turning to dig into his bag, he used his body to shield what he was doing from both her and the patrolling officers.

"My mother would have died if she knew my father worked directly for Fidel, even if it wasn't his choice."

Antonio said nothing, his fingers finding the cool steel tip of his Ruger .380 automatic. He stroked it, checking out the action around him as he did. His mouth suddenly felt dry.

"Maybe she did know. Could that be why my mother left Cuba?"

Jesus, she wanted to ask all these questions *now*? But he needed to whet her appetite even further. She had to *want* to go get her father. "I don't remember much about your mother."

"But you remember a lot about my father?"

Heat rushed into his head, and his temples began to throb. He gripped the gun. Closing his eyes, he tried to breathe deeply to tamp down the memories, but the image of Rebecca's father walking into his front yard materialized anyway.

Antonio had been ten at the time and happy to see Rebecca's father, Arturo Menendez Garcia, one of the neighbors on his block. Arturo always brought the family sugar and fresh milk from his family's farm. The treats made his mother blush, but rendered his father silent. As a boy, Antonio hadn't understood the different reaction by his parents. Now, looking back, he realized that the color in his mother's cheeks had nothing to do with the gifts Arturo delivered. On that particular night, so many years ago, Antonio remembered feeling additional tension between Arturo and his father.

Despite that, Arturo had smiled at Antonio that evening, even rubbed him on the head, so Antonio had let down his guard and had gone back to playing. Not ten minutes later, his father lay dead in the street, blood pooling around the ball the two of them had been kicking around.

Blind fury rushed through Antonio's veins, hot and fast, until his head throbbed like it was close to exploding. His vision blurred. He wiped a hand across his forehead.

"Antonio?" Rebecca placed a hand on his shoulder.

He jumped at her touch; her fingers felt like fire branding his flesh. He shook her hand off. She had Arturo's blood. Finger now on the trigger, he forced himself to remove it and placed the gun back in its container until he could breathe again and act without heated emotion.

"Are you okay?"

She didn't touch him this time, but he still couldn't look at her.

"Let me help you sit down."

"No."

"What is it?"

"This place."

"What about it?"

"It's the root of much evil." Antonio shuddered, the urge to kill boiling in his blood, but unexpectedly, shame also tugged at him.

"What just happened to you? Please tell me."

"I was remembering something."

"What?"

He turned to look at her, close enough to smell the heat of the day on her caramel-colored skin. "The night a neighborhood friend murdered my father."

"Oh God." She paled, her hand fluttering above her heart. "I'm sorry. What brought up that memory?"

"Being here." *With you. With him. In there.* Glancing toward the image of Che, he wondered if the legendary man had ever faltered when faced with the chance to kill an enemy. Probably not. Leaders did what leaders had to, no matter the collateral damage.

"We can leave." Rebecca glanced at him through narrowed eyes, her body perfectly still.

That would be the right thing to do. "Without meeting your father?"

Rebecca twisted around to face the Ministry of the Interior.

He heard himself speak, as if on autopilot, his voice no longer his own. "Don't you want to go inside and ask to speak to the man who should have spent the last twenty-six years being a father to you?" Numb, he'd disconnected himself from his body. "Aren't you curious why he never even tried to contact you?"

She started to walk toward the building, hesitant at first.

"Isn't it important to you to prove you're not all alone in the world now?" He increased his volume and intensity. "That you have value?"

With an indescribable primal sound, Rebecca took off

running.

About damn time. But Antonio wasn't feeling satisfaction. He fingered the pistol, stroking it with conflicted intentions.

He scoured the plaza for any red flags. *Damn it!* One of the young uniformed cops was watching Rebecca with keen interest. Tourists didn't run like hell toward one of Cuba's most guarded offices. She should have known to walk. He shouldn't have provoked her like he had. The officer talked into a walkie-talkie. *Que mierda.* Calling in reinforcements probably.

Rebecca wouldn't make it inside. Quickly, he pocketed the pistol and took off in a well-controlled advance. *Got to stop her before she gets us both arrested.* With his long legs, catching up to Rebecca only took a few seconds.

He grabbed her by the shoulder, tugging at her. "Stop."

"No." She jerked out of his hold. "I'm going in."

"No, you're not." He reached for her wrist, wrapping his hand around her thin bones.

She jerked to a stop. "You're the one who suggested it."

Another uniformed officer exited the ministry, heading down the stairs toward them. *The backup.* "It's too dangerous right now. The police are suspicious of you."

"I'll tell them I'm Arturo Menendez's daughter." Her eyes fired with rebellion. But behind the anger, tears were building. She might lose her cool, and with it their safety. Women could be so emotional. He had to rein her in.

She yanked against his hold with enough ferocity to shake him from his stance, but he held her wrist firmly. "I did know your mother…and your father."

"What?" She stalled, as if she'd run out of gas.

"You lived in my neighborhood, Rebecca."

Her face paled. "I did?" She took a step back. "I don't remember."

"Of course you don't." He tightened his grip, making

sure not to hurt her. "You were just a baby, and your mother left right after your birth." He eyed the cop who had exited the ministry. The young man had stopped to watch them. He also spoke into a walkie-talkie. No doubt the two cops were debating the threat. "I do know why your mother left your father and Cuba. I was there."

"What?"

The shock in her eyes impaled him. "Your father slept with my mother."

She slapped him hard, her free hand spreading a sting of pain across his left cheek. He shuffled backward.

"You're a liar."

The slap startled him, but he didn't let go of her other wrist. "Why would I lie about something as twisted as that?" *Something that ruined my life?*

"They had an affair?"

"When your mother found out, she left your father. Arturo never made an attempt to stop her or get you back." He purposely left out the part about Arturo *murdering* his father in cold blood while he, as a boy, watched but could do nothing to stop it.

Red stained her cheeks. "And you brought me here knowing that?"

He swallowed, instantly hating himself. "I did." The acid in his stomach stirred.

"Why?" she whispered.

Scanning the square, the cop from the plaza was walking toward them again, gaining ground. Antonio's pulse skyrocketed. He'd trained for this. He knew what to do. Still, his muscles clenched.

"I thought you valued me," Rebecca whispered.

"What?" He'd been so lost in his critical observations he'd stopped listening to her.

"I spent my whole childhood feeling worthless. Because

I didn't have a father."

The tears started to roll down her cheeks. *Jesus.* Why did he even give a shit? Because he was getting to know her. *Wanting* to know her more. Still, he couldn't let her blow their cover. "Pull it together, Menendez." His stomach twisted with conflicting feelings.

"You tell me I do have a father, and he's never tried to look for me. Thank you for proving that's exactly what I am. Worthless."

Her words tortured his heart. He knew what worthless felt like. "I'm sorry." The words spilled out, and he stepped back, shocked he'd even said them. Did he mean that? He never said he was sorry. Maybe he did mean it, and the thought made his knees a little weak. For as far back as he could remember he'd been planning for this. She was supposed to be the bait, not the voice of his damn conscience calling him out at the last moment. He wasn't supposed to fall...

"*Oye tu!*" *Hey, you!* The police officer from the plaza called out to them.

Every muscle in his body tensed. *Fuck.*

Rebecca's eyes grew round as saucers.

"We need to go." He let go of her wrist but grabbed her hand. He didn't trust her emotional state right now.

She nodded, but hesitated. "I'm here. I'll never be here again. This is my only chance to prove if my father is alive." She pulled out of his hold. "I'm not leaving."

"If we're detained, you'll never get to see your father. We have to leave now." He reached to grab her again, but her wrist slipped through his grasp. *Damn it.*

She'd started walking, not a run this time, but a very determined kind of gait that left no doubt in his mind that she intended to walk into the lobby of the Ministry of the Interior and ask for her father. The arrogant woman walked right past the approaching ministry guard. *Dios mío...* They were screwed now.

"*Que hacen ahí?*" *What are you doing there?* The young cop who'd been watching her started running after her. The cop who exited the Ministry of the Interior turned on his heel to follow her, too. He kept it at a casual pace.

"*No se muevan!*" *Don't move.* The younger cop was losing his patience with her.

Damn it! Even if she drew her father down from his well-protected office, Antonio wouldn't be able to get a shot off without one of those pigs shooting him as well. And then they'd shoot Rebecca. The realization hit him like a bullet. This was not *her* battle. His father's murder was not *her* fault. He did value her, but no longer as bait. And he didn't want to damage her irreversibly. He didn't want to hurt her at all. He rolled his head, his neck cracking. *What should I do now?* "Rebecca, *mi amor, dígame, por favor.*" *Rebecca, my love, talk to me please*, he yelled across the distance between them.

She hesitated, surely confused at the change in the tone of his voice and his choice of words, but she didn't stop, despite Antonio's plea and the cop's demand.

Sprinting past the police officer closest to her, Antonio reached her side, throwing both arms around her in a lover's embrace. "Play along," he whispered as he pulled her close. "Do it. They're watching us."

"What?" She didn't struggle.

"Have you lost your damn mind? Running like that?" He spoke in Spanish.

"*You're* pushing me over the edge, Antonio." She pitched her voice so low he could barely hear. "Bringing me to this place, hanging the possibility of my father out in front of me. You are driving me to do crazy things."

"Kiss me," he whispered into her ear.

"Now you've lost *your* mind."

He could feel her heart drumming against his chest. He

turned her toward him and forced his lips on hers before she could object or speak. Her lips were warm and pliant, surprising given the crisis they found themselves in. Her body went limp in his arms, as if giving up was exactly what she wanted to do. Or maybe fear had finally immobilized her. Either way, he took advantage of her submission and deepened the kiss. When the tip of her tongue complied, tentatively touching his, he hardened, desire joining the adrenaline already pumping through him. Jesus, he was one sick bastard to be thinking about this right now. They were going to end up in jail. But maybe this playacting was their way to freedom.

"*Buenos días.*" The officer from inside the ministry had reached them. He cleared his throat, probably waiting for them to stop kissing.

Rebecca pushed against Antonio's chest, breaking the kiss first. Fear resonated in her eyes, but he didn't know if that was a reaction to his kiss or acknowledgment of the deep shit they'd just stepped in.

The older police officer had his hand on his gun, eyeing them without expression.

The second officer huffed to their side. "*Porque se movieron?*" *Why did you move?* The young officer must have been pissed they hadn't obeyed his orders, because he had his gun out and aimed right at them.

"My woman. She's playing hard to get." Antonio knew his Cuban Spanish was perfect. Smiling at the officers, he buried his face in the crook of Rebecca's neck, praying she wouldn't freeze and alert them to the fact that she wasn't really Cuba raised. Here, sex was a natural part of life, to be enjoyed and displayed at will. And fighting as foreplay wasn't unusual.

He could feel the blood rush through the artery in her neck, pounding like mad, and sweat trickled down the side of her face, but her body didn't stiffen, nor did she push him away. Instead, she wrapped her arms around his neck and hooked her leg around his.

Good girl.

"Were you heading to the Ministry of the Interior?" the calm officer asked. He must be trained to be the good cop.

"No, señor." He detached Rebecca from his body. "She was running away from me."

"Because you lied to me." She shouted so convincingly, she even fooled him for a second. Or maybe she was being honest. He had lied to her.

Either way, she was playing along. *Smart.* "She was just a friend," he pleaded. Let the cops think they were having a lover's spat.

She slapped him again, real satisfaction lighting up her eyes.

He grabbed her with enough force she had no choice but to tumble into him, but without any kind of violence that would alarm the two cops standing close by. One of them was actually grinning. The other looked angry, but maybe a bit turned on. "I think you're enjoying this," he whispered into her ear. "Don't hit me again." She shivered against him.

"You have no idea how much," she whispered back. "Don't threaten me again."

"Little hellion." He planted his mouth on hers before she could reply. If she wanted to take advantage of the precarious situation they found themselves in to hit him and get him back, he'd do the same. She couldn't pull away. She wouldn't blow their cover. He slipped his tongue into her mouth, savoring the taste of her.

She bit him.

Hellcat. "Ouch!"

A hand on his shoulder pulled him away from her. "Take her home." The older cop gave him a knowing look. "And teach her a lesson."

"Like this, you mean?" He laid another kiss on her. So far the cops were buying their act. Maybe that's because Rebecca was actually kissing him back, this time running her hands through his hair and tugging on it. Jesus, it felt good. He wondered if he were able to maneuver a hand under her clothes, would she be excited? Did danger ignite her fire like it did his? Because right now, as the cops rolled their eyes at each other and walked away, his thoughts were drifting to the hard-on between his legs and how the line between danger and desire, pleasure and pain, was very thin for him.

He pressed her body up against his again, this time forcing her so close she could feel his erection.

She stiffened.

He broke the kiss. "What?"

Her gaze flickered toward the cops.

"They're leaving. We're good." He reassured her.

"You're carrying."

At first he thought she was referring to his erection. Then it hit him. She was feeling the gun in his pocket. *Shit.* It was hard and probably hurting her. He released his hold.

"I'm always packing." He tried a mischievous grin.

"I'm talking about the gun."

"I know."

"Why did you hide it from me?"

So much for desire being a pleasant side effect of the danger. "What difference does that make?" The moment had passed.

"Because I think you're not telling me the whole truth. Come clean, Antonio. What else are you hiding?"

Chapter Nine

Rebecca plopped down on a plastic stool in the bathroom of Uncle Johnny's farm, staring at the steam rising out of a tin bucket. Her bones ached, and she'd become so filthy she was actually able to carve her name in the layers of dirt caked onto her forearm. They'd survived a close call, and now her only plan was to shower, eat, and sleep. "What's this for?" she asked Esmeralda, pointing at the bucket. "To wash my clothes in?" *Please let that be the right answer.*

Esmeralda, who'd taken Rebecca under her wing as soon as she and Antonio arrived at the farm, dragged the bucket to her side and spoke in Spanish. "Hot water for you to bathe with."

Water sloshed over the side, a few lukewarm drops landing on Rebecca's naked toes. "For me to bathe in?" Rebecca stood and ripped back the shower curtain. The tiled area had a drain and a showerhead. "I don't understand."

"We have running water, but it's cold. Ice cold."

Rebecca shivered at the thought. *Great.* She'd been looking forward to powerful bullets of hot water blasting away her stress, disintegrating all this anger and confusion, washing it down the drain along with the dirt. Who the hell didn't have hot water? That was so uncivilized. "Where's Dallas, by the way?" She wondered how *he'd* react to no hot water.

"Helping Maria with something out back."

"You all escaped Angel's wrath, I see."

Esmeralda nodded. "Your guy is a good actor, no? He played along."

"Thanks for watching out for him."

Esmeralda laughed. "The big man watched out for me." She handed Rebecca a thin piece of material, barely thicker than a paper towel. "I brought you a washcloth."

"Oh." Rebecca didn't know what was worse, the rough texture or the moldy smell. "Really? This is all you have?" She wrinkled her nose, disappointment tingling throughout her tired body.

Esmeralda raised both eyebrows, crossing her arms in front of her.

Embarrassed that her tone was coming across as foul as her body, Rebecca looked at the floor. "I'm sorry."

"I think you need something stronger than a shower, something to take the edge off, no?"

Dropping her shoulders, Rebecca turned back to the shower. Smiling weakly, she eyed the bucket again. "I can't remember the last time I bathed."

"This is not just about the bath, no?"

"Well, yes. And no." Her attitude needed a good cleansing, too. Rebecca exhaled, determined not to sound like a spoiled, obnoxious American. "Did you know Antonio carries a gun?"

Waving that concern away like an annoying mosquito, Esmeralda rolled her eyes, "That's what's bothering you? Chica, how's Antonio supposed to protect you without it?"

Antonio had abducted her. He seemed to attract danger and was not afraid to respond with violence. They were in a hostile country. So, okay, it made sense he'd carry a gun. But why hadn't he told her about it?

If she was honest with herself, the hidden gun was only part of what bothered her. After the way they'd kissed in the Plaza de la Revoluciòn, after the way they'd fooled the Cuban police and escaped, she and Antonio should have been celebrating right now. High on life and thankful for the scrape with danger they'd just wiggled out of. *Working together* like Antonio had suggested up on the wall overlooking Havana bay.

But when they arrived at the farm a short time ago, they had both hopped off the bike, barely nodding at each other, and quickly gone their separate ways, like two strong magnetic forces repelling each other. Confusing at best. She shook her head.

Esmeralda raised a finger, watching her through narrowed eyes. "Wait for a minute." Then she slid out of the closet-sized bathroom, a playful smile on her pretty face. "Don't go anywhere."

"Where could I possibly go?" Rebecca asked the empty room. She plopped back down on the stool to wait. An image of the man in the picture Antonio had handed her popped back into her head. Could that really be her father? If so, her *papi* had armed police officers guarding his office building. How odd for an American to see that. What the hell did her *papi* do for the Cuban government?

Looking to keep busy, she occupied herself by checking out the room, quickly groaning at its austerity. Plain white walls, a skinny tiled shower, a toilet bowl without a tank, a sink with no toothpaste or toothbrushes on the counter, and no toilet paper. Really? Did it make her shallow that she longed for more?

And no mirror.

That was probably a good thing.

"*Oye*, I have something that will relax you." Esmeralda danced into the room, balancing a plate of pale orange fruit chunks in one hand, waving a tall, skinny brown bottle in her other hand.

Had to be alcohol. "I don't drink." *But I'll take that fruit, for sure.*

"*De verdad?*" *Truthfully?*

Esmeralda first placed the plate, then the bottle, on the sink counter as if both were priceless china. "Havana Club. The seven-year version. Pretty expensive." She pulled two shot glasses out of her pocket and set them next to the bottle.

Rebecca wished Esmeralda, nice as she was, would leave so she could throw back that delicious-looking fruit, whatever it was, undress, and get on with her lukewarm bucket shower. "Thank you for the food, but you shouldn't waste your expensive rum on someone who won't appreciate it."

Ignoring her, Esmeralda opened the bottle and poured the golden liquid into both glasses. "You may not appreciate it, but trust me, you need it." She handed her one. "Plus, we're celebrating."

"Celebrating what?" Rebecca raised the shot to her nose. The Cuban rum smelled of molasses and sugar cane with a hint of tobacco. Not too bad.

"Our escape from Cuba." Raising her cup in a toast, Esmeralda grinned like a child on Christmas morning.

"Don't you think we should stay sober in case we do have to 'escape' soon?"

Esmeralda's eyes lit up. "Antonio talked with his boat captain. *La Libertad* will be here tomorrow."

Rebecca's muscles tightened. Antonio had shared that information with Esmeralda? But not her? So much for working together. "How does he know that, anyway?" No one here had a cell phone that worked. Rebecca had asked as soon as they'd arrived.

"He talked to his captain by satellite phone."

Of course he did. Antonio must store his sat phone right next to his gun.

"So tonight"—Esmeralda tossed back the alcohol—"we celebrate, and then we sleep."

Rebecca sighed. Sleep sounded delightful, but her mind was racing around like an Earnhardt at Daytona. How the hell would she ever be able to doze off? Her gaze crept over to that shot glass full of rum.

Esmeralda laughed. "You can drink it straight. It's smooth, tastes like vanilla and oak, with a smoky finish that reminds me of a lover's breath."

Rebecca's thoughts drifted to Antonio. "No thanks."

Shrugging, Esmeralda poured herself another, downed it, and then licked her lips. "All right, *amiga*. Take a shower and come to dinner. We have a surprise for you." She rubbed her hands together in what looked like childlike glee. She left the room, leaving the fruit and the bottle of rum behind.

"I don't like surprises," Rebecca yelled after her. Ever since she'd met Antonio her life had been nothing but surprises.

Immediately, Rebecca plopped a piece of the fruit in her mouth. It had a rich, sweet taste, and the texture of a ripe pear. *Yummy.* She quickly ate a couple more pieces, wondering how Esmeralda could live with so little, and yet love so much about life?

After finishing off the whole plate, Rebecca undressed and used the slim bar of soap and the old rag to lather up. She had to use bar soap for her hair as well. Once she had enough suds, she picked up the bucket and poured some of the water over her head. "Aww." That lukewarm water must have been on the surface only, because the water rushing down her back now burned her skin. "You've got to be kidding me."

She dropped the bucket, not caring if the rest of the contents splashed out. Wiping the water out of her eyes, she jerked open the shower curtain, jumped out, grabbed a towel, and sat on the toilet.

Tears, almost as hot as the water that had scalded her, threatened to run down her face as the stress from the trip hit her all at once. Frustration filled up her lungs and burst out in one long, desperate howl. And then she began to cry. How the hell had she ended up here? Her life had been going just as planned. Would it ever be the same?

After a good five-minute deluge, Rebecca decided drinking the rum might not be such a bad idea. Best-case scenario, the alcohol would numb her mind so she could escape this real nightmare and disappear into a blissful sleep tonight.

Grabbing the shot glass, she downed the seven-year rum, swallowing so quickly the alcohol barely warmed her constricted throat. Esmeralda wasn't kidding. The rum went down smoothly, so smoothly she didn't even feel the effects. Maybe a second shot could help her get through an ice-cold shower, since she'd given up on the thought of bathing from a bucket. Rebecca poured and downed another.

• • •

The fingers of a familiar aroma wove their way into the tiny farmhouse bathroom, beckoning Rebecca with the mouthwatering scent of onions, green pepper, and garlic cloves simmering in olive oil. Someone was making sofrito, the basis for all that used to taste good in her *mami*'s West Tampa kitchen. So many different Cuban dishes began with this smell. Her stomach roared in anticipation. The fruit had only been a teaser of an appetizer. She'd barely eaten anything since this whole ordeal had started.

Drying off, she noticed Esmeralda must have brought her clean clothes, panties, and a sundress. *Hope it's the right size.* But no bra. *Great.* But all she could really focus on was the smell of the potential food waiting for her. Was that the surprise? She couldn't imagine anything better right now than home-cooked Cuban food. Bring on the pork, the rice and black beans. Something hardy to pick her up and give her energy.

Dressing quickly, she twisted the water out of her hair, leaned over and messed it up with her hands like she did at the beach. Her naturally wavy hair would dry curly if she did nothing else to it. Good enough for tonight. Her empty stomach protested again, sending rolling hunger pangs through her center. Her mouth was actually watering thinking about what might be waiting for her.

The hall leading to the kitchen remained empty and dark. The sun had set, but blaring salsa music and the voices of adults talking over one another clued her in to the direction she should head. She walked toward an open door at the end of the hallway and out into the softly lit backyard.

A couple of things quickly became evident. First, the temperature had not dropped. The air still hung heavy, like a muggy, tropical-island coverlet. Two, Antonio's family must be throwing some kind of party, odd given the circumstances of the day, but she couldn't deny the signs. Near her, a frosted cake sat on a long card table covered by a bright pink paper tablecloth. The cover looked like the ones you'd buy at the dollar store, and it had the words *Feliz Cumpleaños* on it, the Spanish way to say happy birthday.

Suddenly, a longing to return home rushed over her. She rolled her lips inward.

A couple of young kids, dancing in the center of the farm's courtyard, caught her attention. They were twirling through salsa steps to a song she recognized by Los Van Van, a famous Cuban band. Her *mami* had loved the band and had often played its CDs while whipping up arroz con pollo and sipping sangria on a Saturday night. Rebecca struggled to not get too teary-eyed on memories. The rum must be making her emotional. Maybe two shots had been too many. Maybe she wasn't supposed to have filled the shot glass to the top.

A piñata had been tied up in a tree to the right, white pieces of string hanging down, waiting for little fingers to pull on them. Rebecca closed her eyes, drifting back to her mother's small kitchen in their two-bedroom apartment in West Tampa, where every year her mother had made sure a handful of school friends came over to help her celebrate her birthday. Since they didn't have family in Tampa, her mother had used her famous black beans to lure kids and their parents to fill the empty seats and give the perception of a family gathering. Back when she was young, her mother couldn't afford a real piñata, so she would patch up the ones paying clients discarded at the fancy hotel where she had worked as a maid.

Rebecca's eyes ached, and the bittersweet onslaught of recollections erased her hunger and replaced it with an ache in her belly for home.

She jumped at the unexpected hand on her shoulder.

"Rebecca." It was just Maria. The skinny, small-framed woman had long, beautiful auburn hair but tired eyes. "Happy birthday."

"Oh my God." *This is all for me?* Rebecca's breath caught in her throat. "How did you know?"

"Antonio told me."

"He did?" Her stomach fluttered, but not with hunger.

Maria smiled. "He did."

"I'm—I'm shocked."

"Why?" Maria put her skinny arm around Rebecca's

waist and gave her a squeeze. "Antonio knows a lot about you."

Suddenly uncomfortable, Rebecca shifted out of Maria's hold.

"He's been emailing me for months, telling me all about you."

Rebecca's skin began to tingle. "Months?" She covered her mouth, whispering through her hand. "What's he been telling you about me?" Alarm bells went off in her head. *He's been following me?*

Maria placed a gentle hand on her arm. "He watches your reports, you know."

Okay, he's just been watching me on TV. But she must have had a confused look on her face.

"You're a newsperson, right?" Pursing her lips, Maria looked up, as if trying to come up with the right words.

That's when it registered. Maria was speaking English, and her pronunciation was pretty good. Antonio had probably had a hand in that as well.

"I'm sorry. I don't understand what you do in America. We don't have shows like yours here. We have four channels. One is for education, two are for government, and one has cartoons. Here at the farm we don't even have a TV. But Antonio, he says he watches you on TV every day in America."

Every day? "He strikes me as someone who would look down on the news as sensational."

Maria shrugged. "He told me about the woman who got set on fire."

Stiffening, Rebecca looked at Maria to make sure she heard right. "Adrianna?"

"I don't know her name, but he said you helped a woman being abused. That her husband threw gasoline on her and set her on fire."

The memory made Rebecca shudder. "I covered her story for a year until her ex-husband went on trial."

Maria began to tremble. "Antonio is afraid that will happen to me."

Rebecca froze. "By who? Your fiancé, Angel?"

The skinny woman dropped her gaze, and her hand slid off Rebecca's arm in a silent answer. As Maria moved, her sleeve came up, exposing an ugly purple-and-black bruise.

Rebecca gently held Maria's arm so she could confirm the bruise. "Oh my gosh, did Angel do that yesterday?"

"He's not very nice sometimes. Please, don't tell Antonio."

Maria's voice, barely above a whisper, stung Rebecca, and she couldn't help but see Adrianna's burned features in her mind's eye. Reaching for Maria, Rebecca hugged the young woman. "I won't."

"I don't want to happen to me what happened to the lady in your TV news story."

"I don't want that, either." Now Rebecca had a much better idea of Antonio's drive to get here and get his sister out of Cuba. She'd felt a similar unstoppable drive to help Adrianna.

"You will help me, no?" Maria asked.

"I will."

"I'm thankful for that."

Rebecca's stomach growled. "Oh, I'm sorry. The food smells so good."

"So, the dinner, first?"

Oh God, she couldn't help herself. Even if her mind had forgotten the food, her stomach could not. And the smells were so delicious. "Yes, please."

"Almost ready."

Thank God. "And the piñata? It's all for me?"

Maria nodded, a little bit of joy returning to her eyes.

Rebecca had to blink a couple of times, breathing slowly

to keep the emotion inside. "I don't get it."

"Get what?"

"Why you all would do this for me when you don't even know me." *And you certainly don't have any extra money.*

Tilting her head to one side, Maria smiled. "My brother knows you."

Rebecca swallowed. "No, he doesn't."

"He knows more than you think." Maria laughed and gestured with her head toward the red wooden shack to the right of the courtyard. "He watches you, even now."

Following her gesture, she caught Antonio, mostly in the shadow, leaning against the shack. Their eyes met, and her mouth went dry, her heart palpitating. He'd showered, too, his hair still wet, new clothes on his lean body. He looked so handsome.

He raised his eyebrows at her, but his body remained perfectly still.

Suddenly, she had to know why he'd been watching her for months. Stomach fluttering, she quickly squeezed Maria again and then headed Antonio's way.

He straightened, watching her approach, but his facial expression didn't change, nor did he hide back in the darkness. He looked like he always did, reserved and in control, but one second away from igniting. The tension was evident in the plant of his feet and the way he shoved both hands into the pockets of his pants.

Then a little hand slipped into her empty one and tugged. "Miss America, Miss America," a young voice said in Spanish. "You must do the piñata. Mami says it's for you. I can't play with it."

She turned toward the high-pitched voice.

Little Tonito was speaking in Spanish and pleading with his big brown eyes. "Please? Please?"

She bit her bottom lip, risking a peek at Antonio.

He raised his hands as if asking, 'What does he want?'

She pointed at the piñata.

Antonio smiled, actually smiled at her, and it reached all the way to his eyes.

Heat crept into her cheeks. Quickly she shrugged and smiled back, honestly a little relieved she didn't have to go confront Antonio right now with so many questions tumbling through her head. Playing with a piñata sounded so much easier.

"Okay, Tonito, let's go pull the piñata strings together." She didn't want any candy, but had even less desire to make this cute little boy cry. Like the Pied Piper, she led a line of kids to the piñata. Could they all be family? *Wow*. Her heart stretched. Look at what all she'd missed during her childhood. Stripped of her family by Castro's government.

She shook off the gloomy thought, and in Spanish, told the kids to each grab one of the strings. She counted to three and watched in joy as the young ones pulled so hard the piñata bottom gave way almost instantly, and a flood of candy pieces rained down on the group. A few kids fell on top of one another, rolling around in their effort to grab as many pieces of candy as their small hands could hold. Small M&M's bags and pieces of Sugar Daddys left no doubt in Rebecca's mind who supplied the candy for tonight's party.

She glanced over at the backyard shack, but Antonio had disappeared. Her heart dropped. Shouldn't he at least enjoy the results of his generosity? That man moved like a ghost in the night, sliding quietly in and out of various spaces, never staying any place too long. Never enjoying the results of his good deeds. And she was learning he was responsible for many good deeds. Her heart fluttered at the thought.

"You forgot this." Esmeralda reappeared, handing her another shot of the seven-year rum. "I like it much better than your American candy." She grinned.

Feeling looser than she had in days, Rebecca decided the rum had been good for her, but she declined another shot. Getting drunk had never been her thing.

Esmeralda shrugged, grabbed the shot, and tossed it back. Winking, she leaned in to whisper, "Happy birthday, pretty American." Then she pointed a finger at her, a serious gleam in her eyes. "Don't leave without me."

"I won't."

"Promise?"

Unlike the fragile Maria, Esmeralda's energy burned bright every time Rebecca neared her. She liked this woman and would not leave her behind. "I promise." No matter what the cost. Now, where did Antonio go? She turned to look. She wanted to ask him a few questions about his "research" on her.

"Great! Then we dance to celebrate." Esmeralda grabbed her hand.

Was this woman always so damn cheerful? Before Rebecca could verbally protest, Esmeralda pulled her into the center of the courtyard, another Los Van Van song playing on the 1980s boom box. Rebecca laughed as Esmeralda took the man's position and twirled her around. Wow, she liked this family. They were so unpretentious and kind. And fun.

Esmeralda kept pulling Rebecca into awkward embraces, spinning her around as if they were partners. She giggled, attempting to convince her feet to work—one two three-one two three—but either the rum or exhaustion made coordination impossible tonight, and she tripped over Esmeralda's feet.

Great, I'm going down. Rebecca fell forward, squealing, but before she could hit the ground, two large hands swooped under her armpits and hauled her back onto her feet.

"I think you've had enough rum." Antonio, materializing out of thin air, spun her around so she had to face him.

Her heart bumped against her rib cage. "How do you know?" She wasn't drunk. Hmmm, she leaned in closer to him. He smelled so clean, of soap with just the faintest hint of rum. A strange yearning throbbed in her center.

One of his hands moved behind her back, sliding, as if it were the most natural thing in the world to cup the top of her butt. The heat from his palm transferred instantly through her cotton dress and down into her core. A naughty, out-of-control feeling rose up, making her dizzy. She stepped back to stop from swooning. Yes, swooning. She'd scarcely thought she'd ever have a use for the word, yet alone find herself succumbing to such a thing.

"You can't even stand on your own two feet."

She spun around again, half trying to prove she could dance, half trying to get out of his hold. "That's because I'm tired and hungry." *And because you knock me off my center every time you get this close to me.*

"Another reason why you shouldn't slam rum." He allowed her some freedom, but held on to her hand. Then, like a skilled lead dancer, he twirled her in toward his body.

She banged against him, not very gracefully. "I am relaxed, but I'm not drunk." She laughed at her clumsiness. "I'm just not a good dancer."

His fingers tightened on her waist. "Aren't you?"

A slow smile took over her face. She had to admit she liked Antonio's big hands on her waist, heating up her lower section with a delicious mix of longing and pleasure.

He pushed her at the waist again, spinning her back out, but keeping a tight hold on her hand.

This kind of dancing made her dizzy, and she laughed out loud. He spun her back into his body, directing her until she stood face-to-face with him. Rum danced on his breath. So, he'd been drinking, too. Who could blame either of them? What a day. And it wasn't over. That thought made her cheeks fill with heat.

She devoured his features, gawking at his freshly washed hair. He'd brushed his rock-star curls until the dark strands hit his shoulders in perfect waves. They looked soft, so opposite of everything about him. She couldn't resist testing that theory. She reached up and twirled a piece over her finger. The strand rubbed against the pad of her thumb like satin against her cheeks.

His goatee was still there, but it had been trimmed; neat, but still seductive. She imagined what that hair would feel like if his face brushed against her skin in her most intimate places. She let the strand of his hair go and scraped her fingers slowly, gently against his short beard.

He stiffened and inhaled.

She loved that her touch could do that to him. She smiled at him, stunned to see how dilated his pupils had become and how powerless he looked in this moment. "You knew today was my birthday." She batted her eyelashes at him. "Thank you for all of this."

He stopped dancing, pulling his hands off her. "Yes." His chest heaved as if he couldn't breathe. "You're welcome."

They stood awkwardly in the courtyard, kids dancing around them. Even Esmeralda had taken a new partner and danced as if she had no care in the world.

"How?" Although he'd let her go, he was still close enough for her to feel the heat his body was putting off. And to tell his breathing was faster than usual.

"Birthdays are easy enough to look up."

"Your sister says you've been looking up a lot of stuff about me." She licked her lips, wanting him to pull her closer again, craving the feeling of that rough beard against her cheeks. Deep inside she knew that what she was initiating was wrong. She was a reporter. He was a revolutionary. A stalker. And maybe a criminal. She would never be able to bring this kind of man to her charity events. He'd never fit into her world, and she'd never belong in his. But she'd never known this feeling of reckless desire. Like she'd risk *anything* just to feel Antonio kiss her again, because he kissed with such passion it left her breathless.

. . .

Antonio looked at Rebecca's flushed cheeks and the lips she'd just moistened with her tongue. She looked like a woman who wanted to be kissed. "I needed to study you before I picked you." He had had no idea she'd be this passionate when he was watching her on TV all those months ago, planning her role in his mission, imagining what she'd be like, wondering if she'd live up to his high expectations of her.

She wobbled, and he steadied her with both hands, his big palms resting on the sides of her hips.

Her eyes sparkled up at him. "That's kind of stalkerish, don't you think?"

He couldn't stop the smile. "Is stalkerish even a word?" He reached up to brush a strand of her curly hair out of her eyes. As he touched her, a sting of static electricity jumped between them.

She sucked in a breath.

He wanted to capture that sound with his mouth.

Truth was he had probably started falling in love with Rebecca before he'd even met her. He had been following her, not in person, but on TV and on social media, checking out the kind of stories she did and reading how she responded to viewers. He'd been drawn in at first by her beauty and her strong sense of righteousness and justice. She had always seemed to pick stories that centered on an underdog or a person in need, confronting the injustice, righting the wrong, ending with a resolution for a person who never could have done it on their own.

On social media, she was constantly posting pictures at charity events, and she spent many weekends volunteering her time at a local domestic violence shelter, making him believe her heart was in line with her head, dedicated to serving others above herself.

Then they'd confronted each other in the tent in the Everglades that stormy night. And doubt had rained down on him. And the realization that his lifelong goal was to kill her father made him build up a wall around himself. He'd been determined not to let her in.

The song changed and the tempo slowed. Hesitating, Antonio finally pulled her closer, one hand capturing hers in an old-fashioned slow dance position. *Fuck it.* He wanted her. Couldn't control this crazy physical chemistry. The rest, he hoped, would work itself out.

She relaxed into his hold, as if she wanted to be swept away. "For the first time since I met you Antonio, I feel really good." She exhaled.

He pulled her closer, the hand around her waist drawing her body tight with his until their cheeks touched. "Yes, you do feel good." He intentionally scraped his goatee against her cheek.

She shivered in his hold, her body seeming to melt right into his, like the final two pieces of a puzzle finally fitting together.

"I like this relaxed side of you," he murmured into her ear. He also liked what he'd seen since that first night in the Everglades. First, she'd sacrificed her own safety to help a group of strangers. Then she'd pushed him to allow Esmeralda to come with them back to America, even when he told her she could be accused of smuggling. And just moments ago, when he watched her interact with his sister and nephew, that's when he knew without any uncertainty he'd made the right decision. She belonged here. In his life. In his arms. And tonight he was going to take their relationship one step further. Future consequences be damned.

He pressed his body into hers and waited for her reaction to his brazen move.

Her breath stilled, and she closed her eyes, bringing her lips to his neck, kissing him softly, slowly.

He was hard, and she had to feel it. Yet she was egging him on, baiting him for more.

He strengthened his hold on her, but then hesitated. If they were to take this to the next level, he had to do something very important first. "I…I'm sorry for today." He wasn't the kind of man who was used to apologizing, but he would not take advantage of her. Not now that his feelings for her had deepened. She had to know the truth first, and then decide if she still wanted to kiss him.

She stumbled even though he'd been leading her with confidence. "For what part of today? Everything's kind of blurring together."

"I'm sorry for setting you up."

• • •

Antonio's words sounded like a confession. Her body tingled with his every touch, and right now, as they swayed to the music, his body touched her everywhere. She did register that he was trying to tell her something meaningful and important. "What happened with the cops today?"

Their cheeks touched, and his breath bathed her ear. "Yes."

"You didn't know they'd come after me." With her left hand, she slowly stroked his back, something she'd wanted to do but was too ashamed to even admit to herself. She freed the hand he was holding and placed her arm around his neck, forcing an even greater intimacy between them, because now they had to look each other in the eyes. "We survived."

"We did." His lips moved down to her neck, and his tongue caressed the area where her artery pumped. Just as she'd done to him. Holy cow, she couldn't lie about her desire now. He had to be able to feel how quickly the blood was rushing to her brain. As quickly as his pulse had been pumping.

"You smell so good, Rebecca," he whispered against her skin.

She inhaled, but she couldn't form a reply. He'd literally taken her breath away. Again.

As he nipped and kissed his way down her neck, she sighed at the delicious sensation sizzling through her. "We escaped, and it was kind of fun." She ground her hips into his, hoping to make him even more excited.

He moaned, pulling her closer. "You handled yourself admirably today. But we need to talk about what happened. And why."

She frowned. "I don't want to talk about today."

He broke their embrace. "I need to talk about today. I have to tell you something. Before we do this."

Her heart froze. Whatever he was about to say would ruin the moment, ruin the slow, sexy mood they'd created, she knew it. She gazed up into his eyes, watching as guilt clouded his gaze.

"Rebecca." It was a plea.

She swallowed. "Don't, Antonio." She placed one hand on his chest, right over his heart. It was beating madly, showing her a side of him he'd never revealed in his expression. That scared her even more. "I want to sleep in peace tonight," she whispered, hoping he could hear her over the blaring music. "Whatever confession you are dying to unload, please don't do it right now." She guessed it had to do with her father, and in this moment, she didn't want to know the truth.

He stroked her cheek. "I never expected this."

"Expected what?" Her heart sped up.

"To care." He dragged his thumb against her bottom lip, his eyes following his movement.

A rush of excitement shimmied down her spine. "To care about what?"

"To care so much about you." He parted her lips with his thumb. "To want you so much."

She licked his thumb. He tasted salty. Her head spun. Now she did feel drunk. But it wasn't from the alcohol. She was drunk with lust. Closing her eyes, she allowed the pleasure to wash over her. She sucked his thumb, longing to do the same to his rum-soaked tongue. Yes, she was acting like a crazy woman. But she didn't care. She'd never felt this turned on in her life. And she feared she never would again. She was in Cuba, on a farm, far away from America. Who would possibly know? It's not like they had surveillance cameras or iPhones here. She had to explore this feeling further.

As if reading her mind, Antonio's lips pressed against hers with a need that matched her beating heart. He tasted of the seven-year rum, which she now loved. She gave in and played with his tongue, savoring the flavor. Sucking on it softly at first, she dragged it through her teeth, wanting to, hoping to inflict the slightest bit of pain. Truth be told she wanted to hear Antonio *express* his needs. He was usually so locked up. She was desperate to know he longed for her the way she longed for him.

He inhaled sharply, but didn't yell or stop her. If anything, her naughtiness provoked him further. His big hands moved down to her butt, his fingers gently caressing her there. She could only imagine what it would feel like if those long fingers stroked her underneath her thin little sundress. She willed his fingers to find their way there.

So lost in this glorious sensation, it didn't register at first that the music had stopped. The kiss ended, and Antonio leaned away. Maybe he noticed, too? A round of applause erupted, and a few adults whistled. Oh God, was the whistle for them? She'd totally forgotten where they were. She dragged her hand across her mouth. There were kids here. *Oh Lordy.*

She turned around. Dallas was staring at her with his mouth wide open and his eyes full of disbelief. He had a video camera with him. Was he shooting video of her and Antonio? *Holy shit.* Heat blasted both her cheeks. She felt breathless, just like she had when Ignado had pressed that nasty-smelling rag against her face.

If the police ever saw her making out with her "abductor" that would shoot down any chance she had of getting back into America without repercussions. "Oh my God." Her hand covered her galloping heart. "What the hell have I done?"

Chapter Ten

Rebecca sprinted through the back door, down the hallway, to the closest of three bedrooms in Johnny's farmhouse. She had to get away from Antonio before she crossed the line and became his lover, which would also make her an accomplice and a willing participant, no longer the victim. She'd been depending on using that excuse once she went back to America. What the hell was she going to do now? There was nowhere to run and hide until they could both cool down and realize the folly in taking this attraction any further.

She glanced around. The stark room had one bed in it, a simple unpainted dresser, no closet, and a white sheet hanging over the entranceway serving as a door. Her heart hit the floor. A sheet? That wouldn't keep Antonio out. Not even for one second.

The sound of him stomping down the hall made her back up until the bed stopped her retreat. She held her breath, biting her bottom lip, uncertainty causing her heart to skip beats.

She wanted him.

But wanted not to.

The cotton slip covering the doorway flew to one side, and Antonio marched in. "You want this as much as I do. Don't lie to yourself. Don't lie to me."

She crossed her legs at the ankle, hoping to hide how she was trembling. There was no mistaking Antonio's mood now. He stopped at the threshold, staring at her with the same intensity he'd used before. That glare nailed her feet to the spot and rendered her speechless. She'd fall under his spell again if he touched her. She knew she couldn't resist the physical chemistry that drew them together, so she had to keep distance between them.

"Speechless?" He advanced on her, a dare firing up in his eyes.

She used to be so sure of what she wanted. She wanted to marry a successful man, and live the life she'd dreamed of since she was a little girl listening to her mom talk about the big houses she cleaned on Bayshore Boulevard and of the fine women who lived there. She'd also longed to be a famous reporter, respected for her reports on issues *that mattered.*

"You would never like my world. You would find it too public, and at times ostentatious." But standing here, with her body physically aching for more of Antonio's touch, Rebecca wondered what it was she actually wanted. "And I won't ever understand your world, or what is buried so deep in your heart it's driving you to do dangerous things." She just knew she had never wanted any man like she longed for this one. "I want a simpler life, Antonio. A less dangerous one." *I want these crazy feelings you stir up to stop. Don't I?*

"Don't take the easy way out, Rebecca."

Heat rushed into her cheeks. Why did he always push *that* button? "There's nothing wrong with wishing for wealth and success." *And to remain in control.*

"Money and fame won't be enough to satisfy you." A

knowing smile played on his lips.

"Really?" She gulped down too much air. "And you think you can satisfy me?"

One of his eyebrows arched.

She probably shouldn't have issued that challenge.

"Is that an invitation to show you?" He sauntered toward her, his dark eyes never leaving hers.

"Why did you kiss me in front of everybody?" She crossed her arms. "Why in front of my photographer, of all people, who could have been shooting video?"

"I kissed you because you wanted me to, because you *invited* me to, and because I'm attracted to you, and I wanted to." He took his time, moving on her like a lion advancing on its paralyzed prey. "Obviously, the feeling is mutual." He stopped in front of her, mere inches away, so close when he exhaled she could feel it, yet far enough away they weren't touching.

She placed her hand over her heart, taking a step back, frightened by the power of the energy sizzling off him, but there was nowhere to go.

"I didn't expect to care. I still don't *want* to care." The sound of his voice rang desperate. "But I do care. And I know you do, too."

"We don't need this right now."

"I don't think you know what you really need." Entwining a strand of her hair around his fingers, he used his other hand to pull her closer.

She tripped over her own feet, tumbling into his hold.

"But I'm going to enjoy showing you," he leaned in and whispered, "slowly."

This encounter was spiraling out of control. He was a master at restraint, but she sensed he was seconds away from losing it with her. And God help her, that excited her. What the hell was wrong with her? She pushed against his chest, but barely moved the block of a man. She had to stop this now. "Antonio, you need to leave the room and stop this, before we…"

"Before we what, Rebecca? Say it."

"It doesn't matter. We're going back to America tomorrow." She twisted out of his hold, took two steps backward, and her back hit the bedroom wall.

He followed.

"And then we'll never see each other again." Why start something? Something that could get them both in trouble. Something that might make her long for him forever.

He reached out and stroked her cheek, his touch making the muscles deep in her core clench. She squeezed her legs together. "I don't want you to kiss me again." *If you do, I'm lost.*

"Liar." He moved one hand back into her hair, rolling strands around his fingers, creating a rope, so when he tugged on it, he forced her to expose her neck and arch her back.

Her scalp tingled.

He moved in so their skin touched, cheek to cheek, and his warm breath tickled her ear. "Do you have any idea what I want to do to you right now?"

She shook her head, unable to speak.

"I'm going to show you." His right hand found her left wrist, and he pulled her hand behind her back.

She inhaled.

He grabbed her other hand and pulled it behind her as well. He'd trapped both of her hands between her body and the hard wall. The broken concrete nipped at the skin on her knuckles. "If you don't like it, I'll stop." He shifted his hold on her so his hand protected hers from the rough concrete. "Tell me, Rebecca. If you want me to stop."

It barely hurt, but to her surprise she liked the edgy sensation, a slim balance between pleasure and pain. Her core stirred again, releasing that same delicious wetness. Was this what Antonio was into? A little rough foreplay? A little show of power? And why was she responding? Because no man had ever taken the time to work her up like this. And never in this deliciously slow, torturous way.

He moved in even closer, pinning her whole body against the wall, his erection against her middle. When he nuzzled her neck, his lips brushed the spot where her artery throbbed. He had to know how much he was turning her on. She shuddered at how vulnerable she felt.

"Isn't it exciting to want something so badly, you'd do anything to have it?" Then he whispered, "That's how you make me feel."

She swallowed, too embarrassed to answer.

His lips found that sensitive area right behind her ear. "You'll never feel anything as intense as this, wanting something you know you're not supposed to have." He gently kissed her between words. "You know what this tells me about you?" He kissed her neck softly until she squirmed against him. "In public you're a good girl, but here." He moved his hand down and laid it across her breast. He had to feel her heart pounding. "And here." His fingers slid down the center of her chest, down her abdomen to the vee between her legs, which throbbed now, aching for his touch. He tapped his fingers outside her dress, hitting and missing that one part of her body that had control over her in this moment. "Here, you want to be a bad girl."

She should struggle, fight him, but what he was saying was true. And she wanted to see if he could coax that bad girl out of her. If he could finally get her to let go of the control.

He cupped her against the outside of her dress, and she began to push forward, meeting his fingers. Embarrassment at her neediness should have shamed her, but she didn't care. Antonio was right. This felt so good.

He removed his hand from between her thighs. "But first, you have to tell me you want me, too. I have to hear you say it."

Oh God, was he kidding? "Just touch me already. You control freak." They both were, and this powerful push-and-pull drove her crazy.

Antonio's fingers moved leisurely over her. "Your heart is racing."

She bit her bottom lip again as his finger ran circles around her left nipple. Even with the dress as a shield, the sensation sent electrical spikes of pleasure through her. Leaning back against the wall, she threw her head back and closed her eyes, yearning for more of his touch.

He lifted his head. "Do you want me to stop?"

She shook her head.

His hand moved down to her waist, over her hips, and around to her backside, where he leaned down to gather up the hem of her skirt. "You have a lot of passion buried inside. I bet you've never allowed yourself to let it go."

She shivered, her breathing shallow and fast.

"You're like this ice princess caged inside a perfect little castle. Let go, Rebecca. I want to see the *real* you." As he lifted her skirt, his fingers tickled the flesh of her inner thighs, heightening her pleasure.

"Antonio, please,"

"You can speak." He laughed, not *at* her, as he was obviously enjoying this as much as she was.

"Please what? Please touch you here?" His finger stroked the outside of her cotton panties, teasing her by circling everywhere but the one spot she craved. "I want you undressed. I want to feel you naked against me."

The thought made goose bumps pop all over her skin. The man was physically perfect in clothes, and she could only imagine what he looked like naked. She remembered the ripple of his tight abs as she'd held on to to him on that motorbike. Now she'd have a chance to run her fingers down those waves, slowly, savoring the moment, without the barrier of clothing. And then she'd…

The sheet covering the door flew to one side and someone walked into the room.

Holy shit! Rebecca struggled to right her clothes and cover herself. Blinking, she tried to make out whomever it was that just barged in on them. Heat rushed to her cheeks, embarrassment flushing through her whole system.

"Sorry to interrupt." That was Jose Carlos's voice. The other guy who had kidnapped her. He was standing at the doorway. Jose Carlos cleared his throat.

Antonio quickly flipped around. "You'd better have a damn good reason for barging in here."

Uh-oh. Rebecca knew *that* voice. Why didn't Jose Carlos just leave? He could see they were, well, busy.

"Ignado has the bird in sight." Jose Carlos flashed a quick look her way, and then turned his back, probably to give her privacy.

Her heart skipped. Ignado? Not that asshole. Was he here? What was going on? Why was Jose Carlos talking about a bird?

Antonio strode toward the nightstand.

"The bird is unguarded," Jose Carlos continued. "We have to go now before he flies the coop."

Antonio jerked open the top drawer and pulled out his satellite phone.

"Antonio?" She stepped toward him.

He wouldn't look at her. He dropped his head and started rubbing his temple with his free hand. He gripped the phone tightly in the other.

"Antonio, what's wrong?"

"I have to go into Havana." He sounded tortured.

A chill erupted across her heated skin. "Okay. I'm coming with you." She made sure her clothes were adjusted properly. "Let me go grab Dallas. We can document whatever you are doing."

"No!"

His thunderous explosion after such a loving interlude rocked her. "You can't stop me." They were back to this?

"Yes, I can." Antonio finally looked at her. She could see the conflict raging in his eyes. The look iced her heart and numbed her fingertips. Whatever he was about to do, it was dangerous, and he didn't want her to see it. It probably had to do with her father. Her stomach flip-flopped.

"Jose Carlos will stay here with you and Maria."

"No, *mi amigo*, I'm with you," the kidnapper protested.

"Not tonight. This is my personal mission. No one else can do this for me, and I want to involve as few people as possible."

She ran over to Antonio and grabbed his shoulders. "Oh God, Antonio, whatever it is you're going to do, don't go. I'm telling you I have a bad feeling."

He jerked out of her hold, pushing the satellite phone her way. "Take it."

Reluctantly, she grabbed it.

"Ignado has the other satellite phone," Antonio continued. "I'll get it from him as soon as we meet up. If there's any trouble, call the number. He'll answer the phone, or I will. I promise."

"Don't do this," she whispered, realizing what undone business drew him to Havana this late at night. She started to cry, unable to hold back all of the emotions this one man had stirred up in her in just a few days "Antonio," she pleaded. "Does this have something to do with my father? If it does, I have the right to come with you."

He froze in the middle of the room, his back toward her.

He didn't say a word.

She could fight him, stomp her feet, threaten him, but weak from lack of water and food and spent from almost giving herself willingly to him, she knew she probably wouldn't win. He wasn't going to let her go along. "Please, be careful." She gripped the phone. "Don't do anything that will get you arrested. Or killed." She knew he understood. *Or keep us apart forever.*

He turned, his gaze searching hers. "We leave before dawn, so be ready to go when I get back."

Rebecca couldn't see behind the shield he now wore as an expression.

"This will all make sense to you soon." Without another word, Antonio turned his back to her and stormed out of the room.

Jose Carlos followed him.

It wasn't until after he'd left, and she'd cried for a good ten minutes, that she rolled over on the bed and opened the dresser drawer Antonio had failed to shut properly. Right away she realized Antonio must be expecting trouble here at Johnny's farm.

He'd left her his Ruger .380 automatic.

Chapter Eleven

"*Levántate!*"

Rebecca woke with a start. Her throat was parched. Eyes dry and gritty, it hurt when she blinked.

"*Levántate!*"

Get up? The hair on her neck stood on end at the booming male voice she didn't recognize.

Springing into a sitting position, she jerked the thin sheet over her upper torso. "Who's here?" Her gaze darted across the bed. No Antonio. Her heart galloped, pumping blood to her sleeping brain. Her fingers tingled as she gripped the sheet tighter.

"*Levántate! Ahora mismo.*"

Get up. Right now. What the hell? The dark, windowless room blanketed her in a scary shroud. A trickle of hallway light filtered in through the sheet over the door. "Who are you? What do you want?"

She stilled at the sound of heavy boots scraping against the tile in the bedroom. The person was marching from the doorway toward her. She gulped down a breath to stay quiet. Once at her bedside, a tall man ripped the sheet back. "*Levántate!*"

She gasped as the air hit her mostly naked skin. "*Un momento, por favor.*" She covered herself with her hands as she'd been sleeping in only panties and a barely there T-shirt. "Okay, okay, *permítame vestirme.*" *Let me get dressed first.* Despite the humidity and heat, she was shivering.

The man retreated with a grumble. "*Cinco minutos.*" He threw the sheet back on her and stalked out the doorway.

She jumped out of bed, afraid the stranger wouldn't even give her five seconds, much less five minutes. Digging through her backpack, she pulled out shorts and a clean shirt and threw them on. Should she pack Antonio's gun? *Hell, yes.* She slipped the weapon into her pocket, her hands shaking. She didn't even know how to use the damn thing. The phone? She rubbed her forehead. Where did she put the damn satellite phone? Should she call Antonio? This certainly felt like trouble. *Oh Lord.*

She slipped into the tennis shoes Esmeralda had lent her, found and grabbed the satellite phone off the dresser table, and sat on the bed taking deep breaths.

She dialed the number he'd given her. It rang and rang. "Come on, you promised. Pick up." She shook the phone, but it still rang, a lonely sound, with no comforting words coming from Antonio on the other end, and no way to leave a message.

Boots pounded at the end of the hall, getting louder.

She felt every step with a pounding in her chest.

"*Carajo!*" She couldn't bring the satellite phone. It wouldn't fit in her pocket, and she couldn't risk the man finding and taking it. She buried the phone in the bedsheets and whispered a short prayer.

The silhouette of the man appeared in the hall on the other side of the sheet. It looked like he carried an assault weapon this time. Holy shit, the gun was huge. Her head pulsated with fear. Was it the same guy? Taking a deep breath, she decided to go to him. She had to keep him out of the room and away from Antonio's phone and her identification.

She held both hands up so the man with the gun would think she was unarmed, even though the pistol in her pocket hit her thigh every time she took a step. What she'd give to have Antonio here now.

The man held back the sheet covering the door for her, a surprising move. He grunted and gestured for her to walk down the hall in front of him.

Okay, still alive. That was a good sign. As she turned the corner into the cramped farmhouse kitchen, the rancid smell of sweat, anxiety, and recently butchered pork assaulted her. Too many unwashed bodies had been packed into this small place. Her gaze darted around the room. She counted Johnny the farm owner, Esmeralda, Dallas, Maria, and three men in camouflage-like uniforms. One stood precariously close to Maria. That must be Angel, Maria's fiancé. He had a shaved head and stark, pointy features.

Oh shit. Should she speak? Or wait to see what this was all about? She wrapped her arms around her body, holding her words inside, hoping to stop her shivering.

"Who is *that*, Maria?" The man, Angel, pointed at her. He spoke in Spanish.

Sweat beaded on Rebecca's forehead. She swiped it away. Should she reply for Maria, who looked ashen with anxiety?

"I asked you a question." The man grabbed Maria's arm and tugged her so hard she almost fell.

Rebecca flinched as Maria fought to keep her footing. She suddenly leaned over as if in pain.

The man leaned down, too, bringing his face right to Maria's. "Who. Is. She?"

The hair on the back of Rebecca's neck tingled. This

is how domestic violence escalated. With Adrianna, it had begun with verbal abuse, then this kind of physical control; finally of course, the gasoline and fire.

"She's a new friend of mine," Maria squeaked.

Rebecca's stomach dropped. Abusers like this Angel guy needed to know everyone their victim associated with, and Rebecca knew she didn't add up. She searched for Dallas. Standing in the back corner of the room, he gestured toward the kitchen countertop. She eyed the GoPro camera. It looked like it pointed directly at Maria and the man. Because of its casing, they'd never know they were being recorded, but setting it up must have been a big risk. She nodded at him, but quickly looked elsewhere so Angel couldn't make a connection between her and Dallas or the GoPro camera.

Using Maria's hair as a handle, the jerk pulled Maria up into a standing position. Maria whimpered and kept her eyes cast downward.

Rebecca took a step forward, ready to risk her safety to stop the abuse happening right in front of her. "Who are *you*?" She pointed at Angel. If Antonio had been here he wouldn't have even asked. Angel would be on the ground, and maybe even dead. With her other hand, she fingered the pistol in her pocket.

"Rebecca, this is my fiancé, Angel."

Rebecca caught the warning in Maria's voice. She wanted Rebecca to back down. Rebecca would play this cool to make sure no one got hurt, especially Maria. "Well, great. I've been wanting to meet you." She addressed Angel in Spanish. He had to think she belonged here. "But why now, in the middle of the night?" Did she sound irritated and not afraid? That's what she was going for.

Angel let go of Maria's hair and turned toward Rebecca, planting both hands on his hips. "I'm looking for someone."

"Okay," she shrugged. "Did you find him or her here?"

Keep your voice calm and controlled.

"No, I did not."

"So your friends woke me up for no reason?" She gestured with her head toward the guys in camouflage.

"Do you know who we look for?" Angel's smirk made her chest burn.

"How would I know who you're looking for?" She made eye contact and lifted her chin at him.

Turning back to Maria, Angel gripped her arm again, twisting with such force it made both her and Maria flinch at the same time. "Antonio can't hide. If he's here and you're lying to me, I'll kill him." Angel applied more pressure until Maria cried out for mercy. When he let go, Angel's eyes narrowed, but the smirk on his face lifted even more. Ignoring Maria's distress, Angel shifted his attention back to her. "I want to know *your* name."

Rebecca took a giant step toward him. "I am Rebecca Menendez." Should she play the father card? Did she have any other card to play? "Perhaps you've heard of Arturo Menendez Garcia?"

Angel's eyebrows shot up. "You're related to Arturo?"

"He's family." She watched Angel's face, but he had regained his composure and failed to give away any thoughts with his expression.

"I'm going to visit him tomorrow. I can't wait to tell him why I'm so tired."

Angel's eyes narrowed, and a sneaky smile snaked onto his face. "Let's go, Maria. Get Tony. I will take you both back to Güira."

Maria cast a look her way, regret and longing in that short peek.

Rebecca's heart ached for this young woman, so obviously afraid of Angel and his violence. "I want her to stay here tonight. I came here to see her, and I've barely had a chance to catch up with her. I'm introducing her to Arturo tomorrow. If she's not there, he'll be disappointed." Should she keep talking, making up more bullshit? No, she'd already said enough that could be quickly disproven, but not in the middle of the night out here in rural Cuba. They didn't have the technology available in the U.S.

In the silent pause that followed, it seemed like everyone in the kitchen held their breath, waiting to see what Angel and his gun-toting posse would do now that Rebecca had stood up to them.

The government watchdog glared at her for what seemed like forever.

She swallowed, having no idea what thoughts were spinning through the asshole's head. Maybe he was thinking about whom he could call to check out her story? Sweat shimmied down her spine, but she refused to move and show any discomfort or unease. Antonio would have stood his ground. So would she.

Two other men in camouflage rounded the corner into the kitchen.

"Find anything?" Angel asked, while continuing the stare-down.

"Nothing," one of the men in camo answered.

She exhaled. They didn't find her phone or her driver's license with her American address on it. Thank God Antonio had left. They would have both been in bed asleep, and she'd probably be dead now just because she'd chosen to sleep with the enemy. Glancing at Dallas, she wondered what he'd done to hide the rest of his bulky TV gear.

"It was a *pleasure* to meet you, Rebecca Menendez. I will be sure to learn more about you as quickly as I can." Angel didn't even try to disguise his threat.

She smiled sweetly. "The pleasure is all mine. Do you know Arturo? Shall I tell him you said hello?"

Angel's smile didn't reach his eyes, and he didn't respond to her question. "Maria, I know where to find you. Do not disappoint me." He leaned in to kiss her, but she pulled away. Angel raised a hand as if to slap her, then hesitated, maybe because she was there, or because Angel didn't know if she really had Arturo Menendez's ear. Her father must be a very powerful man to stall a man like Angel. The thought made her nauseous. As soon as Angel and his men left the room, she leaned over, breathing slowly, coming very close to throwing up.

. . .

"They're gone," Jose Carlos exclaimed after trudging back in from outside. He wiped his brow with a dirty rag from the kitchen counter, his face beet red, with horizontal dirt stripes crossing his cheeks.

Maria, who had been holding on to the sink, her head down and shoulders shaking, finally looked up and stared at Rebecca with haunted eyes. "You're Arturo Menendez's family?"

That spooked look on Maria's pale face made Rebecca take a step back. "I'm his daughter."

The energy in the room shifted. Maria's eyes widened, and she stared at Rebecca as if she'd just turned into a demon. Esmeralda's mouth fell open, and Jose Carlos pulled out his *gun* and pointed it at her.

"Whoa." Rebecca slowly put her hands in her pockets, playing casual, but fingering Antonio's gun. "What am I missing here?"

"Antonio didn't tell you?" Esmeralda crossed her arms over her chest.

"He told me my father slept with his mother, and that's why my mother left Arturo." Heat rushed to her cheeks.

What else had he failed to tell her? *Damn him.*

Maria shook her head, her frail body shaking. "No, no, this is not right. Not right. How could Antonio not tell me?"

Rebecca's stomach clenched, even though she had no clue what was making this group suddenly appear deathly still and angry. An affair was bad. No doubt about that. But why be mad at her? After all these years? "Okay. Look, your brother has a way of doing what he wants, while he keeps others in the dark. Part of the reason I came here is because Antonio told me my dad was still alive. I've spent the last twenty-six years believing the Cuban government tortured and murdered my father. Antonio told me he actually works for the government."

"Rebecca." Esmeralda walked toward her with outstretched hands.

"Don't say anything," Maria whispered.

"She needs to know."

"Let Antonio tell her."

"Tell me what?" This back-and-forth between Maria and Esmeralda was making Rebecca's head spin. "If Antonio didn't tell me the whole story, then spit it out, ladies, or I'm not helping either of you get to America." She directed that comment right at Esmeralda. Little white stars spun in Rebecca's line of sight. Boy, she needed to sit down.

"Antonio will take us to America." Maria's pale skin was now painted with various shades of red patches. "When he returns."

"Antonio isn't here." Rebecca patted her pockets, then remembered she didn't have the satellite phone with her. "He went to meet up with Ignado. And he's not answering the phone."

Jose Carlos lowered the gun. "Are you sure?"

"You have another sat phone?" Rebecca asked.

He nodded slowly, still eyeing her warily. At least he had

pocketed his gun.

"Try him again. Maybe I called the wrong number."

Jose Carlos dialed.

"Okay, so if Antonio is gone, what do we do next?" Dallas looked at her with exhausted, saucer like eyes.

"You and I are leaving. Let's pack up now."

Esmeralda took a step in front of her. "I'm going with you. Remember?"

"No answer." Tossing the phone on the countertop, Jose Carlos scrunched up his face. "Something's wrong. I feel it. We should have heard something from Antonio by now."

"Jose Carlos." Now was the right time to make a request of him. Rebecca had planted a seed of doubt, and she could tell Jose Carlos believed her. "You have to take us to the dock in the woods. You're the only one here who knows how to get back there."

Jose Carlos nodded slowly, as if deep in thought.

"We have to leave now." She glanced around the kitchen.

Uncle Johnny had slumped into a chair, his head in his hands. Maria stared down the hall, probably thinking about little Tonito asleep in his bed. And Esmeralda, she was throwing bottled water into a bag. "What's it going to be?" Rebecca continued. "Is someone going to tell me the truth, or are you all going to stay here in Cuba with all your family secrets safely intact but scared to death waiting for Angel to return?"

Esmeralda broke the silence. "I'm sorry, Maria. I'm going to America, and I can't wait any longer. I've got to take this free ride. Even if I can get a government-issued visa to travel now, I still can't afford a plane ticket." The bag stuffed full, Esmeralda put it to the side and walked toward Rebecca. Esmeralda took Rebecca's hands into her own and looked her right in her eyes. "What happened a long time ago is not your fault, *mija.*"

"Okay." Rebecca's ice-cold fingers tingled within Esmeralda's warm ones. Her stomach somersaulted like an Olympic gymnast. What could be so bad?

"Antonio isn't here because he went to go find your father. Arturo Menendez did more than sleep with Antonio's mother." Esmeralda's eyes were watering. "He shot Antonio's father and left him to die in the street in front of their home."

Rebecca gasped. She couldn't breathe. Literally. She bent over, hands holding her stomach. Her father was an adulterer, not a murderer. Those white stars dancing before her eyes doubled, and her lungs tightened. This couldn't be happening. She fell to the ground, knees hitting first.

Instead of trying to stop her collapse, Esmeralda took a knee next to her. "Maria and I don't remember, but Antonio does. He was there, and he watched his father bleed to death in the street in front of his house. The fact that he didn't see the signs and stop Arturo has tormented Antonio all his life. That I do remember. I'm afraid, no matter how he feels about you—and I do believe he is falling in love with you—he won't ever be satisfied until he gets revenge. Antonio won't come back until your father is dead."

Chapter Twelve

Plowing through the woods on their way back to the dock where *La Libertad* had originally landed, the rhythmic sound of boots and tennis shoes crunching through thorny underbrush lulled the group into a hypnotic silence. Rebecca, Dallas, Maria, Tonito, Esmeralda, Pedro—the man they'd met the first day—and Jose Carlos had been walking for a while in the pre-morning darkness. Jose Carlos was leading the way, using a small headlight and a machete to make a path.

Despite her anger over Antonio leaving her to confront her father in Havana, Rebecca had found it impossible to leave for the yacht without Maria and Tonito. Rebecca knew what fate awaited them if she didn't convince them to come with her. It had taken her a while, but Rebecca had finally convinced Maria that this is what Antonio would have wanted had they been able to get a hold of him on that satellite phone.

So here they all were, slogging through unkempt woods, looking for a rickety needle in a very dark and dangerous haystack, a barely-there dock with no roads or signs leading up to it.

Prickly branches, low to the ground, were whipping and tearing into Rebecca's flesh. This continuous flogging by Mother Nature was exactly what she deserved for allowing herself and Dallas to get caught up in this insane scenario. She wished she could have just gone into Havana and hopped on a plane to Miami. But what would she have said when she showed up at customs with no passport or even any luggage? No, they had to go back the way they came. Undercover.

Smacking about the tenth mosquito away, Rebecca trudged ahead. Her desire to get on *La Libertad* and go home was so strong she would have walked across fire to board that yacht.

"You okay?" Dallas was right behind her, his hand on her back, gently pushing her forward.

Rebecca wiped her mouth with the back of her hand. "I'm just nervous." Now was not the time to get into any discussion with Dallas. He'd witnessed the chemistry between her and Antonio last night, and surely assumed they'd had sex. She didn't even want to open the door to the lecture she knew she'd get from him.

Every once in a while, little Tonito would whine, and Maria would reassure him in soft-spoken Spanish that everything would be all right.

But would it? The night and the situation seemed so surreal.

"Look." Jose Carlos stopped suddenly. She'd been so wrapped up in her own thoughts she slammed into his back, almost cutting herself on his damn machete.

"What?" She jumped back, away from the weapon. "What?"

"Lights. Look." He pointed to a spot ahead through the thick trees. "She's here. *La Libertad* is here."

Rebecca's heart leaped in her chest. *Thank you, God!* She spotted the flicker of small lights ahead, kind of like fireflies dancing in the dark. She closed her eyes, exhaled, and turned to the little boy whimpering behind her. "Hey, Tonito, we're almost there." Swinging the little boy up into her arms, extra energy shot through her. "Wait until you see the boat we're going to ride in." *It has air-conditioning, and a bathroom, and all the comforts of America.*

Before she could even take two steps, Maria yanked Tonito out of her arms and plowed ahead, following Jose Carlos.

So, the lines had been drawn. Even though Esmeralda pointed out that any murder Rebecca's father may have committed could not be Rebecca's fault, some family sins apparently couldn't be forgiven. That truth hurt. She was being punished for the actions of a man she'd never even met. Probably never would, now.

Dallas moved up behind her. "I've got the money shots. We got some shiz no one is gonna believe. Now it's time to bounce. I can't wait to get this back to America."

Rebecca squeezed Dallas, then let go, forging ahead, anxious to get to the yacht. Suddenly, a thought stalled her. What would she say if Antonio had already arrived? Would he gloat if he'd managed to murder her father? She shivered. She'd never let him touch her again, not with Menendez blood on his hands, no matter what her father may have done to deserve it.

"Sure you're okay?" Dallas placed a hand on her back.

"I'm fine."

Before Dallas could contradict her or distract her with one of his one-liners, Jose Carlos approached. "We've got company."

"What?" Straining to see around him, Rebecca's heart stutter-stepped. "Antonio?"

"No." Jose Carlos looked though a pair of binoculars. "Looks like a family."

"A family? Let me see." Grabbing the binoculars, Rebecca tried to focus in on the lights. All she could make out were little flames in a circle and some dark shadows. To the right, *La Libertad* sat docked, but dark. *Interesting.* "What do you think?" she asked Jose Carlos. "Is it safe for us to approach? Could this be a trap?" Her ankles throbbed, and her head swam, making her weave as she walked. She didn't know if she was up for a confrontation. "What should we do?"

Jose Carlos appeared to think it over, his features hard to see in the dark. "Let's approach slowly and quietly. We will get close, and you will wait with the women. I'll try to slip on the *La Libertad* and see who is on board."

She swallowed. Should she trust Jose Carlos? He could jump on that yacht and leave them to the mercy of whoever else was out there. Or he could have been in contact with Antonio and Ignado, and Jose Carlos could be leading *her* into *their* trap. She glanced at Maria and Tonito, huddled together, shivering, and clearly afraid. Jose Carlos would *not* betray them. "Okay. We'll follow you."

"Take me as close as you can." Dallas pulled the home video camera with night vision out of his backpack. "Whatever is going on, it's meant to be kept a secret, and that means I'm capturing it on video."

. . .

An older woman, dressed in black, held on to a picture, clutching it to her chest like a prized possession. She swayed back and forth wailing as a half dozen younger people swayed with her in a circle. Each person held a candle, flickering in the already oppressive heat, and they sang together in one strong voice melting in with the hot breeze. "They're mourning someone." Despite her fluency in Spanish, Rebecca could only make out about half of the words from this distance.

"The old woman's grandson," Esmeralda whispered.

"Why are they *here*?" Cradling her son in her skinny

arms, Maria looked as if she'd pass out at any moment.

And then it hit Rebecca. "They're here because this is the last place her grandson was seen alive." As she said the words, an image of Domingo's pockmarked face materialized. The reality of what must have happened to him slapped her and left an invisible imprint that stung.

Esmeralda leaned in closer, her stale breath a reminder they'd been walking in the dust and dirt for hours. "How do you know that? They didn't say that, no?"

Rebecca exhaled, wishing she could clue Dallas in on her thoughts, but he was already too far away. He'd shoot differently if he thought this group could be tied to Domingo, the young boy's story coming sadly full circle.

She pictured Domingo standing with fists on hips, so proud of his boat, so sure it would get him to America. "When we got here, however many days ago, a group of young kids were trying to leave the island by boat, a homemade boat that didn't look like it would make it ten miles out. I guess even though the Cuban government says you can leave now, many Cubans are still trapped by their poverty and lack of resources. I tried to convince them to go on Antonio's yacht." She looked away, suddenly overwhelmed with the urge to cry. "Domingo wouldn't listen. He left on that thing." *Damn it!* The cocky little shit didn't make it. How many others died just like him? Still today? What were all these damn political negotiations worth if kids were still taking to the Florida Straits? She sent a silent prayer that if he did perish at sea, his death had been quick and merciful.

The snap of tree branches made the hair on her arms stand up.

"It's me." Jose Carlos back from the *La Libertad*.

He nodded at everyone as if counting heads. "Where's Dallas?"

"Still shooting video." She pointed in the direction of the

family. "Don't worry. He's not using a light, and they haven't seen him yet."

He nodded. "The captain is on board. But not Antonio."

Rebecca's stomach clenched. Why should she care? Antonio had used her, and then lied to her, and now he was probably betraying her by killing the one man she'd longed for her entire life. She tried to shake the ugly thoughts away, but they stuck to her like a new tattoo. "Why are the lights off on the yacht?"

"For safety."

Right. Antonio had mentioned some kind of government base near by.

"And out of respect for the grieving." Jose Carlos took to one knee and looked right at her.

A ball of regret lodged in her throat. "Domingo?"

Jose Carlos shrugged, but at this close range, she could see the sadness in his eyes. "Maybe." He shook his head and looked back at *La Libertad.* "The captain says he tried to tail the small boat to America, but they traveled too slowly, and eventually he decided to ensure the safety of his own passengers. If he had called the Coast Guard, they would have sent Domingo and his friends back to Cuba." Jose Carlo stood up and brushed himself off. "We need to get Maria and Tonito on board."

Rebecca hesitated, wondering if she should break away and interview Domingo's family members first. The old Rebecca wouldn't have hesitated. It was her job. But no, not tonight. She would trust that Dallas's video would speak for itself. Nothing she could ask would be as powerful as what was naturally unfolding before his viewfinder. "Okay, I'll go get Dallas."

"We board quietly." Jose Carlos offered Maria assistance. She handed her son to the beefy man, flipping a sharp-edged gaze Rebecca's way.

I got the message already. "What do we do next?"

Chapter Thirteen

Standing top deck on *La Libertad*, in the silver light of the moon, Rebecca smelled the onions and sweat first.

The hair on the back of her neck sizzled as soon as the scent whooshed up her nostrils.

"Hey, American."

Rebecca whipped around. *That voice* was coming from the dock below. She ran to the edge of the yacht, looking down. Her heart stalled. Lord, of all people to show up now, why him? "Hello, Ignado." She hated the sound of his name. Hated him.

Ignado stepped out of the shadows, walking right past the grieving family still huddling together like wounded refugees on the dock, and placed his booted foot on the first rung of the ladder leading up to the *La Libertad*. "Going somewhere, America?"

How should she answer that? The way the tattooed man would expect? "Of course not. We've been waiting for you and Antonio." Shooting a quick look over her shoulder, she caught Dallas's eye. Her photographer had been quietly videotaping the family on the dock, keeping his distance by staying on board. He turned toward Ignado's voice, bringing the camera with him. Rebecca knew Ignado wouldn't be able to see Dallas from below. She gestured casually with a nod for Dallas to come toward her. Whatever happened next, she needed it documented on video. "Where's Antonio?"

Rebecca clicked on a flashlight, just in time to catch a snakelike grin slither across Ignado's ugly face. "He's in jail."

She swallowed. Was he lying? "You don't seem too upset about it."

"Turn off the light, America."

"It's Rebecca." *Asshole.* She flicked off the flashlight.

"Antonio tried to kill your father."

The initial sting of those words had already beaten her up. This time when she heard them, she raised an eyebrow, a gesture so subtle she doubted Ignado could even see it in the pre-morning light. "Tried?"

"Ah." Ignado removed his boot from the ladder, resting both hands on his hips. "So you already knew." He nodded, smiling. "I was hoping I could be the one to break the news to you."

Her stomach clenched. "That my father is dead?"

"Actually, he's still alive and well."

Butterflies of hope tickled her insides. But why did *Ignado* sound so happy about that? "And Antonio?"

"Not as lucky."

Her heart flip-flopped. "Where is he?"

"I told you. In jail."

A heavy knot of dread formed in her stomach. She didn't expect that. "He's been arrested?" Stupid question. Why else would he be in jail? Jail was better than dead, but she wanted to hear Igando confirm Antonio was still alive. She clasped a hand at her throat, throwing a quick glance at Dallas. He'd found a place to shoot video from the shadows.

"Want details?" Ignado's voice dripped with honeyed sarcasm.

Dallas nodded, holding out a microphone to show her he could pick up the sound of Ignado's voice.

She turned back toward the big bully. "Of course, Ignado. We can't leave without Antonio." Could he tell she was baiting him? "What happened? When will Antonio be here? And why did you leave without him?"

The wicked grin on Ignado's face stilled her. "We got a tip your dad was visiting a hotel in Havana. I guess he screws his new mistress there every other night."

Nice. Keep a straight face. She bit her bottom lip. *Your father may have given you DNA, but he's no reflection of you. You have his name, but nothing else.*

"We figured we could kill him when he left. He'd be without security. Not wanting the world to know what a *whore* he is."

She choked on those last words. Did Ignado know what had transpired between her and Antonio last night? Was that a subtle jab? Had Antonio, like a typical man, bragged about his conquest? She chewed her bottom lip, hoping she wasn't in the camera's view. Wondering if she was, would it pick up her legs trembling?

"We sprang on him as he left the hotel for his car. But"— Ignado raised his hand, forming a fake gun with his fingers— "Arturo had security waiting, and *bam*."

She jumped. "Bam? Antonio got shot?"

Ignado laughed like an evil man.

She knew from day one something was seriously wrong with the tattooed guy. "He's okay, right?" *Jesus. Shut up.*

"You care so much for the man who wanted to murder your father?"

She dropped her gaze. What should she say? She didn't know which side Ignado was on. As a daughter, she should care about the fate of her father. As a woman drawn to a man, as fucked-up as that might be, she couldn't help but hope Antonio survived with a chance of getting out of trouble. And she couldn't deny her desire to help him.

"You seem a bit conflicted, America."

"Stop calling me that."

"Who are you rooting for? Your father, the Communist, or your lover, the activist?"

Her knees gave out, and she wobbled. A hand on her back gave her the confidence to right herself and stare the evil below in the face. What did Ignado hope she would say? She rolled the dice. "Where is my father now?"

He smiled and held out his hand. "Come with me and find out."

"Don't go, Rebecca." Esmeralda whispered. She'd come topside and must have been the hand steadying her. Rebecca could feel tension even in her fingertips. Perhaps she hated Igando, too?

"Your father wants to meet you."

She didn't believe Ignado. Her father had made no effort to meet her in all these years. "How did my father find out about me? Being here and all?" She hated the fact that her voice shook. She dropped her gaze, breathing deeply to better control it.

"Antonio gave you up when Arturo's security force put a loaded .357 to his head. He used information about you as bait, hanging it out there, reeling the old man in."

She closed her eyes, trying to picture Antonio, the man she'd come to know so well, on his knees, with a gun to his head, begging for his life, willing to sell out anyone to save himself. The picture never came into focus. Antonio would not do that. Rebecca just knew it.

"Antonio betrayed you."

Ignado had to be the one lying.

"He betrayed me, too. That's why I'm here. I made a deal. My life was spared so I could bring you to Arturo."

Rebecca ran a hand through her hair, thinking, trying to figure out what to do. If she went with Ignado, she might finally get a chance to meet her father. Even if her dad were a devoted Castro man, he wouldn't hurt his own blood relative, right? And then she could see if Antonio really was in jail. If he was, maybe she could convince her father to let him go. Because despite everything that had happened last night, her heart ached to help Antonio. "Where would we go? Havana?"

"You've got to be joking." Dallas burst out of the shadows. "I knew I shouldn't have brought my ass over here with you. I'm ready to go home and now you want to play the Walton family? Well, good night Jim Bob, we're outta here. We're not going to Havana."

"I agree with Dallas," Esmeralda whispered.

"You two aren't. I will go with you, Ignado. But on one condition." This was her chance to protect Dallas, Maria, Tonito, and Esmeralda. It's what she had to do. "I will get off the *La Libertad*, but once I do, the captain gets to leave right now with everyone else on board. Once he's gone, I will go with you."

"Oh, hell no," Dallas barked.

It *was* a risk. She would be walking with Ignado, a man she didn't trust, into the great unknown. But she knew the captain of *La Libertad* wouldn't leave Antonio here in Cuba for long. He'd come back for them both. Jose Carlos would, too, after he secured Antonio's family's safety in Miami or Tampa. And Dallas would stir up more media interest in their whereabouts.

Ignado threw his head back and laughed. "You would risk your life to help Antonio's family? Knowing he would not do the same for you?"

Yes, Antonio would. Instinctively, she knew that. But

better to play along. "I want to meet my father, Ignado. You know that. That's what this is about." And she did, but she also wanted to do more.

Antonio had not killed her father. That she knew now for sure. So she had to try to help Antonio. She was under no illusion it was going to be easy. She wasn't James Bond, and this wasn't an action-adventure movie. She couldn't just storm the jail and break him out. But before she could come up with a game plan, she had to know what was really happening in Havana.

But she did not trust Ignado.

Not at all.

As if he could read her mind, he whipped out a gun. "Let's go then, America." His hands were steady. Always steady.

"I don't need a metal escort. I am agreeing to come of my own free will." *And I'm armed, too, sucker.*

"You don't really think I'm going to let the rest of your crew go back to the United States, do you, America? They could cause big problems for Arturo. And me."

So that's whose side Ignado is on. She should have figured. "Get below deck, now!" Rebecca fumbled in her pocket, praying she wouldn't shoot her own foot before she could draw Antonio's weapon and bluff Ignado. "This is between you and me, Ignado." She pulled the gun out and took aim, hoping he wouldn't call her bluff and pull his trigger first. "If I stay, they leave. Otherwise, we're all leaving. Right now."

"Don't be naive," Ignado snarled. "You don't think I'm going to let you call the shots? I am not Antonio. And I was not stupid enough to come alone."

And with that, the trees began to dance, swaying as men in dark camouflage exited their hiding places, armed and ready to shoot.

Jose Carlos burst out of the shadows, his gun drawn.

"Get below deck, Rebecca! Now!"

A series of shots fired.

Rebecca screamed. Backing up, she racked the slider on top of Antonio's gun, loading a bullet.

A projectile whizzed by her ear.

Shit. They're really shooting! That's it. Lowering the gun she didn't really know how to use, she turned and ran like hell to the opening leading below deck.

The motor kicked in. Thank God, the captain wasn't on Ignado's side.

Hand on the doorway into the galley, she flipped around, and the whole scene before her slowed down. Ignado rose above the deck line. He had climbed the ladder and was now stepping on board. She raised Antonio's gun, hands quaking.

A *pop* sounded and Ignado grabbed his chest, his gaze landing on her, wide-eyed and frozen, shocked maybe by the pain or maybe by the fact that a bullet had gotten him before he could kill her.

He hovered on the top rung of the ladder. First, his weapon slid from his long fingers, then his arm of tattoos dropped to his side. His body, stained now with a growing red splotch, wobbled. His eyes rolled back and he fell, disappearing from her view.

A splash.

Then a flurry of bullets.

Shit. Ignado's posse was still attacking the boat.

The motor screamed, and the yacht jerked forward, taking a part of the rickety dock with it.

A bullet pinged the side of the hatch where Rebecca stood. She ducked and was pulled back into the cabin suddenly by Esmeralda. "*Tu eres loca?* Get below."

Rebecca felt crazy. "Where's Dallas?" Last time she saw him, he'd been shooting video on deck, barely concealed.

The *La Libertad* bucked like a bronco being held behind

a rodeo gate, and then suddenly, released, it surged forward.

Rebecca couldn't breathe. She couldn't think. She stumbled toward the closest seat and fell into it. The hand holding Antonio's weapon was shaking so badly she feared the gun would go off. She tried to place it gently on the table, but it rattled as it hit the glass. "Oh Jesus." Laying a flat hand on top of the gun, she started to cry. "I don't know. I don't know. Did I shoot Ignado?"

"No, I did." Jose Carlos jumped from the top deck, grabbing on to the counter as the yacht kicked in to a higher gear. "Traitor."

Rebecca slid down the couch as the yacht jerked to one side. The gun flew off the table, hitting the floor and sliding into the kitchen. Jose Carlos stuck a foot out to stop it. He glared at her. "Let me handle the weapons. You're going to get one of *us* killed." He knelt and picked up the gun, pocketing the weapon.

"Think the Cuban Coast Guard will chase us?" Esmeralda had gone pale. She sat next to Maria, who held Tonito up against her chest like a blanket. The little boy sucked his thumb, his chest rising and falling in silent sobs.

"We'll know in less than ten minutes," Jose Carlos said.

"Why?" Did she want to know the answer?

"If the Cuban Coast Guard takes off from the pier at Mariel, that's how long it will take them to catch up to us."

The heat rushed out of Rebecca's face.

"Find the life jackets and have them ready," Jose Carlos shouted as he leaped through the door. "The captain will be running full-out."

Chapter Fourteen

Sitting in an edit bay in her Central Florida television station, Rebecca had but one goal for the next two hours. Take control of *her* story.

After barely escaping Cuba in the early-morning light, they'd made it to Miami in less than six hours. The captain had dropped Esmeralda, Tonito, and Maria off at the marina and had waited with them for members of the local Catholic church to come pick them up. An advocate Jose Carlos knew at the church had offered to help the family with the immigration process. Rebecca hadn't wanted to leave them, but knew they were in good hands.

She also knew when she'd caught Miami's local news in the marina lounge that she and Dallas were still headline news.

Just like Antonio had predicted.

She and Dallas had jumped into a car the captain had waiting for them at the marina and drove the four hours back to Tampa, only stopping once at a McDonald's drive-through to grab a burger, extra fries, and some soda. A ridiculous choice—yes. But Dallas had insisted, and after the events of the last forty-eight hours, she owed him at least a Big Mac. She'd learned a long time ago, a full photog was a happy, productive photog. Thank God the captain had thought to give them cash. But they still didn't have their iPhones.

When the cashier recognized Rebecca, she knew she had to get straight to her TV station and take control of the information that was about to explode onto the public stage.

Rebecca knew from experience that the first words and pictures to hit the internet would be the ones to go viral. She wanted to make sure *she* was the one putting those words and images out. She didn't want the announcement of her return posted first on some cashier's Instagram. That's why, despite her still-bloody, dirty clothes and her scratched-up legs, she and Dallas had come straight to the TV station. And called their news director in, immediately.

It was a little after 9:00 p.m. They had just enough time before the eleven o'clock news to put a story together that would explain how she and Dallas ended up in Cuba, and how they managed to get away. After that, they'd archive all the raw video, just in case the Tampa police requested to see it. Truth was, Rebecca had no idea how the legal ramifications of their trip to Cuba would play out. Dallas had been on his game the whole time, documenting everything. And she bet that video would save them from any legal charges. Just like Antonio had said when she first met him. Video does not lie.

Dallas was searching through video he'd uploaded onto his Mac laptop. "Let's start with video of Ignado's shooting and our escape. 'Cause that video is the shiz, like a freaking James Bond action spectacular, if I do say so myself."

His unique humor had grounded her through their years working together and most certainly in these last days. "Hey, Dallas," she whispered. "Thank you."

The big guy shuffled a bit before giving a slight nod. A

moment later, he turned his full attention to the video screen.

The sound was up fully, and hearing her own scream gave Rebecca chills. "I can't believe how giddy you are about what has happened."

Dallas shrugged, his back to her while he started editing their video. "Man, just glad to be back in the good ole US of A. That Big Mac made me a happy man. That shower on *La Libertad* helped, too."

They'd both showered, but had no new clothes available to put on. Least of her concerns right now. "Dallas, stop the video right there." She stared at her own image standing on the deck of the *La Libertad*, arms straight in front of her, Antonio's gun in her hands. Dallas had been shooting from behind, so it was obvious she was pointing the gun at Ignado. "We need to make it clear Ignado is the man who kidnapped us in Tampa and that, although he's now dead, I didn't shoot him." She leaned over and tapped the computer screen. "You've got me on camera pointing a gun at him, then he falls overboard."

"Hey, hand me some more fries, will ya?"

"Dallas." Was he serious? He'd already polished off his own bag.

"I got ya." He turned and reached behind him, plopping a handful of her fries into his mouth. He chewed and swallowed.

She tapped her foot.

"Damn, Mickey D's can make some fries. You never see your gun go off, so relax, Jesse James. Any good cop will know from the video you didn't shoot Ignado, someone else did."

Jose Carlos. And he was probably already on *La Libertad* heading back to Cuba to search for Antonio.

"You think Ignado dying will clear Antonio of kidnapping charges?" Ignado was the one captured on video kidnapping her and Dallas from the Tampa courthouse. They'd seen that video replayed on the news while in Miami. "And we've got him falling overboard with a bullet in him. Maybe Antonio…"

Dallas abruptly stopped editing and swung around in his chair. "You sleeping with that cat?"

Rebecca held her breath. "Is that what you think?"

He turned back around. "I think you're hot for the guy."

Hot doesn't even begin to describe the range of feelings I have for him. "If I am, does that make me crazy? He's not really a bad person. You know that. He risked his life for his sister and her son, he is loyal to his friends, he is…"

"You don't have to sell him to me. I'm a fan, too."

She let her shoulders drop. "Can we keep that between us for now?"

"What? That I'm a fan?" Dallas chuckled and then made another quick edit. "Look mama, what you do behind closed doors, or behind the white sheet over the door, is your business."

Oh my God. He knew. Had she and Antonio been loud or something? "Okay, after you finish that edit, let's see what video we can use to set up the real story. People will want to know *why* we were kidnapped. We can show…"

"Why *were* you kidnapped?" Stan Delamonte, the station's news director, pushed into the edit bay, all six four of him.

She jumped up.

Stan pulled her into an awkward boss-employee hug, pushing back quickly and glancing down at her bloodied clothes. "You okay? Do we need to get you to a hospital?"

"No, no." She took a step back, running a hand over her hair. She hadn't even considered what a mess she must look like. "We took a shower on the boat, but didn't have clothes to change into."

"You have blood all over you." Stan's gaze raked over her.

"It's not mine, Stan." Well, some of it was. From the scratches all over her skin made by the brush in the woods. She glanced down. Yep, she looked like the victim of a horror movie. They didn't have Band-Aids and Neosporin readily available in Cuba.

"I'm calling an ambulance."

"No." She blocked his exit. "I'm fine. So is Dallas. We have to keep editing this video. But I'm glad you're here to see and approve it."

"Yep, all good here, mate." Dallas fast-forwarded the video back to the place where Ignado had been shot and had fallen overboard.

"That's the man who kidnapped you?" Stan's mouth dropped open when he saw the part with Rebecca holding a gun. His gaze slowly turned to her. "So, why were you two kidnapped? And where did you get a gun?"

Oh boy. It was going to be a long-ass night. "A man on a mission wanted our help documenting a rescue."

"Is that the man on a mission?" Stan pointed to the computer screen. "The dead man whom someone shot?" Stan was rubbing his chin, his brows pinched together. "Not you, I hope."

"See, Dallas." She slapped his shoulder. "People are going to assume it was me. I didn't shoot him, Stan." *But I would have.*

"Good to know. So, where is this man on a mission now?" Stan folded both arms across his chest.

"In a jail cell in Cuba," she said.

"We think," Dallas added. "If I know Antonio, he's escaped or something."

Stan plopped down in a seat in the corner of the edit bay. He ran his hands through the little hair on his head. "Okay. I need some caffeine. This is going to be an all-nighter. What about this rescue? Who was he rescuing and why?"

Just like her news director to cut the bullshit small talk and get right to the point. "His sister—from an abusive relationship with one of Castro's government watchdogs."

"Castro's watchdogs." Stan sighed and leaned forward, studying the video as Dallas edited. "This story is also political, then? You know this is going to stir up a shitstorm of controversy at a time when the United States is trying to appease Cuba and smooth over relations."

So? What was with Stan tonight? "You love controversy. Look what Samantha Steele's story on those adventure-vacation murders did. Made *national* news. You've always told me to report the truth. People aren't seeing the whole truth of what's currently going on in Cuba."

"I'm listening." Stan leaned back in his chair, bringing both arms up, hands resting behind his head.

She smiled. She had him hooked. Just like she'd hook her audience. "We've captured the story of two different families and how difficult it was for both to leave the island. One didn't make it—the others did. All were willing to risk their lives to leave Cuba. Even today. Despite all the changes. That's the story I want to tell."

"And you think you can pull that together to air in less than an hour and a half?"

"I think I can at least put together one story."

"We have enough for a ding-dong documentary," Dallas chimed in. "Mr. Emmy say my name, say my name."

"Well, I'm glad to see your sense of humor made it back from Cuba, Dallas." Stan put a hand on Dallas's shoulder. "But tonight's story is you, Rebecca, whether you like it or not."

"Stan." *I do not want any more attention on me. I have to help Antonio.*

He lifted his other hand—like a bossy crossing guard. "You are the story. You have no idea how much media attention your kidnapping has generated. I've already called *Good Morning USA*, and they want to interview you live on the morning show. So tonight we stick to this. How you were kidnapped, using video of your kidnapping outside the courthouse. Then we answer why. You can explain about this man on a mission. You have video of him?"

"Yes." *Antonio won't be happy that I'm using it, but watching him fall to his knees in front of his grandmother will win the public over. They will see him as a wounded and compassionate soul, and anyone with relatives in Cuba will instantly connect with him and his cause.*

"Great. And you have video of how you escaped."

Dallas snorted. "Oh, do we. This shit will get millions of clicks on YouTube." Dallas turned the audio up, and Stan watched the yacht tear out of the dock in Cuba. You could hear gunfire popping even over the yacht's motors.

"You were shooting video on deck that whole time?" she asked. She'd been so freaked out in that moment, she hadn't noticed where Dallas was.

"Damn straight."

"Dallas Jones, you are crazy."

Stan was shaking his head. "You are crazier than George."

George was Samantha Steele's photographer. Whether Dallas was crazier than George was definitely debatable.

"Rebecca." Stan cleared his throat. "Are you going to wear those clothes on the air tonight?"

Really? After what she'd just been through, what she was wearing seemed so insignificant. "Yes. I think it tells the story better than any words can."

"Police are going to want to talk to you." Stan was looking at her like he wanted to gauge her reaction.

"Fine. I didn't do anything wrong. I'm the victim here." *But was she?*

"Where is this family you rescued?"

"I didn't rescue them. Antonio did." She wanted to make this all about Antonio. If she were to use her resources and influence to get him out of Cuba, she'd have to paint him a hero. Which he was. Once you looked past his "unusual" practices. "They're in Miami." She glanced over at Stan, who was still watching her with a boss's focused attention. "We did it the right way, Stan. We didn't break any laws. They're going to have to go through the proper channels to stay here. But I am going to help them. I've got friends at immigration here in Tampa."

Stan shook his head. "You sound pretty in control for someone who was just kidnapped."

Shit. Okay, play the victim. Just for a little while longer. "I'm just so thankful to be back home." Which was true. "Stan—there's another story I have to tell." She didn't even let Stan respond. She just dived in. "It's the story of a man who risked his life to save his family and how the Cuban government is now holding him. His name is Antonio Vega, and he's been wrongly imprisoned. I have to help him. We have to help him. He's a hero."

Stan rocked back in the chair, hands still behind his head, watching her. "He is, huh?"

She swallowed. Why was it getting hot in here?

"What part did Antonio Vega have in your kidnapping? He's the one who wanted you to document the mission, right?"

"He didn't force me into that van. Nor did he force me into Cuba. He gave me a choice." She purposely left out the whole "at gunpoint" thing, and the deal concerning her father. As far as she was concerned Arturo Menendez was dead to her. Again.

The edit bay grew quiet, the only sound Dallas's fingers beating keys in an effort to edit the video quickly.

And her pounding heart. But Rebecca assumed only she could hear that.

Finally Stan spoke. "People are going to think you're suffering from Stockholm syndrome. You know what that is, right?" From the way he stared at her, she suspected he believed she truly did suffer from some misguided feelings for her captor.

Let the public think whatever they wanted, as long as they helped her win Antonio's freedom. "I do."

"Until you have a doctor check you out, it may be a good idea to let people think that. It will create public empathy for you and your traumatic experience and explain why you are gung ho to help your kidnapper."

Stan couldn't know what was going on. Could he? "Antonio didn't kidnap me. I'm going to call Senator Nelson's office first thing in the morning."

"Rebecca," Stan cautioned.

But she was already in her head planning. "The mayor is my friend. He knows people in Washington. We can embarrass the Cuban government into freeing him."

"Rebecca." Stan's voice raised a couple of notches.

She blanched. And shut up.

"One story at a time." Stan rocked forward, using his momentum to stand up. "Tonight we focus on you and Dallas, the fact that you are back and you are alive. If I were you I'd go home and clean up after the eleven p.m. newscast. And brace yourself. You're about to get sucked into the media vortex that is now your life. You are famous now. Internationally."

If he was trying to scare her, it wasn't working. That's exactly what she needed. An *international* audience. "Good. I'm about to throw a very big spotlight on a government that is holding an American citizen hostage." Antonio was an American citizen, right? She didn't even know. He had to be after all these years in America.

"Okay. Okay." Stan stepped to the door, looking back at her. "I want to see a script in ten minutes. I have the final say. You both look…tired. Then after this, you go straight home. I'm sending over a doctor, just to make sure you're okay."

Love that you'll wait till I get the video on the news first. "Thanks, Stan."

"And the Tampa police are going to want to interview both of you about this kidnapping tomorrow. I've already called the chief. Homeland Security also wants to talk to you. It's a mess. A real mess."

"Got it." *Good.* Let them question her and Dallas. They were on the same page. They'd synced their stories on the way up from Miami. They wouldn't lie, but they weren't going to throw Antonio under the bus, either. They could paint him as a hero. Get the public on his side. *Help him.*

"I'm watching you, Rebecca."

"I'm fine." *I know what the hell I'm doing.*

"I hope so." He hesitated. "If this gets to be too much— you let me know."

"I will." But she couldn't stop to reflect or rest now. Images of Antonio that first night in the Everglades flashed into her head. Her hot rebel dictating to her what would happen. *Everyone will want to know who kidnapped the pretty TV news reporter and why.*

He was right.

He'd always been right.

She had a new mission now.

And the power and platform on which to work from.

She was going to find and rescue Antonio Vega.

Chapter Fifteen

Two weeks had gone by since she'd returned from Cuba, but as soon as Rebecca stepped out of the limo onto the temporary red carpet outside the Bayshore mansion of Florida's current governor, a series of flashes popped off.

Rebecca's heart slammed against her ribs, and she froze, instantly regretting her decision to come with Dallas, Samantha Steele, and Sam's fiancé, Zack Hunter, to this glitzy, high-profile charity event. But she'd promised Sam. Rebecca just had to smile and get through the night.

If she wasn't the lead story on the 5 p.m. news, Rebecca was still making the top news block, every damn day. Especially after her one-hour documentary on their controversial trip to Cuba aired three nights ago, to the highest news ratings her TV station had ever seen. The national morning news was still picking up clips, making Rebecca even more of a national celebrity.

Just as Antonio had predicted.

But Antonio, or the image of him, was becoming famous, too. Wonder if he'd counted on that?

Her stomach seized. Not one day had gone by without Antonio's words ringing in her ears. She couldn't get him out of her head no matter how hard she tried. She kept hearing his voice and looking for his face. But despite trying like hell and pulling every string she had, she still had no information on his whereabouts. Senator Nelson's office told her the Cuban government was denying they had an Antonio Vega in custody. And Maria and Esmeralda told her they hadn't heard from him, either. But then, they might not trust her to tell her if he had made contact. Antonio couldn't have just vanished. And she refused to believe he was dead. If the CDR made an example of him, wouldn't it face repercussions from the United States?

More flashbulbs. Rebecca stumbled and raised a hand to cover her face. *Jesus.* Didn't the media ever rest? Last year she would have been on the other side of the red carpet, ordering Dallas to shoot whoever made the news of the day. Be it good or bad. *No mercy.* Tonight, her friends and colleagues were feasting on her.

Dallas slipped a friendly arm around her back. "Smile for the camera, girl. You used to eat this shit up. Now you look like you're sucking on a lemon."

"I know." She'd been dying to attend this party before her trip to Cuba. Now Rebecca felt, well, guilty. She should be at home working the phones. Trying new sources to help find Antonio.

She exhaled, thankful Dallas was with her. His big physical size and his over-the-top personality would deflect some of the attention away from her, and maybe he'd even make her laugh tonight.

The foursome had stopped in front of a decorative white background. The names of about a half dozen party sponsors were imprinted in bold colors on the sign behind them. Zack, Sam's gorgeous man, pulled her in tight, and the four posed for the cameras. Rebecca managed to pull off a fake smile and a hair flip right as the flashes went off.

"Look at those lights." Dallas struck a manly stance, one hand grabbing his tux jacket, the other casually placed in his pocket. "They're soaking all this up, this big, beautiful, chocolate thunder."

That forced the corners of Rebecca's lips up. "Oh God, Dawg, lower your voice." Dallas had become quite the star as well, earning accolades for the gripping video he'd managed to shoot while undercover in Cuba.

He lifted an eyebrow and posed for the photographers. "Get some of this. Get some of this." Dallas shifted his weight left and right. Then, unexpectedly, he pulled her into him. "Don't leave my little Cuban pepper out."

Rebecca laughed. "You are enjoying this way too much. Let's get inside." She twisted her ankle as Dallas pulled her away from the cameras.

She righted herself as they entered the foyer and were greeted by the host, the governor, and his wife.

"Hello, Your Governorship." Dallas pulled off a light bow. "Quite a spread you have here."

The governor, a tall, elegant man with attractive silver hair and a perfectly fitted tux, grabbed Dallas's hand and shook it, but he was looking at Rebecca, a curious light in his wise old Republican eyes. "Glad you could make it, my dear. I must say I want to talk to you, Rebecca, about that documentary you aired the other day. You expertly pointed out that much of this talk going on between our countries is just bull...hockey. Neither Castro nor his brother wants the embargo lifted. They lose their ability to isolate their people with every additional American dollar that comes in. And the president knows we won't vote with him to lift it, so this is all for..."

Rebecca's throat tightened. *Here we go.*

Dallas rolled his eyes in a way only Rebecca could pick up. "Excuse me, Your Governorship." Then to Rebecca, Dallas said, "I'm going to go find Sam and Zack." And Dallas was off, leaving her to face the music. Alone. He hated all the political talk.

"Terrence." The governor's demure wife, who always smiled but rarely spoke, placed a delicate hand on Rebecca's shoulder. "We must let Ms. Menendez join her friends in the great room." The woman turned slightly and winked at her. "We're so honored you could join us. Especially after the trying time you've had. We'll let you go enjoy the party and discuss your masterful report later."

The understanding anchored in the first lady's eyes made Rebecca's heart swell with gratitude.

Rebecca had really tried to keep both her personal experiences and the politics out of her documentary, focusing instead on the emotion of two families desperate to escape Cuba, why it was still difficult today despite a fast-changing political climate, and what was stopping them still. She'd highlighted Domingo and his sad fate, and Antonio's family, clearly illustrating in the process that despite an opening of travel restrictions, and even some lifting of economic sanctions, the Cuban people remained trapped by their poverty and by a government that seemed to ask for much more than it was willing to concede.

She took the first lady's hands in both of hers, hoping the fine woman wouldn't be offended by the iciness of her fingers. Rebecca was still a bit nervous about making her first public appearance since returning. "We support the charities you're raising money for tonight and"—Rebecca threw in a genuine smile—"you have a reputation for throwing the finest party in town."

The first lady beamed, her eyes sparkling at the compliment.

Rebecca gave both a quick nod and turned, searching for Dallas and Sam.

"Nicely done." Zack Hunter was right beside her, tall as hell and commanding in his presence. "Sam sent me over to rescue you. But once again, looks like you can get out of an uncomfortable situation without much help." He grinned down at her.

Zack's confidence reminded Rebecca a lot of Antonio's strength and power. Her heart fluttered at the thought of Antonio. But Zack was a more flirty kind of guy, winking and grinning, very unlike Antonio, who was always so intense and serious. "Thanks."

"We're over here." Zack gestured toward the door to another room.

"Did you have a chance to check on the case for me?" Her cheeks heated. She knew she shouldn't be putting Sam's fiancé on the spot. He was an agent for the Florida Department of Law Enforcement and could get in trouble for talking to a reporter about information in an active case.

Instead of looking pissed, Zack just smiled. "Yes."

Yes, and? "I know I shouldn't ask you, but…"

"You're going to anyway." Zack winked at her. "Sam warned me you would. Here's what I can tell you. Off the record, of course."

"Of course."

"The FBI's kidnapping case is still open." Zack casually led her through the crowd, nodding as they passed people, looking cool and in control. No wonder Sam lived for this guy. "Since we can only assume the other kidnapper, the one caught on tape throwing you in the van here in Tampa, is dead in the waters of Cuba, and Antonio Vega is still in Cuba, the FBI's case will remain open for a while, but I wouldn't worry about it." Zack's eyes crinkled at the corners. "You were clearly the victim in all of this."

Was I? She exhaled. "Well, right, I'm not in trouble. I just don't want Antonio to be either."

Zack stopped dead in the middle of the room. "Really?"

Now her checks were flaming. One thing she'd left out of her documentary was her growing attraction to and relationship with Antonio. "Well, he has a family here now to support and…" In fact, she hadn't shared all the details with Sam, either.

Zack threw up a hand. "Then *your friend* should stay in Cuba where our federal law officers have no jurisdiction." Shaking his head, Zack motioned for her to move through the door first. "The man still masterminded a kidnapping that resulted in a murder."

"He didn't kidnap me, Zack." Rebecca wished she had proof of what happened to both Ignado and Antonio, but even Esmeralda hadn't been able to get info from inside Cuba. Rebecca furrowed her brow, a slight headache coming on.

"You okay?" Sam walked up, handing Rebecca a much-needed glass of white wine. "You look stunning in your Alexander McQueen."

"Oh, right." Rebecca glanced down at her black rented gown. "Thanks." She'd forgotten how excited she'd been to wear it here tonight. That was before her trip to Cuba and before Antonio. "I'm fine. Thanks for the wine." She raised the glass in salute to Sam, Dallas, and Zack, her friends all gathering around her in support. "Salud. To a great night." She must concentrate on what was good right now. Friends, fame, and food. Unlike in Cuba, there would always be plenty of food here.

Dallas rolled his eyes. "You get any happier, and that face is gonna fall off."

She sighed. Dallas nailed her with the truth. Once again. "I'm just feeling a little guilty." Why not tell Sam the truth, too? "Antonio is probably being roughed up in some Cuban jail cell, skinny and sick." She turned to look at the man who would definitely understand. "And Dallas, we're here, drinking and being celebrated for exposing his poor family on national TV." There. She'd said it. "And if Antonio ever comes back to America, I'm the reason he'll probably be arrested."

Zack Hunter cleared his throat. "You did nothing to seal that man's fate. He's a grown man who made his own decisions. You are a *victim*."

Maybe in the beginning, but I became a willing participant. And now I miss Antonio. Damn it. She missed every damn thing about him. She especially missed the way Antonio made her question her every decision. He'd forced her *to think*. He'd been the force behind her growth. And she was a better person now for it. She felt enlightened.

Zack's features registered a real disgust, but Rebecca knew if the two men ever met under different circumstances, they would surely respect each other's strengths and intelligence.

"Protecting this guy in the future would make you an accomplice."

"Zack." Sam stepped in between them.

"An accomplice to what?" Rebecca asked, fearing Zack's answer.

"To whatever illegal activity he's involved with."

What did Antonio do when he wasn't rescuing family members or running from police? She sighed. Vega was a wanted man.

Wanted by the law here, despite her efforts to crown him a hero. The public was on his side, but the FBI still wanted to question him about the international kidnapping. She'd never testify that he made her go to Cuba. She'd told FBI investigators that.

The law in Cuba also wanted Antonio.

She also wanted him.

Despite it all.

Sam moved Rebecca's glass up to her mouth. "Take another drink and stop thinking about him." But the look on Sam's face told Rebecca her friend understood how you could have feelings for the most unexpected person. Sam had confided in her about the rough start for her and Zack.

Dallas halfheartedly nudged her in the arm. "I think if Antonio, the ole boy, was here, he'd be thanking your ass. First of all, you went out of your way to get his family to Miami, and you signed paperwork as their sponsors. Then you got Maria and Tonito into a domestic violence shelter here in Tampa, and you helped Esmeralda land a good job. You did what he wanted to do, but couldn't do himself, so I think you're off the guilt hook here. Let's have ourselves some fun, okay?"

America's "wet foot, dry foot" policy had allowed Maria, Tonito, and Esmeralda to stay legally because they were Cubans. The U.S. government hadn't changed that policy yet, and the Catholic Church was still offering direction and help so the Cuban immigrants could start to file the proper paperwork to achieve citizenship. If the two women followed the law, they could become legal citizens one day; Tonito, too. That had been Antonio's grand plan, and his promise to his grandmother.

Rebecca had hooked the group up, not only with the shelter, but also a local Catholic church in Tampa. The threesome seemed to be settling in. After her documentary aired, donations had come pouring in to the TV station. Rebecca and Dallas had hand-delivered food, clothes, and even money to the three yesterday.

An unexpected wave of longing washed over her, making her feel a little dizzy. Off center. Would Antonio ever know what she'd done for his family?

What she'd done for him?

"Isn't that the mayor?" Zack asked.

The Cuban American politician approached them, his lovely wife on his arm.

Zack and the mayor shook hands, but before they could launch into a conversation, the mayor's wife, Carmelita, grabbed Rebecca by both shoulders. "Rebecca, I must ask a huge favor."

"Well, of course." Rebecca had always liked Carmelita because she'd been a "commoner" when she married a wealthy, prominent man. On many occasions the two women had bonded over the difficulties of earning acceptance into the very exclusive South Tampa society of old money. "Whatever you need."

"Good, because Samantha is now off the market." Carmelita smiled, but nervousness flashed in her eyes. "Linda Joyce, you know the neurosurgeon's ex-wife, she has a sick child and couldn't come tonight. I'm helping Marilyn with the fund-raising, and my responsibility is the live "first dance" auction. Linda had agreed to be part of the auction." Carmelita put both hands on her shoulders. "I need you to fill her spot."

"A dance auction?" Dallas's eyes widened, and he broke out into a full-out grin. "You all want me to bust a move to some Ace of Base. Old school. 'It takes two to make a thing go right.'" Dallas broke out a few break-dance moves.

The thought made Rebecca's stomach so uneasy she didn't even laugh at Dallas's antics. "Thanks for asking me, but…"

"Why not?" Sam asked.

"Just what you need to get your mind off Mr. Cuba." Dallas did his best Michael Jackson spin. "Go be a thriller."

Carmelita cocked her head, giving Rebecca her best *I*

need you look. "It's a dance to raise money for local *charities*. You'll get to pick the charity. Think about that."

Her breath caught. Dallas was right. This *is* just what she needed to do tonight—throw the spotlight on herself for a positive reason, prove her intentions were good, only to help those in need. Rebecca knew exactly which charity she wanted to raise money for. "I'll do it." What could possibly go wrong with this plan?

Chapter Sixteen

"Ladies and gentlemen, our next volunteer is one of my good friends and a friend to our community." Carmelita stood stage right in the large ballroom of the governor's mansion, holding the microphone and acting as emcee. She waved for Rebecca to move toward center stage and away from the half dozen other Tampa socialites still waiting to be auctioned off.

Hesitating, Rebecca stepped forward into the spotlight. A relay of sweat droplets slithered down her back. Stomach churning, she attempted a smile, the corners of her mouth shaking as they tipped up. She wouldn't be up here long, right? She usually didn't get this nervous in front of a crowd.

"Rebecca Menendez is a reporter for Eyewitness News in Tampa, but we've all seen her on the *national* news lately."

A polite flurry of applause erupted. Rebecca licked her lips, suddenly unnerved by being the center of attention, again, this time by choice.

"She covers the courthouse and the political beat, and just returned from a fascinating undercover adventure in Cuba."

Adventure? Really?

"In case you didn't see her outstanding documentary, you can find it on the station's website. Who will start the bidding for the charity of Rebecca's choosing, *La Casa de la Libertad*?"

A few audible gasps preceded the polite applause.

Rebecca bit her bottom lip. Must be in response to her choice of charity, a foundation run by Catholic nuns that aided Cuban immigrants when they first arrived in the United States. Probably not the brightest choice, because there were some in the audience who didn't really support all the extras Cubans got if they touched American soil, extras other illegal immigrants did not receive, but she hadn't known Carmelita planned to announce it in front of everybody. Why in the world had Rebecca chosen to subject herself to this public scrutiny tonight, with her legs still shaky underneath her?

"Two hundred dollars."

Zack's voice. She blushed. He was just being nice. Rebecca looked over at Sam, sitting at a table with Zack in the second row, and flashed her a smile of thanks for allowing her fiancé to get the ball rolling and put her out of her misery up here. She hadn't realized how embarrassing waiting for the first bid would be.

Sam winked at her.

Rebecca smiled, glad her friends were here.

Most of the bids had started in the hundreds, despite the mostly affluent crowd. The highest bid so far had been five thousand for the beautiful twenty-something daughter of a local banking magnate.

A couple of bids came in from men Rebecca couldn't see in the crowd. Didn't really matter. She was just doing this to raise money for a group that was already actively helping Maria and Tonito.

Rebecca cocked her head at Carmelita, waiting for her to

close the bidding at five hundred, where it was now, and get her the hell off the stage. Sweating like a cool glass of iced tea on a hot Florida afternoon, Rebecca suddenly appreciated the strapless gown she had rented.

"One thousand dollars."

The smile slid off Rebecca's face at the bid from a voice in the back of the room. Tiny drops of sweat beaded on her forehead, but she resisted the urge to wipe them away. She recognized that authoritative tone. But it couldn't be him. She was hallucinating.

Heart fluttering, Rebecca scanned the crowd for the bidder. She rolled her lips inward. It took every ounce of willpower not to fidget or take a step farther downstage, out of the light and closer to the crowd, so she could see.

Someone else made a bid. Rebecca didn't even register the amount.

"Six thousand dollars." As the man upped the bid by six times the amount, he slowly walked out of the crowd, but not yet into the light.

Rebecca tried to swallow, but her mouth had gone dry.

Carmelita's cheeks appeared flushed, and her eyes danced as her gaze landed on Rebecca. "Six thousand dollars. Going once."

Rebecca held her breath.

"Going twice."

What if it was Antonio? Would he dare show up here looking like Che, in fatigues and a beret?

"Going three times." More applause erupted, but a few cynical snickers could be heard above the clapping. A rippling of heads turned in the opposite direction searching for the extravagant bidder, too.

God, Zack was here. He'd know. Antonio would stand out in this crowd. Would Zack arrest Antonio? Zack was FDLE, not FBI, but didn't all those agencies work together?

Annoying stars started spinning in front of her. She should have eaten dinner.

"I would like to thank you, sir." Carmelita crossed the stage to stand next to Rebecca, Carmelita's excitement at the strange turn of events palpable. "Please pay at the table in the foyer. The dances start at nine o'clock."

But Rebecca knew she couldn't wait one second longer to find out if the man who spent six grand on a dance was the same one who had, without spending a dime, engraved an unbelievably deep mark on her heart.

Chapter Seventeen

Quickly slipping off the stage in the ballroom, Rebecca intended to find the mystery bidder right away. Before any of her friends did.

Avoiding Sam and Zack's table, she slipped through the buzzing crowd now breaking up after dinner.

When the mystery man suddenly broke through the gathering, her breath halted in her lungs.

Antonio stopped when he saw her.

Their eyes locked, and her heart pounded as if injected with adrenaline. She shot a hand to her head, fingering a strand of hair that had fallen loose. Antonio had cut his glorious long hair, almost shaved it all off, into a preppy cut typical of most South Tampa millionaires.

She slid her other hand across her mouth. Slowly, she pulled her fingers over her lips and across her chin. Freshly shaven, Antonio's goatee was completely gone, his features no longer looking dangerous, but regal instead. The man walking toward her looked younger than she remembered, and he'd traded his fatigues and beret for a beautifully fitted, expensive-looking black tuxedo and a simple black bow tie.

Wow. She took a step backward, knocked out by Antonio's new appearance. He looked, quite literally, like a young James Bond. Like a freaking million bucks.

Quickly Rebecca walked into the crowd and away from Sam, Zack, and Dallas. Antonio swerved and followed, his dark eyes never breaking the stare. Those black orbs hadn't changed at all. They still flamed with intent. Antonio ignored several people trying to stop him, his stride purposeful, as if he couldn't wait to get to her.

As if no one else in the room mattered.

Loud voices, many close by, blended together into a distant buzz. The room shrank and her vision narrowed and all she could see was Antonio.

The closer he drew, the more of her body tingled with anticipation.

He'd made it back, alive! Part of her wanted to run to him, throw her arms around his neck and squeeze him until the whole length of his body melted into hers. She wanted to scream how happy she was that their leaving without him hadn't resulted in his death. But another part of her realized what a threat his return posed, and he probably didn't even know it. Closing her eyes, her hand came to rest on her neck, her jagged pulse the proof of her apprehension.

She swallowed, wondering what he'd do next. They were in the middle of a roomful of people, people who had heard Antonio's name on the news, seen video of him, although he did look quite different now. And no one would expect an escaped revolutionary to score an invite to the governor's exclusive soiree, but she was still nervous someone might catch on. Namely Zack. What should she do? She had to think first. Okay, maybe *breathe* first.

"*Buenas noches, mi amor.*"

She opened her eyes. His heat washed across the nape

of her neck. He was right behind her. How did he do that? Move around and shift positions so swiftly? "Good evening, Antonio." She stared at the bustling crowd of dancers and partiers mingling around as if nothing mattered. None of them had any idea a society scandal was brewing, about to boil over right before their eyes.

"Rebecca, look at me."

The strain in his voice made her breath hitch. "Jesus, you're alive," she whispered, turning toward him. Tonight, he smelled not of seven-year rum but of expensive top-shelf whiskey.

"Yes, I am." He raised one brow, a confident smile on his lips.

"And you're *here*."

"You should close your mouth." His eyes twinkled, locking with hers. "People are beginning to stare."

Her gaze automatically brushed the couples standing closest to them. A few pairs of eyes *were* on them. "I can't believe it's you." Like a moth to the flame, her gaze flew back to Antonio. Her sexy, disheveled revolutionary had vanished. This man looked like he'd spent the day at a men's spa, instead of returning from a Cuban jail cell. A lump formed in the back of her throat.

He reached out to brush a strand of hair away from her eyes. "The look on your face tells me you've missed me."

"I have." She sighed. "I have, but Antonio, please." She brushed his hand away. His fingers left a trail of heat. "Not here."

"Are you serious?" The cockiness drained out of his eyes, and hurt moved in. "That's how you greet the man who came all this way just to thank you?"

"Oh God, I'm sorry." The dam holding back her emotions cracked. "I'm so sorry we left you." Placing a hand over her heart didn't stop the leak. "We didn't have a choice. That damn Ignado betrayed us all." She dropped her head, unable to bear the wounded look in his eyes. "I'm glad you're alive." And she was, but she also feared what his appearance here might do to his future. "But you have to go now. For your own safety." She glanced up at him.

His left eyebrow cocked up. He glanced at one couple in particular, who looked as if they were already spreading rumors about them. He nodded politely and turned back to her. "I believe I bought myself at least two minutes with you on the dance floor. I'm not leaving until I collect."

"Don't be crazy." She took a step back, her gaze darting toward the table where her friends had been sitting. They weren't there anymore.

Antonio thrived on crossing the line and facing the consequences later. If she agreed to the dance, she'd keep him away from Zack, who would be itching to take Antonio in for questioning once Zack found out Antonio was actually here. The dance floor was filling up. "Okay." She couldn't look at Antonio. He looked so damn good, and she'd already fallen prey to that physical chemistry once. "Let's get this dance over with."

"Well, when you put it that way." Antonio reached for her hand and pulled her toward the dance floor. He didn't say another word as he led her into the center of the tangled web made up mostly of South Tampa couples. A number of people stared with raised eyebrows as they walked by. Her stomach clenched at their judgmental glances. But they couldn't know who Antonio was. They wouldn't recognize him like this. She was just being paranoid.

Once Antonio got her deep in the center of the moving crowd, where they simply blended in with the wave of dancers, he drew her to his hard body, pulling her so close she could feel proof of his excitement at seeing her again. Jesus, did he always have his testosterone level turned on high? The crowd of people staring her down melted into an unimportant blob, and once again her body automatically reacted to his.

"You're trembling."

"I'm frightened."

"Why?" he whispered into her ear. "I'm not going to leave you again. I promise."

"That's what scares me."

He stiffened and stopped dancing, pulling back enough to look into her eyes. He wasn't smiling.

"I'm not going to lie to you," she said. "I'm thrilled to see you. I've been worrying about you every day. But in all honesty, it would be better for you if you would just leave. We can meet and talk about this later."

Another slow song started. "I have a better idea. Let's not talk at all." He pulled her into a more intimate embrace, easily sweeping her into his arms.

Her body fit into his so effortlessly, just like it had the last time they'd danced at Johnny's farm. "Oh Antonio, it's not going to be that easy."

"I suggest you start calling me Tony. That's how people in Tampa know me."

She stopped midstep. "People in Tampa know you?" Glancing over his shoulder, she exclaimed, "*These* people?"

"Well, many have heard of Tony Vegas." Swaying, he forced her to move in time with the slow, sensual beat of the Latin ballad. "I have a reputation for being a shrewd businessman, but I admit to being a bit of a recluse in the past."

Tony Vegas? Heat spread throughout her body. What game was he playing now?

His fingers found that sensitive area at her waist, right above her hip bone. He pressed in with both his fingers and thumb.

She shivered and pushed his hand away. "Stop it. Why

Tony Vegas?"

"The Miami sisters who placed me with a Catholic family when I first arrived here thought I'd stand a better chance with a more American name."

Moving his fingers casually back to her waist, he stroked her in small movements that no one dancing near by would be able to pick up, but the tiny electrical jolts shooting through her body left her breathless. "Please, Antonio, stop teasing me."

He continued to touch her in an intimate manner.

She quivered, like she had the last time he played this control game, and for a moment she couldn't breathe.

"Don't be fooled by this polished appearance. I may have cleaned up, but the man inside has not changed," he whispered. "You know I believe in doing what I want. And right now, what I want to do is you. I've missed you." His voice broke as he said it.

The flat of his palm on her lower back and the seriousness of his words sent longing soaring throughout her already-aroused body. "Why are you here tonight? Why not talk in private?" *Tell him. Tell him the truth. That there's another reason he has to leave. The police know his name. Zack knows his name and what he looks like. They will arrest and charge him despite the public outcry or her efforts to stop them.*

"I decided I needed to reenter society and stop hiding under all that hair and all that old anger."

Oh my God. "You're different."

His body twirled in a small circle, taking her with him. "You've changed me. I knew you'd be here, and I wanted to thank you personally for taking care of my family while I couldn't. You have no idea how much that means to me."

Her breath stilled and her heart swelled about three times its normal size. She bit her lip, trying to hold back the wave of joy tiding in her. Antonio knew she'd gone to Miami and had claimed his sister and family members. "A six-thousand-dollar donation is thank-you enough, I think."

"Money means nothing." His eyes smiled down at her. "But the charity you selected is a good one."

"How would you know?" Antonio and charity didn't really add up.

"I helped the nuns start that charity six years ago, after I sold my company."

"What?" Rebecca tripped over his left foot, forcing them to bump into an elderly retired doctor and his wife dancing next to them. "So sorry," Rebecca murmured, her attention immediately pulled back to her own partner. Would he continue to surprise her like this? "Your company?"

"I used to ship Florida produce to other countries, including Cuba."

The irony of his statement didn't escape her. "You sent food to Cuba, where they have endless fertile farm land, but not enough to eat." She shook her head.

"That sounded a bit cynical." The corners of his mouth tipped up. "I think I'm rubbing off on you, Rebecca Menendez. Perhaps you did see Cuba through my eyes, after all."

Her heart skipped beats, and the heat in her cheeks flamed hotter. Antonio was doing it again. Slowly seducing her with his words, his passion and his politics. *Stop it, Rebecca. Get a grip on yourself.* She'd gotten out of this whole thing without any repercussions on her life. She should listen to Zack and stay away from Antonio. But selling produce wasn't illegal. She needed to hear more about Antonio's life. He *wasn't* a criminal. Was he?

She looked to her right. Another doctor's wife was watching them with an inquisitive look on her face as she and her husband slow-danced nearby.

"My company was quite successful. I sold it for millions, took the money, and took time off to plan and execute our trip to Cuba."

Our trip. She shook her head. *Don't let him pull you in. Keep some distance between you two.* "So you actually run in these circles?" The owner of a chain of successful jewelry stores and his glamorous wife danced past them, both flashing smiles. At least they weren't judgers. "Why haven't we met before this?"

"I've chosen not to attend these events, until now."

"Why?"

He sighed. "I used to believe most of these people represented everything I hated."

"And now?"

He dropped his gaze, paused, and then twirled her full circle, her gown sweeping across the floor. "I'm opening my eyes and my heart to new possibilities."

Stumbling and catching herself, she looked up at him, conflicted emotions raging in her center. "Because of me?"

He nodded, holding her up and settling them once again into a slow, sexy groove. "I know this world is important to you. Unlike most here, *I* understand why." He pulled her in, his cheek brushing hers, his skin hot and fevered. "I'm willing to give this world a chance if that's what you really want."

. . .

"We could do so much good together." His lips found her skin, and he whispered against her cheek, "When I first saw you tonight, you literally took my breath away." She smelled so good. *Felt* so good. He caressed her shoulder, stroking her exposed flesh, moving his fingers in circles, hoping to send electric pricks of pleasure throughout her body. "I don't think I can let you go. Not right now. Not ever again." God, he missed her. He missed the fire in her eyes, the passion in her voice when she stood up to him, and the way her body melted into his, just like it was doing now.

He pulled back and stared at her, feeling a longing so intense it made his center quake. "I thought about you and what might have happened to you and my family every single day I was away. You have no idea how surprised and thankful I was when I learned from my uncle you convinced my sister, Esmeralda, Pedro, and Tonito to come with you to America. Esmeralda told me you actually offered to go with Ignado to Havana to try to help me. That you'd risk your own safety…" He swallowed. No one had ever risked so much for him. "I can't explain what that means to me. And you took care of my family while I've been gone. You may not admit it, or even realize it yet, but you did that because you care about *me*."

"Oh Antonio, I have to talk to you."

But the way Rebecca was looking at him made him think she wanted nothing to do with words. Neither did he. He wanted to touch her whole body, run his hands through her long hair all fancy and piled on top of her head, mash his lips on top of hers.

"Please, take me out of here. Off this dance floor."

It was as if she could read his mind. That's exactly what he wanted to do. Get the hell out of here. He grabbed her hand and led her off the dance floor.

She stumbled.

He looked back.

She was staring across the dance floor, but it was hard to see whom she was focused on. His blood pressure raised a notch. He didn't want her focused on anyone but him right now. It hadn't been easy getting out of Cuba with so many looking for him. But he did it, thanks to Jose Carlos, in large part to get back to her. Make sure she was okay. He wanted Rebecca's full attention now.

She turned back to him. "Your six-thousand-dollar, two-minute dance is over. You have to go now."

He smiled, wondering how she could have forgotten so quickly who was in charge. "Follow me then." He grabbed her hand. "Because I am not leaving this dance floor without you."

She knew better than to resist. He may have polished his looks, but the rebel still raged inside him, and he'd cause a scene if he had to.

Maybe she realized that, because she nodded and finally let him lead.

Silently he pulled her through the moving crowd, the human sea parting in front of them, and an ocean of inquisitive glances tiding the floor in their wake.

Chapter Eighteen

Pulling her behind him, Antonio strode through the mansion silently, exiting the main ballroom and heading down a hallway. A few people nodded, recognizing Rebecca, but the looks of appreciation from other women as Antonio passed by made her stomach turn. Was this what jealousy felt like? Or was it simply anxiety stirring her insides?

She kept glancing back, waiting for Sam and Zack or Dallas to descend on them, but so far her friends must not have made the connection to her disappearance and the mystery bidder. Someone who had noticed her and Antonio dancing would eventually tell them. It was only a matter of time. What the hell was she doing? Why did she continue to let Antonio persuade her to follow him when she knew the result would be nothing but disastrous for both of them?

Every nerve in her body vibrated, like a tightly strung cord rocked by a jolt of electricity. She felt *alive* when she was with Antonio. That's why she was following him now.

Antonio moved through a pair of doors into a smaller version of the big ballroom. How many rooms did the governor's mansion have? Looking up to see whom she might know in this room and whom she might need to avoid, she stopped as the opulence of the decor stole her breath away. The entire room looked like a fairy-tale fantasyland, with white linen treatments from windowsill to floor, white trees with crystal lighting hanging from fake branches, and more than a dozen long dessert tables, dressed in white linen with various sweet delicacies displayed in between large carved ice sculptures. This room looked like a snow queen's ice palace, just the kind of fancy venue she'd dreamed of for her own future wedding reception.

"What are you thinking?" Antonio walked up to where she'd paused, near a large dessert table. He was staring at her with both eyebrows raised.

Antonio looked deliciously handsome, and conflicted emotions turned like a screw inside her. With only a few inches between them now, high-voltage energy surged through her. Her fingers tapped against the tablecloth.

"Tell me. What's going on in that head of yours?" he asked, his eyes narrowing but the corners of his lips turning up, like he already knew where her mind was wandering.

"I'm all knotted up." She stepped away, catching her breath, taking in the rest of the room. She had to change the subject or she'd just throw herself into his arms and be done with it. But she had something to prove to Antonio first. "I wonder if the taxpayers are footing the bill for all of this? And even if they're not, this is an example of what's wrong with America."

Antonio took a step back, cocking his head to one side. "Not exactly what I expected to hear from you right now."

She bit her bottom lip, well aware of how off-the-charts her comment must sound, but there was something deep inside her that longed for Antonio to see how the trip to Cuba *had* affected her. "Look at all this extravagance." On the table nearest to them, she plucked up a square brownie, with a liquid red middle and a smear of nuts and caramel on top. It was bigger than her whole hand. "The brownie is big enough to feed Esmeralda, Maria, and Tonito. For dinner. Ridiculous. And at the end of the night, they'll throw over half of this expensive food away." She sighed. "They always do."

Antonio chuckled under his breath, strolling around to the other side of the table. "It's a party, Rebecca." Picking up an even bigger brownie, he took a bite, chewing slowly.

Her stomach turned. "It's a *charity* event. Paid for with tax dollars, most likely." Suddenly appalled by the waste that had been her life practically every Saturday night recently, she raised the obnoxiously large brownie in a salute and casually tossed it into the nearest trash receptacle. *If you can't beat 'em then join 'em.* "The governor let the Tampa Ladies Club, of which his wife is a member, use his home to raise money for the less fortunate, but I bet they're spending more money on food and entertainment to entice these big spenders than the same big spenders will donate and leave behind tonight. That just doesn't make sense, does it?"

"Oh, I don't know. I donated six grand. And I know my money is going to a good cause." He grinned, looking suddenly normal, not like the angry rebel at all.

Antonio had chocolate on the corner of his mouth. She longed to reach across the table and wipe it off, but that would be too intimate of a gesture, and she didn't want to draw attention to Antonio yet. Rebecca glanced away, self-conscious. "And look at that older man slurping champagne while staring at that young girl's cleavage. Is he really here to help charities like yours?" She glanced back.

Wiping the corner of his mouth, Antonio sucked the frosting off his own finger. "Now you're being too cynical. Many of these people are your friends, and I'm sure their intentions are good." But then he winked at her.

Her cheeks flamed; she knew he understood what she was trying to say to him. She finally got it. She finally got him and his mission. He'd won. He'd changed her. Forever.

Antonio walked around the table, and as he brushed past her, his fingers grazed hers, barely touching her skin.

She shivered.

He gestured with his head for her to follow.

"I think we need to go outside to finish this conversation," she whispered, not even sure if Antonio heard her.

"My thoughts exactly." His eyes were dilated again.

She'd seen that naughty intent in Antonio's gaze before at Johnny's farm. He wouldn't be stopped back then and probably wouldn't tonight, either. *That* kind of energy still crackled between them. Another reason she had to get them both out the door quickly.

As she pushed the back door open, she glanced over her shoulder and noticed Carmelita standing in the entranceway, staring at them wide-eyed. *Freaking great.* Rebecca waved at Carmelita, having no choice but to acknowledge her, but Rebecca couldn't seem to get enough air as the invisible noose, made by her own actions, began to tighten. "We've been spotted." She shot a quick look Antonio's way. "Meet me in ten minutes out back, in the garden maze by the greenhouse. It's behind where the men are smoking cigars."

"No. We're finishing this conversation now." Antonio's eyes flamed.

Carmelita started walking toward them. She was the second-biggest gossiper in South Tampa, next to the plastic surgeon's wife. Rebecca turned to face Antonio. "I promise, I'll be out there in ten minutes. Let me deal with *the mayor's wife*, first."

"Rebecca," he stopped. "You know me well enough to know I don't give a damn about *the mayor's wife*." Antonio attempted to grab her hand. "But I do give a damn about you. *You* are coming outside with me. Right now."

She jerked out of his reach. "I can't. I have to ward off trouble for both you and me."

"I'm not afraid of trouble."

"Don't I know it."

This time when his fingers wrapped around her wrist, they locked on, and he tugged her, forcing her to move her feet in order to not fall over.

Glancing behind her, she swallowed. Carmelita stood ramrod straight staring at her and Antonio. Carmelita's mouth was wide open. Rebecca signaled to her across the room and mouthed the words: *I'll be right back.* How stupid was that?

Antonio pulled her onto the porch, tugging her through the crowd of well-dressed men, smoking stogies and drinking sherry and expensive port. He led her down a set of stairs and through a garden gate, until they were suddenly alone in a dark corner of the governor's garden maze.

He pulled her into a small, unlocked greenhouse. The windows were partially covered with half-open shutters; the door was now shut behind them, and the noise of the party but a low buzz in the background. The only light filtering in was coming from both the party and the moon.

Once again she found herself trapped with Antonio in an enclosed place, with little light to see and electricity popping around them. But this time it wasn't from Mother Nature.

Antonio turned to face her.

Her eyes quickly adjusted to catch the seriousness of his features.

"Maria told me how hard you've been trying to find me."

Her heart fluttered. "I tried everything I could think of, but…"

"It's okay. I'm fine." He placed a finger over her lips. "But

I do want to know why you wouldn't give up the search."

"Antonio."

"You care about me, that's why, but you don't want to admit it. You're afraid if you love me, these people might not approve, and this fancy life will go away." Antonio gestured to the stocked greenhouse. Then he moved in on her, backing her against a table in the center lane of the glass house.

She couldn't take her eyes off him.

"But I can give you this life, too." Gripping her face in his hands, Antonio kissed her, his lips firm and unrelenting.

The old Antonio, the demanding revolutionary, was back, and his powerful confidence was injecting her with the euphoria of an illegal drug. She pushed against his chest, creating needed space between them. "That's not what concerns me. You don't understand. The police are looking for you. You're a wanted man. I don't want you to be arrested. Your whole world will change." She said it all in one breath, and feeling dizzy, stumbled.

He caught her, both hands on her elbows. "Both of our worlds have already changed." His black eyes flickered, like they had that night in the tent in the Everglades. "Cuba changed you. *I* changed you." His grip on her elbows tightened. "Isn't that what you've been trying to prove to me tonight with all your talk of waste and extravagance?"

He was right. She swallowed.

He pulled her closer. "And *you've* changed *me*."

She knew what was coming. She took a deep breath, her whole body tingling in anticipation.

"Enough with the talking already. You know how I prefer to communicate." His lips pressed down on hers again. His tongue shot into her mouth, capturing hers, suffocating her until she feared she'd pass out. He kissed with a fierce intent other men had always lacked. She wondered if it would always be like this.

Then Antonio pulled back, grabbing her chin roughly. "You will never look at your old life the same way again. And no one will ever satisfy you the way I do."

He's right. But she still feared his complete control over her. Other men didn't make her swoon. Only he did. "Maybe my ignorance was bliss."

"No, ignorance is just ignorance." His chest was heaving up and down. As they stared at each other, both trying to catch their breaths, she witnessed some of the fire dissipate in his eyes, replaced by uncertainty and then what? Fear?

He let go of her, and as he stepped back, the warm Florida night air failed to replace the heat of his rock-hard body. "I hate these fancy penguin suits." He struggled to undo his bow tie.

This Antonio looked and sounded more like the one on his knees before his grandmother, his vulnerability so rarely on display.

"No, no. Antonio." Love rushed through her veins. She'd do anything to protect this wounded man. Anything, now that she understood him so much better. "I'm appreciative of how you've changed me, and how you make me feel." She placed a hand on his chest. "And I love you in a tux."

Antonio's voice sounded husky, his tone dropping a notch. "You love me, period. Maybe you need to be reminded of how much." He reached for her, enveloping her in a hug. His lips found her neck and traveled from the base slowly up the side.

His fingertips skimmed her back just above her strapless gown line. He inhaled, than exhaled slowly, his breath leaving a warm imprint on her flesh. "I missed the smell of your skin." Then his hand moved from her back to cup her right breast. His deft fingers tugged down her gown enough to expose her.

She froze, frantically glancing around to make sure no one else had joined them in the greenhouse. Did the governor have surveillance cameras? Would they work in such low light?

It was dark enough that maybe no one could see.

Still.

This could get her fired.

God, would Antonio always drag her into dangerous situations?

And would she always respond like this?

She tried to pull her gown up. "I have to go back inside before Carmelita starts wondering what's taking me so long."

"Rebecca." The way he whispered her name indicated a warning she knew she should heed. "Stop talking."

His hand snaked into her perfectly styled hair, and this time he wove his fingers into her curls with such force that the little white pearls popped out and the carefully pinned strands came undone. He wrapped her locks around his skilled fingers and jerked her head toward him, meeting her halfway with a kiss meant, no doubt, to shut her up.

And it worked. She exhaled into the kiss, giving in, admitting finally to herself that this man was *the* man. The one who made the hair on her skin rise, made her heart swell with longing, and made her brain fire off like fireworks were stuck inside. Coming up for breath, Antonio whispered, "You have no idea how much I've missed you. How much I've wanted to do this."

Oh, but she did know. And she wanted it, too. And now she was going to do something about it.

He shuddered as her hands found his abs and her fingers rolled down his hard stomach, moving south. He grabbed her hand and forced her to feel the length of him over his clothes.

"I want to hear you tell me how much you want me, too." He released her hand and quickly pulled up the bottom edge of her designer gown, his fingers finding her naked skin.

She sighed as his fingers traced circles on her thighs.

Teasingly, he moved his fingers higher, on a path to a place wet and full of longing.

"Antonio," she pleaded. "You know we shouldn't do this here. I've already drawn enough attention to myself. And I don't want people to be asking questions about you. Let's go somewhere else."

His fingers found the lace edge of her brand-new panties and hovered there.

"Please, Antonio."

"Please what?"

"Please…please, please." Oh God, he wasn't going to stop until she told him exactly what he wanted to hear. What the hell was she thinking? He wasn't going to stop at all. Heat rushed to her cheeks.

"Please what? Touch you like this?" He slid one finger under her thong.

"Ah." She arched and tightened her muscles.

He stroked her with a controlled feather light touch. She arched her back to meet his fingers, wanting more. "That feels great." *He's so skilled at this.* All she could think about was the physical release she knew was moments away. But she wanted him inside her.

"You need this," Antonio whispered, his lips against the throbbing artery in her neck. "You need me."

"I do." The time he'd been away had been so taxing. She'd been so desperate to find him. He had no idea. And now that he was here, she couldn't risk not having another chance to tell him, "I love you." She sighed. "And I need you inside me." Holy shit, did she just say that?

Apparently, that's exactly what Antonio had been waiting to hear, because he unzipped his pants and sheathed himself so quickly she barely had time to open her eyes and register what he was doing. Not sure how he was balancing them both, he lifted her onto the table and pushed up into her.

Slowly at first, he began picking up the pace, his movement so consistent and so right, the orgasm started to build. "Let go, Rebecca."

She wanted to. God, did she long to let go. Of so much she'd been holding on to for so long. And she'd do anything he asked right now. Anything. Because she loved him.

"I know she's here."

Through the fog and haze of her own lust, Rebecca picked up Carmelita's distinct Spanish inflection. She was walking this way! Rebecca's heart stopped. She tried to put her feet on the ground.

Antonio held her fast, his hot breath quickening on her flesh, his pace picking up.

"I saw her leave with him. *Everybody* did." Carmelita's voice grew louder.

Antonio moved back an inch, his eyes meeting hers. His gaze locking onto hers. He whispered for her to remain quiet.

"Leave with who?"

Jesus. That was Zack's voice. Sam and Dallas had to be with him. Rebecca couldn't swallow. They were going to get caught!

"I don't know him. A handsome guy, though. And it was obvious they know each other." Carmelita was sure stirring the pot tonight.

Rebecca's throat went dry. She reached down to stop the illicit act.

Antonio shook his head, mouthing the words, "Don't say a word." Then his body continued its slow assault, his gaze never leaving hers. He moved just enough to keep her right on the edge.

Antonio leaned in closer. "You will never feel this way with anyone else, Rebecca." He intensified his movements.

Her whole body tingled as she first pushed away, and then into him.

By the sound of their voices, Carmelita and Zack were only a few seconds away.

A ripple from deep in her center spread outward, the waves of pleasure drowning her like a tsunami. She couldn't stop now if she wanted to. And she didn't.

"I think he's the man who bid on her." Carmelita's voice was so close Rebecca swore they were right outside the door.

"Are you thinking what I'm thinking?" Zack must be speaking to either Sam or Dallas.

Antonio pulled her hair, forcing her head to one side, pushing her over that orgasmic edge with that little infliction of pain. "No one will ever know you this intimately, or satisfy you like I will. No matter what happens next, I want to make sure you don't forget that."

A groan escaped her firmly pressed lips.

"Rebecca, I love you, too."

Every hair on her body tingled. He said it. He loved her, too.

"Who's there? Rebecca?"

She shut her eyes, trying to block out the suspicion in her friend's voice.

The muscles in her upper thighs clenched as the wave of an orgasm crashed over her. She bit down on her lip to keep from making any more sounds. Burying both hands in Antonio's short hair, she couldn't find much to grasp. She missed his long, rebellious curls, but she pulled at his scalp as if to share the intense sensations bursting through her.

Antonio shuddered.

"Over here." Carmelita's voice had an odd satisfied ring to it. "I think I heard something right inside here."

Antonio pulled away.

Rebecca jerked down her dress, quickly smoothing it into place, little tremors of an earthquake still rocking her.

Antonio adjusted her dress, tucking her back in.

Remembering how Antonio had pulled at her hair, she smoothed back the errant strands and twisted it all up into a loose bun, her insides burning now with a dread that made her shake. Looking down, she made sure she was covered.

"It'll be okay, Rebecca," Antonio whispered. "Trust me."

Trust him? Jesus, she couldn't trust him or herself. The crazy things desire made you do. Anchoring her gaze on the man who'd just seduced her in a somewhat *public* place, her heart fluttered with wings of worry. She'd never done anything this naughty or risky before.

Okay, maybe *everything* she'd done since meeting Antonio had been risky.

And exciting.

And addictive.

She put a hand over her heart, taking a deep breath to slow it.

Antonio jammed his shirt into his pants, readjusted his belt, and ran a hand over his hair. He then turned to her and smiled in a knowing way. Much to her surprise, he walked casually to the door, opened it and stepped forward, out of their dark hiding place into the moonlit, party-filled night.

Her pulse skyrocketed. What the hell was he doing?

"Remember, trust me."

Chapter Nineteen

Antonio stepped out of the dark greenhouse where he'd just made love to Rebecca. His blood was still pumping, but a deep sense of satisfaction calmed his nerves. Rebecca was his. He'd felt her shift and give in to it, this crazy connection they'd had almost from the start. He would let nothing stand between them ever again. "Looking for me?" Not even this crew of her friends, standing outside the greenhouse.

Dallas Jones, in a tux, stood next to a tall man with dark hair and knowing eyes whom Antonio didn't know. A petite, attractive woman he'd seen before on Rebecca's TV station and the mayor's wife were walking up.

When Dallas saw Antonio, the photographer stopped talking, rubbed his chin, then his eyes popped wide. "No way." Dallas stepped back. "That really you, man? Damn, son, you look fresh." Dallas's worried gaze flickered to the man he'd come with. "It's clear you didn't come back on a flotation device."

Interesting that Dallas didn't call him by his name. Or try to shake his hand. Or even smile like he was glad to see him.

Instead the photographer stood in front of Antonio, stiff, shifting onto a different leg, looking around, probably for Rebecca. So the guy with Dallas had to be a cop. No other reason for Dallas to look so uncomfortable. *Good to know.*

Dallas's eyes raked over the greenhouse where Rebecca was still hiding. "Have you seen Rebecca?"

The energy prickled on the top of Antonio's skin. "Yes, I have."

"See, I told you, Samantha, this is who Rebecca left with." The mayor's wife was eyeing him like he was a jewel thief about to steal the pricey piece around her weathered neck. "He does know her."

"Well, where is she then?" The reporter called Samantha had both her hands on her hips now, engaging Antonio in a stare-down. "Who are you, and how do you know my friend?"

"Am I being interviewed?" Antonio had watched Rebecca's documentary, so he knew she had aired video of him. He also knew how different he looked tonight. No one here except Dallas knew who he was and what his real connection to Rebecca was. Antonio planned on keeping it that way for a little while longer.

The dinging of a cell phone text alert went off.

All eyes turned to the greenhouse where Rebecca was still hiding.

First, a light came on, as if Rebecca was checking her phone. Then she darted out the door, her hands out in front of her, the phone in her hand pointed right at him. "This has to be a sick joke."

"Rebecca?" Sam's features dropped as Rebecca entered the light.

Carmelita gasped. "Are you okay?" The mayor's wife brought her dainty, jeweled fingers to cover her heart.

Both women looked shocked, but as Antonio drank in Rebecca's appearance, he could only beam.

He loved the strands of her hair out of place tumbling around her shoulders, her lips full and red like she'd just been kissed, a lot, and her skin all flushed with a tone that only meant one thing. Her clothes were still not adjusted correctly, and it looked like she was trembling.

There was no question what had been going on in that dark greenhouse. He couldn't help but grin. *He'd* done that. Taken her breath away.

"Damn, girl." Dallas raised both eyebrows. "It's obvious you've been slapping uglies."

"What?" Rebecca and Sam asked at the same time.

Antonio laughed, knowing exactly what Dallas meant. "Last time I checked, slapping uglies isn't illegal." Antonio stared at the cop. Let him say something.

At the uncomfortable silence, Antonio turned back to Rebecca. She was clutching her throat, not responding to either Dallas or his playful banter. It was the fear anchored in her eyes that quickly made Antonio realize something was seriously wrong. "What is it?"

She looked down at her pink-encased iPhone, but then took a step back and stumbled, bobbling her phone from one hand to the other.

Antonio watched as it teetered at the end of her fingers. *Jesus, don't drop it.* Antonio grabbed her. "Take a deep breath and tell me what's wrong." He steadied her with two hands on both elbows, but he couldn't stabilize the phone. It tumbled to the ground, hitting with a thud.

Rebecca looked up at him, her words skipping out in a stuttered mess. "Who else knows about him? Who, who?"

Beads of sweat bubbled on her skin, but Antonio didn't think he'd done that. "Knows about who?" Antonio swiped the phone off the ground. "What are you talking about?"

She inhaled, but it looked like the air had stopped and lodged in her windpipe. She couldn't speak.

Antonio glanced down and read the prominent text message. The heat drained from Antonio's face. "It's a joke, Rebecca." It had to be. *That man* wouldn't have the fucking nerve to show up in Tampa.

"He's *here*." The words squeaked out of Rebecca's throat. "How?" She took two steps back. "Did you…"

"No." Antonio stopped her retreat. How could she even think that? "I didn't bring him."

"Then who did? And how would he know to come here?"

"All right." The cop with Dallas grabbed the phone from Antonio's grip. "What the hell is going on here?" The man moved his lips as he read the message, then his gaze locked onto Rebecca's, focused and inquisitive. "Who is Arturo Menendez Garcia? One of the Cubans you sponsored?"

Antonio jerked the phone out of the man's hands.

"I'm an agent." The man bowed up.

"Fine." The cop had no idea how interesting things were about to get if this text was true. "Then go get a warrant, *agent*." But Antonio wasn't going to make it easy for him until he knew for sure what was going on.

"Oh, Zack." Rebecca's pale cheeks wore red splotches. "There's so much I have to tell you."

Great. She was going to confess. What Rebecca didn't realize was that at this point, it didn't matter. If Arturo was really here, the shit was about to hit the damn fan.

"All right, it's okay, Rebecca." The man walked over and put both hands on her shoulders. "First of all, I need to know. Did this man just hurt you?"

Antonio tensed, balling his fists.

As if sensing his reaction, Rebecca put out a hand, warning him to stop. "No, Zack. I'm fine." She glanced at Antonio and smiled. "He's my…my…well, I love him."

The group fell silent.

But Antonio's heart soared. She had just vocalized her

feelings. Made it public.

Another *ding* from her phone.

"Zack." Rebecca turned back to the cop. "Arturo Menendez Garcia is my father, although I haven't met him yet. Apparently, he's a big man up in the Cuban government. As you read, he says he's waiting for me at a home on Culbreath Isles. He's left Cuba, and he says he's here seeking political asylum. And I am going to meet him."

"Oh hell no, you're not." Antonio reached out and grabbed her wrist. "Not without me to protect you."

Chapter Twenty

Rebecca sucked in the warm night air and widened her stance, keeping her gaze locked onto Antonio's. *Here it goes.* She stood toe-to-toe with him on the side of the driveway of the governor's mansion, away from the crowd waiting to get their cars from the valet. What could she say to Antonio to convince him she had to face her father alone?

She knew if Antonio followed her, which he kept insisting on doing, either Antonio or her father would die. Or maybe the life Antonio had anticipated on his return to America would perish. She wrapped both arms around her body. Either way, she wanted to protect Antonio. God help her. But he was such a stubborn man.

She swallowed, watching Antonio's eyes narrow, knowing the hard-core revolutionary in him would not likely give in easily. "You can't go with me." Stepping forward, she prayed the caustic truth about to spill out wouldn't irreparably damage their new relationship. "There may be a warrant out for your arrest."

Antonio's eyes widened, and he shifted his weight,

the only indication he recognized the seriousness of her admission.

She stared up at him, the words still burning in the back of her throat. "I had to give a statement to the police when I got back." Heat rushed into her cheeks. "I told them Ignado kidnapped me at first, but you gave me a choice. I told investigators I went with you to Cuba willingly. But they, the police, they think I'm suffering from Stockholm syndrome, you know, where the captive bonds with or sympathizes with her captor."

"I know what Stockholm syndrome is. That's not what you're feeling." He shook his head, paused, and blinked a few times before looking down. "You gave the police Antonio Vega's name, right?"

His voice was low, and Rebecca couldn't figure out if he was angry. Her stomach churned. "Yes. Yes. I'm sorry. But I also showed them the video of Maria being abused. Dallas recorded Angel using violence with her the morning we left. There's no doubt she's a victim of domestic violence and no doubt you did what you did to save her. But I don't know if I've done enough to protect you. Zack, Sam's fiancé, says you're a principal to my kidnapping. I think that's what he said." She pressed her lower palms against both temples, massaging the tension away. "I don't want you to get in trouble." Moving her hands across her face, she covered everything but her mouth. "That's why I'm telling you not to come with us. Zack is an agent with the Florida Department of Law Enforcement. You heard him say he's coming with me. What was I supposed to say? No, you can't?"

Antonio gently pulled her hands away from her face, exposing her to his drilling gaze. "Where are your friends now?"

"Getting the car." As they'd exited, Zack had flashed his badge and grabbed the keys off the valet stand. Sam and

Dallas had gone with him, at her insistence. She needed this time alone with Antonio. "Go get your family and leave," she implored.

A disgusted sound rumbled from deep within him. "I'm not running. No one is chasing me out of this country. I've done nothing wrong. My family will never be uprooted again."

She threw her hands up, breaking the hold he had on her. "You could live anywhere."

"We *live* in *Tampa*." Leaning into her, his eyes flared. "We aren't leaving."

"But *I* can't *live* with the guilt if Zack arrests you. I fear I won't be able to stop him."

"He won't." Antonio's body remained perfectly still, except for his chest, which was moving in and out at a quicker-than-usual pace.

"Oh, Antonio, stop fooling yourself." She placed a hand on his chest, wanting to feel him breathing. "The publicity has gone too far. I know you believed all this media coverage would protect you, help your cause. But really, all this constant media speculation has done is force my friend's hand. He's already suspicious you aren't just my new boyfriend." Lord, the whole damn country had watched her documentary, learning all about Antonio and his family. They'd catch on eventually, despite Antonio's new look.

An amused grin lit up his face. "This Zack will arrest me and charge me with what? You, yourself, told them I didn't physically kidnap you. They have no physical proof I committed any crime."

"A technicality." She wanted to shake him, make that self-assured look slide off his face, so she could actually help him. "They are saying you ordered and paid for my kidnapping. And the police think you're a human smuggler. That you have a pipeline bringing Cubans to America."

"I didn't actually smuggle anyone into America." He pointed a finger at her, but not in an aggressive manner. "Not like you did."

"But they believe you orchestrated the whole plan." She smacked his hand away.

"From the Cayman Islands."

"What?" His unexpected response caused her heart to hesitate. "Why does *that* matter?" She forced herself to take deep breaths.

"After I sold my company, I moved to the Cayman Islands."

"To hide all that money?"

He smiled, the twinkle back in his eyes. "To plan my attack and protect my ass."

She fanned herself with a gala program, glancing nervously behind her, expecting Zack to drive up the driveway at any minute. The last thing she wanted right now was another confrontation. "I don't get it."

"Then let me spell it out for you. If I didn't commit the crime I'm accused of *in Tampa*, or *in the United States*, then your FDLE friend has no jurisdiction and can't arrest me, even if I admit I'm guilty." He unbuttoned his tux jacket, and his thumbs hooked into the belt loops of his pants.

The gesture not only took her breath away, but also made her completely believe him. "Are you sure?" *Please tell me you are.*

"Call your friend and ask him." Antonio pulled his cell phone out of his tux jacket and held it out for her to take.

"Jesus, you thought this all out."

"Of course I did." Taking a step closer, he lifted her chin with two fingers. "One day you'll stop underestimating me."

Oh God, he looked so solid, standing there in that damn expensive black tux, with his bow tie off and his white shirt partially unbuttoned. But Zack would be bringing the car around any second, and she had to think about more than how much she lusted after this man. She had to concentrate on how much she loved him, and how she could save him from himself and his dangerous obsession with revenge.

Keeping Antonio a free man was the only way his family would survive here. "I still don't think you should go."

Antonio raised his hand to stop her words. "The truth is coming out, Rebecca, and I want it to. I'm not afraid."

"But I am."

"I have to go with you." The resolve in Antonio's voice made her shudder.

"Why?" But she knew.

"You know why."

"Please, tell me I'm wrong." She closed her eyes, bracing herself by wrapping both arms around her stomach.

"I have unfinished business with Arturo Menendez Garcia."

"Antonio," she groaned.

"Get used to calling me Tony."

She dragged a hand down her mouth. "You had a chance to kill my father in Cuba. You should have done it there." She threw her hands up in disbelief. "I can't let you kill my father *right in front of me."*

His hands balled up. "I did not have a chance to kill Menendez. Ignado set me up before I had a chance to even meet him again. You know how much you want to meet your father? We'll, I've been dying to confront him face-to-face for much longer." Antonio reached for her, but stopped, his hand outstretched. He turned away, as if disgusted. Maybe by his own conflicted feelings? "Do you want to know what saved me from getting arrested and jailed in Cuba?"

Where was he going with this?

"Ignado's phone kept ringing, and all I could think about was how you were calling me for help."

Of course she remembered. With his back to her, she couldn't read Antonio's features, but his shoulders remained high and tight. "I called over and over, but Ignado never answered. Neither did you, Antonio."

"Exactly." Antonio flipped back around, his eyes harried. "When Ignado ignored the phone, after seeing the number, and then he refused to give the phone to me, I knew something was up. I tricked Ignado and escaped before we got to our destination in Havana."

So Igando had been lying that night on the yacht. Right before Jose Carlos had killed him.

Both hands on his hips now, Antonio's voice lowered in timbre. "I have no doubt that your phone calls saved my life. If I'd gone with Ignado, I'm sure I would have walked right into a trap set by your father." He pointed right at her. "He is a very dangerous man, Rebecca."

"So you want to kill him here in Tampa and go down for murder?" Should she slap Antonio and wake him up? "Then Zack will definitely have a good reason to arrest you."

Running his long fingers over his shortened hair, he appeared to let that comment sink in. "I'm not going to kill your father."

"Right," she whispered, suddenly aware of the stares from those in the valet line. Maybe she'd yelled the word "murder"? Great. More suspicious gawking. They hadn't walked far enough into the shadows.

"I'll admit when I started this journey with you that was my intent, to use you as bait to draw Menendez out, kill him, and escape Cuba." He ran his hand over his chin, stroking it as if his beard were still there.

The gesture pulled at something deep inside her. "And you'd never suffer any consequences because Cuban officials have no jurisdiction here." Now Rebecca was getting it. She took a step toward him, aching to get closer, knowing she shouldn't dare with all these people potentially watching. "What changed your mind?" *Please tell me what I need to hear.*

"I knew if I killed your dad, you'd never forgive me, regardless of what you learned about him. I left my gun with you that night at Johnny's farm as a way of proving to you my intentions had changed."

Her breath caught in her lungs. "So, you planned to do what? Arm-wrestle with my dad when you saw him in Havana?" She wanted to believe Antonio so much that she physically hurt.

"Confront him." He took a step her way.

She back-stepped.

"I wanted to tell him that I knew he killed my father and devastated my mother by leaving her, too. She died of a broken heart because that father of yours has no heart."

Something in Rebecca's brain registered. "You still hate Arturo." She watched Antonio's pupils dilate, realizing a need still burned deep within him, and nothing she could do or say would change that. "You still want to make my father suffer." The last was barely a whisper. If Antonio killed her dad, he'd go to jail. He'd be gone from her life and Maria and Tonito's for good. She had to stop him. "You can't go with me."

"You can't stop me." Antonio's words were barely audible, his lips narrowed like his eyes. "I know the address of the house where he's at, remember."

Her stomach turned over and beads of perspiration bubbled up on her own forehead. "I'm bringing Zack with me. The Feds are on their way. Zack called the CIA, Antonio. The freaking CIA."

• • •

She was trying to save him. He saw the fear in her eyes. He didn't doubt her good intentions, or her love for him, but she didn't realize how dangerous Arturo was. He was not about to let her confront that man alone. "He's going to disappoint you, Rebecca."

Rebecca stood perfectly still, watching him with wide eyes, a sheen clouding them.

"Zack? Or the...the...CIA?" Air wouldn't support her words.

"No, your father." Taking two quick steps forward, Antonio faltered and stopped. "He'll shatter every dream you've ever had of him. If you bring the FDLE or the CIA with you and he finds out, he's going to kill you. Or them." Intuition turned his gut sour. "This night is going to end badly. And I will not let you end with it. Even if it means I'm taken in for questioning."

She took a step back. "I think you're being a bit dramatic." Her hand flew to cover her heart. "My father is seeking help, remember?"

Antonio arched one eyebrow. She showed such naïveté when it came to her dad. But he understood her false hope. "You don't know Arturo Menendez. He doesn't need anyone's *help.*"

"Antonio, that's the point. I have to know him. I have to take this chance."

He nodded, leaned in, and brushed kisses across her burning cheeks. This standing here arguing would result in nothing good. But he would protect her, while letting her believe she had won, therefore protecting him.

He had another plan.

Then without even looking at her again, Antonio turned and stalked away, into the dark pit of the governor's overly landscaped lawn.

Chapter Twenty-One

Rebecca walked down the oak-lined sidewalk of the exclusive bay-front neighborhood under the muted lights of the aged streetlamps. The flapping of her Cuban sandals beating against the concrete sidewalk was her only companion.

A light wind whipped through the tall palms and sprinted past her ears, but other than that, the neighborhood remained eerily silent.

Made up primarily of well-to-do families with old money, and young professionals who worked long hours for their new money, she figured most of the people who lived here would probably be asleep already.

Licking her lips, she wished she'd grabbed her bottle of water. Her mouth had gone dry as soon as she'd left the group. Dallas, Zack, Sam, and a group from both the FDLE and the CIA had stayed behind in a home three doors down. They'd set up a mini command post with the homeowner's reluctant consent.

She'd stood in the house sweating bullets while the CIA had put a wire on her, practicing deep breathing exercises, anything to stop the drilling of her heart against her rib cage. She'd been so conflicted by the request she wear a wire. But it was the only way to protect herself and Antonio. Right? Because her dad was a member of the Cuban government, allegedly seeking asylum, the CIA had gotten involved. Maybe her dad would prove everyone wrong. Maybe he really was reaching out to her for help.

Finally, she'd gotten the nerve to move forward with their plan.

Now her heart was thumping again as she walked. Could they pick up that sound?

Zack had promised her a few of his men would be close behind her all the time. And he'd assured her the CIA had a SWAT team moving into place. She didn't even know the CIA had SWAT teams. Zack told her she wouldn't see them or hear them unless she ran into trouble, but they'd always have her in their sight.

She glanced to her left. No cars moved on the darkened two-way street. Glancing to her right, she pulled a few strands of windblown hair out of her eyes. Thick oleander bushes lined the driveway up to the house. The wind rustled through the leaves. Anyone could be hiding in the landscaping.

Even Antonio.

He'd left so abruptly. She had no way to call him. Fill him in on what was going on.

She stopped, the air catching in her lungs. She hoped the bushes sheltered the undercover officers and not one of her father's henchmen. The howl of the hot late-night sea breeze continued to ruffle the greenery, making creepy sounds that brought out a blush of bumps on her skin.

She counted to ten, her gaze glued on the bushes. No more movement, so she continued walking. She turned down the winding driveway leading up to the mansion. It was set far back from the road. "I'm—I'm at the house now. Uh, walking down the driveway." She tried to sound brave for the group listening three doors down, but she knew her voice probably sounded as tight as the muscles in her upper back.

The driveway should have been well lit. Lamps lined each side, but not one of them had been turned on. No cars were visible, at least not by the glare of the moon. Up ahead, she noticed the house was dark. Strange her dad would call her here. She shivered, the hair on her arms tingling. Did anyone even live here? Maybe her dad had chosen an abandoned house to hide in? No, mansions in this part of Tampa weren't abandoned or foreclosed on like the homes she grew up next to in West Tampa. And how the hell would he know what house to pick from all the way in Cuba? Can you say red flag?

"I'm afraid this might be a trap. It's way too dark here. Doesn't look like anyone is home. It doesn't feel right." She spoke in a low tone, but loud enough to make sure Zack and the rest of the group could hear her. "I'm scared," she whispered, this time to Dallas in particular. She knew her backup had no way to talk back and reassure her. But it made her feel better knowing Dallas would hear and understand.

This whole night had taken such an unexpected turn. First, Antonio had shown up. Alive. Looking so damn healthy and sexy. He'd made intimate love to her in a semipublic place. Then her father had texted her. And Antonio had left. With Zack there, she'd had no choice but to let the FDLE and CIA gather their resources together and weave her into their undercover plan to find out what Arturo really wanted by coming here to America.

So here she was.

Undercover.

Again.

This time in her own country.

Wishing this was all over.

And to think she'd been *dying* to be the investigative

reporter.

Not anymore.

An unexpected chill rippled through her. Pulling out her iPhone, she searched for the flashlight app and turned it on. A shard of hard white light hit the pavers.

She squealed as a furry black object darted across her path. A low, mean hiss trailed off into the darkness. "Holy shit." She covered her heart with her free hand. "It's just a cat. A cat. Oh boy, a *black* cat." She kept walking, imagining Dallas back at the house, rolling his eyes over her fear of a silly superstition. He'd offered to come with her, but she'd told Dallas that Arturo had insisted she come alone, and the head guy from the local CIA office had agreed she should do so, at least in appearance. Where were those damn undercover cops? They were slick, because she hadn't heard a peep from anyone.

And where was Antonio?

She shivered remembering his words. *Tonight is going to end badly.* Antonio was always right.

Always right.

She should have listened to him and let him come.

For what seemed like an eternity, only the lonely sound of her sandals kept her company, until finally, she reached the front door. The massive two-panel wood entranceway had a large old-fashioned brass knocker. Beating it against the door, the sound of metal against wood echoed in the silence, and the door, left slightly open, squeaked and moved inward. Nervous energy spiked through her. She knocked again, the move propelling the door open even further. Spooked by the sudden movement, she stumbled over the raised entranceway and tumbled into the silent house, throwing her hands out to catch her fall.

Her iPhone slipped out of her hand, dropping on the marble, bouncing once and then skidding across the floor, her only light going out with a thud. "Shit!" She banged her fists against the cool flooring. Then she bit down on her bottom lip, pissed she'd made a noise.

Sprawled across the floor, face planted against the cool stone, arm stretched out in search of her phone, it was her sense of smell that raised the first flag of warning. Was that onions and sweat? The odor entered the room like wicked fingers of warning. She'd known only one man who smelled like that. She stiffened and sniffed deeply, but the aroma disappeared. Maybe she'd imagined it. Fear must be playing tricks with her head.

Laughter erupted, but from a distance. She froze for a split second, and then pushed up onto her knees, turning in the direction of the voices. Moonlight filtered through the sliding glass door leading out to the backyard. Beyond that was a walkway leading up to a dock. A sleek sport-fishing yacht was docked, and a handful of men were loading something on board.

One man stood out among the others.

He was tall and lean, and dressed in camouflage pants and a white shirt. One foot balanced on the edge of the boat closest to her, his other foot rested on the boat's deck. He waved a cigar around as if either telling a story or giving orders. Either way, his bold gestures left no question in Rebecca's mind who was in charge out there.

The fluttering of her heart escalated, and a trickle of sweat sizzled down the center of her back. This was it. The moment. The one she thought she'd never have.

Beyond curious, she crawled toward the sliding glass door, too afraid to stand up and be noticed in a moon-driven spotlight.

The man in camouflage had a head of gray hair, a boatload of it, and the texture was thick and wavy, just like hers. His bronzed skin looked a bit leathery. She wasn't close enough to see his eyes, but she'd bet all she owned they were chocolate brown like hers. Despite his age—he had to be at least fifty-five—he had a lean, muscled body, like a marathon runner. He didn't smile. Not once. Nor did he laugh.

Still on hands and knees, she pressed her hot forehead against the cool sliding glass door. Closing her eyes, she tried to recall a memory with that man in it. She imagined her birthday party when she was a toddler, maybe two or three. He wasn't there. She jogged her brain for the memory of a family dinner. He wasn't there. She couldn't re-create his face in her mind.

She imagined playing in the front yard of her home in Cuba. Zero. Her mom was there. That man wasn't. Maybe there was one night when he sat at her bedside and read her a good-night story? She felt like a car sputtering on empty. Her heart seized, and for a moment she couldn't breathe. Was he her father? Didn't a child instinctively feel love for a birth parent? Why did she feel so depleted and lethargic?

She pounded a fist gently against the glass window. Realizing what she'd done, she popped open her eyes and crawled away from the window, her hand leaving a temporary print on the glass as she moved away. She held her breath, waiting to hear any voices or warnings that she'd been spotted.

"I'm okay. I'm okay," she whispered half to herself, half to make sure Zack and the rest of the law enforcement team didn't take her silence or whimpering for a signal to come out of hiding, guns blasting. "I think I've found my father. Or the man Antonio showed me the picture of…" She couldn't finish, her air cut off by a tsunami of buried emotions.

She mumbled something, knowing she had to reassure Zack and Dallas she wasn't being hurt in any way. "I'm going to confront him now. Have to find my iPhone first. I dropped it when I first got into the house, which was unlocked, by the way."

Crawling away from the sliding glass door, Rebecca moved slowly, patiently, led by the moonlight, toward the corner in the direction where her phone flew. Still on her hands and knees, she felt safer closer to the ground, knowing the bustling activity going on outside would stop once she'd been spotted. Her shoulder hit the side of a couch. Reaching under the corner of the couch, she felt for her phone.

"Hello, America."

Her fingers froze. Swallowing, she jerked her hand out from under the couch and flipped around so her back was against the piece of furniture. Her chest tightened. Checking to the left, then to the right, she tried to make out a figure in the shadows that danced between the blocks of moonlight scattered across the living room.

Holding her breath, she listened for any sounds of another person breathing, footsteps, anything to prove she really did just hear *that* voice. She bit down hard on her bottom lip. Only one man ever called her America. And he was dead. She'd watched him fall overboard.

"Too afraid to talk to me."

"I would think you would know my name by now, Ignado," she whispered, hoping that Dallas would warn Zack who Ignado was and how his presence here was a dangerous game changer. "Are you alive, or are you a ghost haunting me?"

"I've come back for you, America."

No mistaking his voice this time. She stood and bolted toward the door. Hand on the door handle, her chest heaving up and down, she froze. She needed to bait Ignado, call him out where she could see him. Get him to talk since she had a mic on and the police were recording.

"Come out, Ignado." She flipped around to face him, yet found nothing but the moonlight dancing on the floor in front of her. "Come out. Show yourself." She pressed her back against the front door, her hand still on the knob. Just in case he was armed.

In the pause, she heard her own heart beating, then laughter from the group of men out back, but nothing more from Ignado. She swallowed. Was she going crazy? She lessened her grip on the doorknob.

"Talk to me," she whispered.

The tinkle of a porch wind chime broke the silence, the melody sending shivers throughout her body. He was taunting her with his silence. *Always an asshole.*

Then an idea hit her. Searching the room, she located an old-fashioned house phone. Walking over to it, she picked up the receiver and dialed her cell phone number. Not half a second later, her phone rang, the sound coming from a darkened corner of the room to her right.

She froze, wishing to God she had a gun.

Or Antonio as her backup. Antonio was the only one who could control Ignado.

"You have my phone, Ignado." She swallowed, the words sticking in the roof of her mouth. "I'd like it back."

The chuckle that followed caused goose bumps to erupt all over her skin.

Ignado stepped out of the dark corner, her phone, still ringing, in his hand.

He pretended to answer it.

She flipped on a table lamp, ignoring him.

"I underestimated you, America."

I underestimated you, too. "I saw you get shot."

"You watched me fall overboard. I swam to shore."

"With a bullet in you?"

Ignado pulled his white shirt up, exposing his abdomen. On his left side, a red scar was visible. "Jose Carlos is not a good shot. Not as good as I am." The moonlight bounced off Ignado's crooked teeth as he smiled. "He missed all my vital organs." Without warning, Ignado launched her phone at her.

As soon as she caught it, her gaze darted back to her enemy, just in time to see him whip out a gun and point it at her.

Her throat started to close, but she squeaked out, "You're going to shoot me? Before I can meet my father?" Her way of letting Dallas and Zack know Ignado was now armed. "What will my father say? He called me here." The CIA guy would be able to alert his SWAT guys, right? She had to buy them time. If they were close outside, she had a chance. She'd left the front door open, hadn't she? Shit. She couldn't remember. The muscles in her legs began to cramp.

"Your father will tell me to kill you unless you do exactly as he says."

Her heart crashed. "So, that man…" She turned back toward the sliding glass door. "The one ordering everyone else around. That's my dad?"

"Yes."

She did an about-face.

"You look like him. Don't you think, America?"

The big man—her father—had taken a seat on the bow of the boat, still waving his arms in grand gestures of authority. Like a general. Or a dictator.

She flipped around, pointing a finger at Ignado. "I thought you worked for Antonio."

The corners of his ugly mouth curved. "You're a silly bitch." He shook his head, but the gun he held remained steady. "You screwed Antonio. Then he screwed you."

Heat rushed up her neck and into her cheeks.

"He used you. In many ways."

"Shut the hell up!" She wanted to smack Ignado's face. Only the gun he held stopped her. "I can't believe Antonio ever trusted you. You've betrayed him."

"Your father sent me to America years ago to find and

befriend Antonio. His counterrevolutionary group was small but dangerous, even then. Your lover made it so easy for me. Antonio was desperate to get to Cuba and trusted anyone who spewed the same hatred. His plan was already in place. I only added one important piece."

"What was that?" She hated herself for asking, knowing that's exactly what Ignado wanted. He was baiting her, slowly, carefully. Her stomach knotted, rumbling in distress. But she needed Dallas and Zack to record Ignado's words, so she had to keep him talking. And she could buy time for the SWAT team to mobilize.

"The plan to kidnap you."

Her heart flipped. "*You* planned my kidnapping?"

"Surprised, America?" He cocked one eyebrow at her.

"Yes. I thought it was Antonio's plan." Now who was baiting whom? She had to get this confession recorded. It could free Antonio for good. She bit her bottom lip, well aware she was verbally wrestling with a viper, and it could have deadly results.

"He wanted to use you as bait to draw your father out, but he thought he could convince you with a phone call or an email."

"And when I didn't respond?" *Keep talking. Keep him talking.*

"I took you forcibly. I knew the violence of it would catch the media's attention. I also knew I'd enjoy it." Walking toward her slowly, his gaze never left hers, and his gun never dropped an inch. "And I did."

That she believed. She shuddered, remembering the smell of that nasty cloth he'd pressed against her mouth. She began to tremble. "Why did you come back for me?" She backed away from him, wishing she'd left the front door wide open.

The arrogance in his eyes evaporated, and his brows pinched together. "I was supposed to take you to your father while you were in Cuba."

"And you failed." She continued inching back. The front door had to be right behind her. "So Arturo came with you this time." Her hands behind her, she had both palms out, waiting to touch either a wall, or the door, or something. "To make sure you got it right."

He hissed at her. "Bitch."

"What happens if you fail again, Igando?" There! Her hand felt the knob of the door right as she backed into it. "Will my father kill you if I leave again?" All she had to do was turn around and bolt.

But he must have read the intent in her body language. She turned around and pulled the door handle, but he was on her. His tattooed arm snaked around her neck, squeezing her. The air whooshed out of her lungs, but she couldn't inhale more. The tip of his gun chilled her temple. The sound of her own pulse rocked in her inner ears. She was getting light-headed, and knew she had only seconds before she'd pass out.

"If you come with me right now, I will not kill you, America. I must take you to your father. Alive." He let go of her and she dropped instantly to the floor.

But before she could recover, Ignado grabbed her by a fistful of hair, jerking her back up. The pain pierced her scalp as he pulled her headfirst toward the sliding glass door. She opened her mouth, intending to scream. Instead she whispered, "I'm okay. I'm okay." Her way of telling the SWAT team to stand down. Despite this unexpected development, she was seconds away from meeting her father, and no one was going to stop her.

No matter the consequences.

Chapter Twenty-Two

Ignado threw Rebecca toward the yacht with such force she tripped over her own feet and fell forward, sprawling out on the concrete pavers leading up to the dock. The breath whooshed out of her and she gasped for air.

A hand appeared in her line of sight, the palm turned up and open in a friendly gesture of help.

She couldn't help but notice how big and tan this man's hand was and how perfectly groomed the short, clean nails looked. She blinked. "Are—are you my...my father?" This was not how she imagined meeting her dad, on her knees, breathless, stuttering, and afraid.

"My sweet child, I *am* Arturo Menendez Garcia. I am your father."

She swallowed. He'd admitted it. He was real. He was *here*! Her heart leaped and all those warnings Antonio had delivered disappeared as real joy swept through her.

Grasping her father's hand, Rebecca allowed him to help pull her up. She slapped a few concrete pebbles off her indented knees, wanting to look as good as she could.

Silly, but she'd been dreaming about this moment since she'd learned her father was still alive.

She took a step toward him, but her legs wobbled beneath her. Her father reached out and steadied her.

She stiffened, and her breath hitched. How should she react? Her heart felt as if it had stopped beating. She looked up at the tall, lean man, really *seeing* him for the first time.

Arturo Menendez Garcia, *her father,* had weathered golden-brown skin, and his dark brown eyes glistened with intelligence. His abundant gray hair looked messy, but still elegant. The material of his white cotton shirt seemed expensive. He certainly didn't look like a man who'd just crossed the Florida Straits running away from a precarious or dangerous situation. She exhaled, dropping her gaze.

He released his hold on her. "*Mi niña*, so many years we could have had together were wasted."

Was he kidding? She looked up, wanting to see the veracity in his gaze. This man had no way of knowing her lifelong insecurity stemming from not having a real father. How she'd waited every birthday for a phone call or a visit, every first day of school for some sign he knew she'd advanced to another grade and maybe even felt proud of her minor accomplishments. Every Christmas she'd prayed for even the smallest present. Until her mother told her he'd been murdered. Now she was learning that was a lie. All of her childhood had been a lie. So, what had her mother told this man? Maybe he had longed for her, too. *Oh my God, was this possible?* Could she get her happy reunion, too?

"Your mother took you from me." Arturo spoke, hands on his hips, exuding the confidence of a man telling the truth. "And later told me you'd died. We should both ask her why she lied for all these years."

Rebecca's stomach rolled. "She told me you were a hero. She told me you were arrested for speaking out against the revolutionary government. That you'd died a man of honor." The evidence was standing right in front of her.

Arturo raised his eyebrows at that. "I *am* a man of honor. But I am very much alive. Let's ask your mother about this. Together."

She wished they could. "My mother is dead."

No reaction. Not one flicker of remorse in Arturo's cold eyes.

That brought tears rushing to the back of hers. "What is going on here?" If her father didn't know her mother was dead, wouldn't the surprise have registered on his face?

"Come on board, *mi niña.*" His tone softened. "You need to hear my side of this story."

"Wait a minute." She stalled. "I'm confused." What did this man really want? "If you're here so I can help you seek asylum, why not leave with me now? Why would we get on the boat?"

"The truth is I came here to take you back with me to Cuba. *I* need *your* help now."

Her father's words sent chills up her spine, her mind racing with ire. He'd lied to her to get her here. "I have no desire to go back to Cuba." So he was a deceiver, too. What else would this man tell stories about? She backed away.

He grabbed her wrist, encasing it like a handcuff. "Do you think that you've been fair with the pictures and images of Cuba you've shared with America? Are they a true and accurate portrayal of your birthplace, especially at a time when our governments are trying to repair the damage of the past? You could help us bridge this gap and lay the foundation for a better future."

"I can't believe this." Once again she was being used because of her job, because she had a platform from which to speak to an international audience.

"Believe this. Your viewers are buying what you said in

your documentary, that relations are better on the surface only. Your documentary made it seem like our people are enslaved by poverty. That they want to leave, but can't."

"That is true for many," she said.

"You insinuated that Cuba is not changing. But there's more to this story that you conveniently left out." Arturo pointed a finger at her. "Like how the American embargo has held Cubans like those in your story in handcuffs for decades. That embargo still exists because your leaders are being held hostage by the anti-Castro voters in Miami, who continue to control Florida's electoral votes. Those people think they are hurting Castro and maybe even me with this embargo, but they are only starving their own relatives. And then, like hypocrites, they play the part of the heroes by sending money and feeding their families, all while blaming the Cuban government for the lack of food."

Rebecca snorted. She'd seen firsthand all the fertile farmland with no crops growing. How was that the fault of the Cuban Americans in Miami?

"Then your fanatical Cuban Americans expect their poor relations in Cuba to fall to their knees in gratitude for their great American saviors." Arturo threw a hand up in what looked like disgust. "Who, I ask you, is controlling and manipulating whom? And for what?" He took a step closer, his eyes alight with purpose and passion.

Just like Antonio's always were.

"Your president and mine are trying to end this nonsense, and I think you are the key. You have the attention of the nation. You are the key to unlocking the padlock on the past. But first, we must change public perception."

"We? I don't need to change public perception." She wrenched against his hold, heated anger rising into her cheeks. How dare he insult her like this? "I shared the who, what, why, and where of what I witnessed while in Cuba in my documentary. I told the truth of what I was able to document and see there." He would dare to question her ethics? This man who lied so easily? "I told the truth as I saw it."

"I will give you full access to our country."

"I had full access to *your* country."

"There is so much more to see and understand, Rebecca. Surely as a journalist, you have a responsibility to investigate further. To tell the *whole* truth."

She dropped her gaze, unable to look at him as she realized how very little he cared about her as a person. "That's why you came?" If she threw up now, it would only show this asshole how much he was able to hurt her. "You came here to convince me to come with you so you could feed me the story you want me to share. To show the world the Cuba *you* want them to see." She gagged on the nasty taste of disenchantment. *The bastard.* She pulled her wrist free and pressed both hands against her temples. She hated him. *Hated him.* He didn't care about her as a daughter at all. "Oh my God." She shook her head. Antonio had been right. Again. She would never doubt him again.

She glanced over at the tree line, looking for any movement. Nothing. The head CIA guy had told her to get Arturo to talk if she could, talk about why he was here, what he might be trying to accomplish. How it might affect the security of the United States. Because the government had no notice a Cuban diplomat was visiting Tampa.

In the dark of the night.

Her breath stalled in her throat.

Keep Arturo talking.

No pressure.

She glanced across the yard again.

Arturo snapped his fingers at her. "Who are you looking for?"

She jerked back to attention. "I thought I heard

something."

Her father glanced at the tree line, right where a large oak stood out in the perfectly landscaped yard. Then he snapped his fingers again. "Manuel, go check it out. You." He pointed a finger at her. "You are, above all else, a journalist. You came here to do your job. Now do it."

She turned on her heel, but two steps down the pavers, her anger erupted, and she flipped around, stomping back toward the boat. "I observe, and I report what I see. Whether anyone likes it or not. I am an American! I don't do what I'm ordered to do by you or anyone else." She was pointing a condemning finger at him now, and her father took a small step back, and she swelled with the small victory. "Ironically, the only person involved in all of this who expected me to report the truth, *whatever* the truth might be and despite the consequences, is Antonio Vega, and he's the damn criminal in everyone's eyes." *Oh shit.* What had she just done?

The hot night breeze whipped past her, splashing her hair across her face, blinding her momentarily. The slight hum of the boat's idling motor was the only other sound. Jerking her hair out of her eyes, she glanced around, realizing her rant had brought every person buzzing around on the boat to a halt. There had to be half a dozen big men looking back and forth from their leader Arturo to her. Dragging her gaze to her father, she shuddered when she saw the chill that had settled in his eyes. His fists had balled up, and he opened and closed them as his arms hung stiffly by his side.

"Antonio Vega is here? Right now?" Her father's gaze darted back and forth across the backyard. "That's who you were looking for?" He ran a hand through his windblown hair. His lips drew into an unpleasant line.

Rebecca couldn't stop the smile that tipped the corners of her mouth up. So, Arturo Menendez feared Antonio. She couldn't help but feel a little proud that this monster of a man respected Antonio enough to look at least a little worried that he might be here, hiding.

A flurry of movement at her dad's side caught her attention. He jerked his shirt out of his pants, uncovering a gun.

Her breath caught in her chest.

The click of hammers being pulled back on a half dozen weapons made the hair on her arms stand. His men all followed his lead and now stood armed and alert. *Shit!* She had to warn the SWAT team who may be hiding close by. Just in case they couldn't see. "You all can put down your weapons. All of you. Antonio isn't here." Her throat tightened until she could barely breathe. "Why are you still looking for Antonio, anyway?" Anxiety ripped through her at such an intense speed now, her heart raced painfully. "He didn't kill you."

"But he won't stop trying," Ignado shouted out.

"Can you blame him?" Rebecca shouted back, and then addressed her father. "You murdered his father." She held her breath, waiting for some kind of verbal confirmation or explosion. When Arturo offered none, she shook her head, disgusted. "Even if I knew where Antonio was, I wouldn't give him up to you."

Arturo lowered his gun, threw back his head, and laughed.

She beat her fists against her thighs. "What the hell is so funny?"

"Why would you protect Antonio, when he was so ready and willing to give you up to me?"

Was he? Antonio told her he'd never made it to Havana and never actually met Arturo on their trip. No. She knew Antonio. Loved him. "Giving Antonio up would be like giving up my own freedom. I won't tell you where he is."

Her father lifted his chin, a signal she assumed to Ignado.

Slowly, she dragged her gaze around toward her enemy, who was standing close behind her.

"You don't have to, Rebecca." Ignado grinned.

The tattooed man's hot onion breath hit both her nose and her right ear at the same time, but it was the icy cold barrel of his gun pushing into her temple that dropped her heart into her stomach.

"Antonio will come looking for you. Even if it means traveling back to Cuba."

Chapter Twenty-Three

Ignado shoved Rebecca forward, pushing her twice until she stumbled, falling to her knees.

"Get on the boat, bitch," he snarled.

"No! I'm not going with you, Ignado." She screamed this time, praying to God she'd alerted Zack and the CIA SWAT team.

The roar of an approaching boat engine caught her attention. Maybe they were arriving by water?

Ignado gripped her by her hair, dragging her with such force she feared her scalp would rip. She shrieked as the pain intensified, radiating through her head and down her spine. She planted her feet and threw a backward punch with her elbow, not sure what part of Ignado she'd hit.

"*Puta*!" He grunted but didn't pull the trigger. "If your father was not here, I'd kill you with my bare hands."

"Bring her on board," her father roared. "Igando has assured me Antonio's need for you is almost as strong as his need to kill me."

Ignado's arm wrapped around her middle, and he

squeezed until the air zipped out of her. Lifting her off the ground with a loud grunt, he flung her over his shoulder and stormed up the stairs and onto the boat.

Heart thrashing wildly against her rib cage, she kicked and screamed, pummeling his backside with her fists. "Help me! Help!"

Topside, Ignado dropped her. She landed awkwardly on her feet. Twisting one ankle, she went down.

The roar of the boat motor stopped and a slew of expletives in Spanish erupted.

And then everything happened in one slow-moving second.

Arturo sprang up and ripped his gun out of its holster.

Ignado turned his weapon away from her.

She looked to where both were pointing their guns.

Antonio was jumping off a speedboat at the dock next door. He'd arrived by water? She knew he wouldn't have let her come alone. He'd told her he wouldn't. Antonio had a gun drawn and pointed directly at her father. But he was still too far away.

The vibration of many footsteps pounding on the deck rocked her bottom.

"CIA!" A dozen team members, heavily armed and protected, burst from different sides of the house, taking various positions around the backyard. "Drop your weapons!"

A series of gunshots pinged, like the first kernels of corn popping in the microwave.

Arturo's boat motor roared, and the vessel started moving away from the dock.

The wind picked up as the blades of an approaching helicopter roared overhead.

She pushed herself up despite the pain ripping through her hand. "Take cover. Run!" She barely had time to locate Antonio in the chaos unfolding. He was running her way. "Antonio, we're moving." She was still close enough to swim for the shore. Should she jump?

An arm shot out and pulled her back. Her father!

A bullet whizzed by, close enough she could hear it.

Her father yelled. He stumbled back, taking her with him, but his left arm loosened, and she wiggled out of his grip. Another round of shots fired. He pulled her up against him again. Using her like a shield.

A burning fire ripped through her left shoulder.

She jerked once and spun around, red pumping out of a hole in the left side of her white cotton shirt. "I've been shot!" By a bullet meant for her father. She clutched the side where the round entered her body. Why didn't she feel anything?

Arturo stumbled away, but as he did, he shoved her. She stiffened, hesitating at the edge of the boat, her father's hand moving in her direction again.

Was he finally reaching out to help her?

"Rebecca, *por favor.* Forgive me."

Then her father shoved her forward, harder, using both hands.

Help me! She teetered on the boat's edge forever it seemed, before toppling over the side. Her body splashed into the warm bay, and she glided down, sinking into the black abyss. For one moment, she allowed her body to relax and fall away. No worries, no fear, just falling. If she didn't breathe, this would all end, this horrible nightmare that had taken over her life.

Something disrupted the water, making a muted splash. She had to still be close enough then to make it to shore. Her heart slammed against her ribs. Maybe her dad had jumped off the boat to rescue her after all. He couldn't let her die. Kicking hard, she moved her hands in a heart shape, pulling herself skyward, mostly with her right arm. She'd find him. Eyes open, the darkness made her dizzy with vertigo. Oxygen starved, her lungs tightened.

Something warm touched her. She flinched. Her daddy's hand? She threw her arm out in the direction of the warmth. Hot fire roared through her shoulder now, the pain becoming too difficult to ignore. Breaking the water's barrier, she pushed her head out of the surf and gasped for air. Inhaling hurt, but the air gave her renewed hope.

Dog-paddling at a rate she knew would tire her out quickly, she dived under again, swimming this time with one arm wide. She flailed around in the dark of the night sea, pressing her palms against the liquid, but to no avail. Finally, her left shoulder gave out on her. She had to surface, or she'd surely drown.

Kicking again, she felt the cooler air as she broke through the surf.

"Rebecca! Stop."

Antonio. Of course he would be the one to jump in and save her. She inhaled instinctively, ingesting both air and seawater at the same time. The water slid down her windpipe, causing it to seize. She threw back her head and coughed, hoping to spit out the water.

Tired, arms trembling, Rebecca failed to keep her body above the surface and slipped under. Eyes wide and lungs burning, she struggled to right herself and find her way up. *Air, she needed air.*

That's when two hands grabbed under her armpits and pulled her upward. She moved her weak legs in an effort to help. Pressing her lips together to suppress another effort to cough out the water in her windpipe, she prayed. *Please, God, let me surface. Let me breathe.*

With a forceful shove, the hands pushed her head above water. She sputtered. Slapping her good arm against the surface of the bay, she fought to stay afloat, despite the fact that the left side of her body wasn't cooperating.

"Rebecca."

"Antonio." The muscles in her arms burned as she circled them repeatedly.

"I knew this would happen, that son of a bitch."

Water splashed up in her face.

Antonio grabbed her arm and then pulled her to him. "You have to relax and let me save you."

She gasped, kicking her legs so hard she kicked his side accidently, their arms and legs entangled as they fought the dark bay.

"Rebecca, you're making this difficult," Antonio huffed. "Don't fight me."

She stilled.

"Don't talk. Roll over on your back and float if you can."

She did as he asked, her heart skipping beats because she realized at this moment that of all the men here tonight, it *was* Antonio who truly cared about her. Why else would he have risked what he'd risked to be here? He'd jumped in to rescue her despite all the flying bullets.

"I'll pull you to shore. Don't do anything. Just let me do the work."

She could see the lights of the house, but it would be a good swim. She could feel Antonio struggling to pull her and swim at the same time. She heard the strain in his shallow and swift breathing. "Antonio, I can try…"

"Don't argue with me." He could barely get the words out.

Her legs were starting to cramp from dog-paddling, pain burning through her whole body now, not just her shoulder, and she was struggling to get enough air. Suddenly, she feared dying, because she had something new and powerful to live for. She prayed Antonio would have the strength to see this moment through and save them. She wanted desperately to live now—no matter what repercussions were waiting for them both on land.

Chapter Twenty-Four

Crawling onshore, her lungs screamed for more air. She collapsed, falling into a bed of rocks, her shoulder throbbing. Rolling over, she coughed until she puked up bay water, the effort to exhale the liquid so violent she could hardly breathe.

"Let it out. It's okay." Antonio collapsed to his knees, falling down by her side, pulling big chunks of her wet hair away from her face. "Just breathe, Rebecca. Breathe." One of his hands found her back.

The comforting tone of his voice calmed her enough to do as he said. She took shallow breaths until she was able to breathe deeper. Then an image of her father pushing her overboard blinked like a strobe light in her mind. She jolted upright, a sharp pain ripping through her shoulder as she moved. She screamed from the distressing sting. "That bastard tried to kill me."

"Rebecca." Antonio's voice had an odd ring to it. "Your father is gone. Not dead. Gone, as in left, probably heading back to Cuba."

She wobbled to her knees, looking around for any sign of

her father or the vessel he'd been on. She saw neither, but her eyes had trouble focusing, and she was so damn light-headed and nauseous.

Antonio stayed right beside her. "Don't worry. The Coast Guard will run after them. Take deep breaths, Rebecca. Just concentrate on breathing. Forget everything else."

Forget everything else? An ironic truth slugged her. "Antonio, why did you come when I asked you not to?" He couldn't have known ahead of time that her father would try to kill her. Antonio had come here for another reason.

"Rebecca, I told you I was coming whether you liked it or not. I did not lie to you. I knew the bastard would try something."

"You shot my father, didn't you?" With a spurt of energy she didn't know she had left, she staggered up onto all fours. "He was bleeding, too. You came here to kill him." She could only take in small puffs of air again. Her lungs were failing to expand like they should. "But you shot me instead."

She rocked back on her heels before catching herself. Yes, Antonio cared about her, but he loved his revenge even more. In trying to kill his enemy, he'd almost killed her. She raised her arm, but it sagged before she could point an accusing finger. Would this back-and-forth between them ever end?

Antonio jumped up as if a lightning bolt had struck him. "I didn't kill your father. I wanted to. That son of a bitch was using you as a bulletproof vest. I didn't shoot Arturo because I didn't want to miss and hit you, and I didn't want you to do this—accuse me and never forgive me."

Her father had pushed her overboard, of that she was sure. She'd never forget the look in his eyes, or the terror in her heart as he forced her off the boat. She grabbed her left shoulder, which throbbed terribly.

"Then who shot my father?"

"I shot him." Zack Hunter broke out of the mess of people

now bustling across the backyard. Most of them uniformed cops.

Zack rushed to her side, taking a knee next to Antonio.

"We need help here." Antonio grabbed Rebecca's wrist and held it. "She's been grazed. Pulse is still fine."

A blast of air blew out of her lungs. "This is my fault. It's all my fault."

"Rebecca, are you okay?" Zack looked concerned. She must be dying.

"We need a paramedic here." Antonio yelled over his shoulder, gesturing for one.

When had the ambulance arrived? Jesus, her clothes were wrapped around her like wet leaves, suffocating and heavy. She couldn't move, and her world was blurring.

She tried to sit, but her wiggly arm gave way. Antonio caught her. She watched Zack's gaze move to Antonio.

"I think it's time you told me exactly who you are." Zack's narrowed eyes were burning question marks.

Rebecca's eyes locked with Antonio's, her heart crashing. Antonio was going to tell Zack everything. She read the intent in his eyes. She shook her head, silently warning Antonio to not say a word. At least not right now. Fear pierced her center.

Antonio hesitated, looking at her with sad eyes.

Her insides exploded. "Don't do it," she pleaded. "Don't say anything to him. He's a cop."

Zack gave her sharp look. "Rebecca, I'm your friend. Let me help you."

Zack still didn't trust Antonio. She couldn't have these two men face off right now.

Zack was staring at Antonio. "You are?" The detective rested one hand on his holstered weapon.

Antonio held his head high, and his back stiffened with that proud posture she'd come to know as her determined lover. "I am Antonio Vega."

She shook her head, her heart aching almost as much as her shoulder.

"Tampa Police have been looking for you." Zack's voice was neither accusatory nor celebratory.

"I know." Antonio was looking at her, an odd look in his eyes. "We need to get Rebecca to the hospital."

"Wait—" She struggled to sit up. "I've told you, Zack, Antonio didn't force me to do anything."

"Rest, Rebecca." Antonio pressed her back. "I'm going with her, agent."

"Mr. Vega, I'm going to need a statement from you."

Oh no. Please, no. She tried to swallow and then speak, but she didn't have enough moisture in her throat.

"And I'm going to need you to contact my lawyer. His name is Don Fitzjohnson."

"He's your lawyer?"

She couldn't see Zack's eyes, but heard the concern in his voice.

"And Barry Lohen is representing Rebecca now."

Antonio had hired the best in Tampa. Of course he had. But did he need to? If Ignado confessed that he was the mastermind, and Zack had admitted to shooting her father who was using her as a bulletproof vest, than Antonio should be in the clear, right?

"I see." Zack made no move to stop or cuff Antonio. In fact he leaned over and winked at Rebecca.

At least that's what she thought she saw.

"Yes, I'm glad you do." Antonio pulled wet hair away from her mouth. "You can call either of them to set up an interview. I'll be at the hospital with Rebecca. I'm not running away. Tampa is my home. I've done nothing illegal."

"Well, Mr. Vega, I'm sure I can trust you, but just in case, we'll be sending a patrol officer to Tampa Hospital with the ambulance."

Another man in a gray shirt dropped down next to her. He began to cut off the shirt around her injured shoulder. "Looks like the bullet grazed you. Missed the bone. That's good news. Transport has arrived. Let's get her in."

The paramedic guy began to move her onto a board; her whole body burned as he lifted her. She moaned.

"Rebecca, focus on me."

Antonio's voice.

"You're going to be okay. They're just putting you on a gurney to take you to the ambulance. It's a flesh wound. Don't be afraid."

Was that his hand on her face or the paramedic guy's? At least she wasn't going to die. They started moving, and every bump was torture on her shoulder.

"Before you pass out I need to tell you something." Antonio grabbed her hand. "I have my family here, thanks to you. They're safe. You've made it so my story has been heard all over the United States. The spotlight is now on Cuba and not on me."

"Ignado confessed, Antonio."

"He's gone now. I don't want to spend another second of my life wasting energy on either Ignado or your father."

"I'm not feeling very good."

"I'm here with you." Antonio, walking along the right side of the gurney, squeezed her hand.

His flesh was warm against her clammy skin. "I know." She wanted to squeeze back but couldn't get her fingers to move.

"I'm here with you, and I'm not leaving this time."

She exhaled, giving up and letting her grip on his hand relax. "Good."

He smiled down at her as he walked alongside her. "You're finally listening to me." His eyes were wide, and his face looked paler than usual.

"Don't count on it." She tried to smile, but now even her face felt numb.

She felt the paramedics raising the gurney. "We're going to lift you up into the ambulance. It might hurt for a moment."

The lift and shove forward did send a jolt of raw pain through her injured shoulder. If this was a graze, what the hell did a bullet jammed in your body feel like?

The paramedic jumped up and returned to her side. "I'm going to give you some pain medicine through an IV. It will lessen the pain and make you sleepy."

Like she wasn't about to pass out already. "Okay." She wheezed the word out.

Antonio hauled himself into the ambulance and reached for her hand. His fingers entwined with hers, sending a rush of warmth through her veins. Or was that the drugs in the IV?

He squeezed her hand gently. "I'll be with you, by your side, until you wake up. Trust me."

She wanted to laugh. "I do."

"You do?"

"I do." She closed her eyes, aware the vehicle had started moving. Red lights flashed against the darkness of her closed lids, and a siren wailed, rocking her pulse and causing it to beat in her ears like a bass drum. "Do you think the police will catch Arturo?" She opened her eyes, wanting to read Antonio's features.

"I think that's as uncertain as the future relationship between our two countries." But there was no uncertainty in his eyes.

He knew.

She did, too.

The pain was lessening. Thank God. Maybe this was all a sign. A physical indicator of what was to come. "I want you to know when I agreed to wear that wire tonight, I was choosing you. I chose you over my father. If you can let go of your obsession with him, I can let go of mine, too." She smiled to herself, knowing she would survive this latest crisis, but when she woke up, a hurricane of change would be brewing. She blinked, staring into the dark black orbs she'd grown to love. The way his concerned gaze bored into her made her heart melt.

"I'm still here. You're going to be fine. *We're* going to be fine. I love you," Antonio whispered.

I love you. Antonio said it again, and she knew he meant it. Those three little words settled her nauseous stomach and took away the sting of anxiety. Maybe the drugs were helping, but she felt warm and safe. "What a story we have to tell."

She barely felt his warm lips on her forehead, but understood the sentiment behind the gesture.

The ambulance made a sharp right turn. Her body shifted, but she didn't feel any new jolt of pain. She felt soft, like the inside of a pillow.

"We have a common cause, and I believe we were brought together so we could help each other. When I heard you'd left Cuba with my sister and her son, I knew then you loved me, too. You risked your job, your reputation, and your future to help me."

She blinked back tears, understanding completely. She'd agreed to go undercover in Cuba with him for the same reason. She just knew, even if she wasn't able to clearly see it at that moment in the Everglades, she just knew he was *the one*. The one who would change her life, and save her from her past by providing her with a future. She'd gone undercover to expose a wrong, and in the process, found something so right.

"You have seen the real me, Rebecca. The good, the bad, and the ugly. And you still love me. You love the *authentic* me. What more could a man ask for?"

"And you have seen the worst of me, and yet you risked it

all to come make sure I was okay. You saved my life tonight, Antonio."

"My life is entwined with yours now." Just as his fingers were securely wound within hers.

Now, although her life was totally uncovered for the entire world to see, and she had no idea what tomorrow would bring in terms of her job, her reputation, and her health, she'd never felt safer. "Stay with me, Antonio."

"That's my plan."

"Your plan?"

"We'll be in and out of the hospital, quickly." He winked at her.

She smiled. The man always had a plan. Knowing that, she closed her eyes and drifted into a blissfully pain-free darkness, her future looking brighter than it ever had before.

Acknowledgments

I want to thank my many critique partners and beta readers who helped me with *Cuba Undercover*. Thanks to Laura McElroy and members of the Tampa Police Department for their advice and information on proper police procedure, and to Eric Moore, who helped me give Dallas "Dawg" Jones a real voice.

Thank you to my editor Vanessa Mitchell for patiently working with me to make this story the best it could be for our readers.

And a special thank-you to my husband, Jorge Figueredo, who listened to and influenced every word of *Cuba Undercover*. He's my real-life Antonio Vega, whom I met while reporting in Cuba back in 1995. *Cuba Undercover* was inspired by our love story. I hope you enjoy it as much as I did. :)

About the Author

Linda Bond is an Emmy award winning journalist by day and an author of romantic adventures by night. She's also the mother of five, four athletes and an adopted son from Cuba. She has a passion for world travel, classic movies, and alpha males. Linda currently lives in Florida, where the sun always shines and the day begins with endless possibilities. You can become a Bond girl and share in her continuing adventures at www.lindabond.com.

Also by Linda Bond...

ALIVE AT 5

FLATLINE

CPSIA information can be obtained
at www.ICGtesting.com
Printed in the USA
LVHW010939230821
695886LV00002B/133